"Mrs. Quinn?" Armande said, his hand covering the mouthpiece. "There is a very hysterical woman on the phone asking for you."

The look on his face told me that half a glass of whiskey wasn't going to do me any good. I picked up the phone. "Hello?"

My sister's sniffles echoed in the background. "Nina?"

"Maria?" I whispered so my mother wouldn't hear. I glanced over my shoulder at her. She continued to slug courage from her glass. There was no need to worry her about this Nate business.

"What's wrong?"

"I shot him."

My glass slipped from my hand. I heard my mother murmur something to Ana about me not being able to hold my liquor. I turned so they couldn't read my lips. "Nate?" I whispered. "You shot Nate?"

"Good god, no." I heard more sniffling and a few hiccups. "The man."

I rolled the phone cord around my finger. "What man?"

"The man who broke into my house."

Longingly, I looked at the whiskey staining the floor. "Call the cops," I said. "I'll be right there."

Nina Quinn Mysteries
by Heather Webber

TROUBLE IN SPADES
A HOE LOT OF TROUBLE

TROUBLE in SPADES

A NINA QUINN MYSTERY

HEATHER WEBBER

AVON BOOKS

An Imprint of HarperCollinsPublishers

AVON BOOKS
An Imprint of HarperCollins*Publishers*
10 East 53rd Street
New York, New York 10022-5299

Copyright © 2005 by Heather Webber
ISBN: 0-06-072348-3
www.avonmystery.com

First Avon Books paperback printing: May 2005

Avon Trademark Reg. U.S. Pat. Off. and in Other Countries, Marca Registrada, Hecho en U.S.A.
HarperCollins® is a registered trademark of HarperCollins Publishers Inc.

Printed in the U.S.A.

10 9 8 7 6 5 4 3 2 1

For my family.
All my love.

TROUBLE *in* SPADES

One

"Thou, Nina Colette Ceceri Quinn, shalt come back as an only child in any future lives." I added this commandment to my ever-expanding personal list.

And I was putting it near the top. Because if I *were* an only child, then I wouldn't be standing here in my sister's backyard breaking another commandment of mine. The one where I made no exceptions to my company's carved-in-granite policy.

My unique business, Taken by Surprise, Garden Designs, had flourished in the two years it had been in existence. The appeal, I knew, lay in the fact that my crew arrived very early in the morning and was gone by nightfall, leaving the customer with a vastly different lush and beautiful landscape.

The added twist to my company was that someone, usually a clueless spouse, had no idea a garden renovation was going on. Oftentimes the change was met with happiness. Less frequently, anger. And that was usually only after the clueless spouse found out how much the garden cost.

Surprise makeovers weren't cheap.

Rarely (actually never) had I made an exception to my in-and-out-in-a-day rule. I'd been in the typical landscaping and lawn maintenance business for years before creating

TBS and didn't particularly want to go back. Though my hours were still long, and it was pretty much the same back-breaking work, the rewards of designing surprise make-overs were addicting.

But then Maria had gotten engaged.

And demanded an exception.

Maria. My baby sister. As much as she annoyed me—and had since the day my mother brought her home from the hospital and she spit up breast milk on my Holly Hobby doll—I loved her. I also had a bad habit of being unable to say no to her.

I'd reluctantly agreed to do a backyard makeover for Maria and her fiancé Nate. Okay, so the guilt from my mother helped sway my decision. That, and transforming Maria's backyard, counted as her wedding gift.

Also because watching my twenty-five-year-old sister throw a tantrum of epic proportions wasn't something I needed burned into my psyche.

I already had more than enough shocking images in there to see me clear through the bottom of many, many boxes of Nilla wafers.

Honestly, I really ought to look into buying Nabisco stock.

And go on a diet.

Looking down at my watch, I winced. As usual I was running behind schedule, but this time it wasn't entirely my fault. Maria was late for our meeting, making my already overloaded schedule that much more crowded.

It was closing in on three o'clock, and I still needed to head back to the office to interview prospective employees before chauffeuring my stepson Riley to his new job.

Sitting on the hot concrete patio, I stared into the flat, barren backyard. It was early June and hot, hot, hot for this area of southwestern Ohio. It seemed we'd been in a heat wave for weeks now with no relief in sight.

This time of year I usually worked sixty-hour weeks, but my usual weekday workload sagged under the weight of completing Maria's yard on time. Not to mention that my day-planner overflowed with a long laundry list of extra to-dos just so I could take the following weekend off for her wedding.

Which was another reason it would serve me well to stick to my newest commandment.

I was Maria's matron of honor.

If it weren't so horrifying, it would be laughable.

Truth be told, I wasn't sure why Maria had even asked me to be in her wedding at all.

Except to torture me.

Hmmm.

Beyond the fact that Maria and I weren't all that close, my marriage to Kevin Quinn, Freedom PD's lead homicide detective, was in shambles. Who was I to stand up for anyone at a wedding? I'd fought tooth and nail against being involved, to the point where, with the wedding twelve days away, I had yet to see—or be fitted for—my dress.

Unfortunately, my reprieve would end that day. One of my many to-dos was an appointment at the bridal shop that night.

As much as I wished I could grab Riley and hop the first plane out of town to avoid the festivities, I wouldn't. I'd recently learned the hard way how important family was. Even when they were as crazy as mine.

A slight breeze swept dust across the bleak backyard. A knot of worry twisted in my stomach. Would I be able to get this job done on time?

Just under three weeks. That's all the time I had to implement my monumental design plans. I'd called in favors, made lofty promises, and pretty much begged my usual contractors to get the help I needed to transform Maria's backyard. Luckily, I wasn't footing the huge bill for the work—that fell on the wallet of Maria's soon-to-be father-in-law, a former Kentucky governor.

Maria had tested my design limits by wanting an enormous Japanese-themed garden. Seeing as how water was such a huge design element in a Japanese garden, digging had already been completed for the huge koi pond that sat slightly off-center in the middle of the 1.5 acre backyard. Grading, utilities, and irrigation were up next. It was going to be a crazy three weeks.

Stanley Mack, the carpentry contractor I often used for elaborate work, was busy building a half-moon bridge for the koi pond and a zigzag bridge for the dry creek bed that would be filled with small black pebbles. He was also working on a Japanese teahouse-style garden shed. He'd assemble them in his huge woodworking shop and reassemble them here closer to the completion date.

The game plan was to be done with the yard by the time Maria and Nate got back from their honeymoon in Fiji. I had twenty full days to complete the makeover, and with all that Maria wanted done, I would need every minute of it.

My cell phone buzzed inside my backpack. I rooted around for it, flipped it open.

"Nina," Tam Oliver whispered, "there's a scary bunch of men here waiting for you."

Tam was my secretary, or as she liked to call herself, my executive administrative assistant. Luckily for her, she had just the right amount of haughtiness to get away with such a title. Despite being just two years older than me, she looked—and acted—more than a bit like a young Queen Elizabeth, and would be a dead ringer except for the lack of a British accent. There was no mistaking that Tam had been born and bred in the Midwest.

"How scary?"

"Very. One of them keeps winking at me."

"Well, you're cute."

Her voice rose. "I'm a whale."

Tam was almost seven months pregnant and stressing over every second of it. "Whales are cute. Especially those Beluga whales. Very sweet."

Her tone took on that regal edge. "I am not amused."

I smiled. "You are too."

"Okay. Maybe a little. But what do I do about these men? I can't hide behind this water cooler forever, not that I'm doing all that good a job of hiding, seeing as how my belly's sticking out."

I wanted to laugh at the mental image, but didn't want to risk Tam quitting on me. "Ask them if they want anything to drink and please tell them I'll be there as soon as possible."

"What!?" She gasped, then her voice dropped. "Tell me these aren't the men Ana was sending over."

My cousin Ana, beyond being my best friend, was also a probation officer. Each one of my employees had come to me through her—including Tam. I was a sucker for the down-and-out, and every once in a while it paid off.

"They are."

"Oh boy."

"Books and covers, Tam."

Tam tsked, sounding disgusted. "You did it again."

I groaned. Tam was on a mission to break me of sounding like my mother, who tended to abbreviated clichés and trite expressions.

"Oh, and Robert MacKenna called. Again. When are you going to call him back?"

I wasn't. "Soon," I lied.

"Liar."

Robert MacKenna was Riley's vice principal. We'd met about a month ago, and there had been instant chemistry. Of the Big Bang kind. Two problems. One, he was married. Two, I was still kinda-sorta in love with my adulterous soon-to-be-ex. Ack! I hated that about myself! Now *there* was a commandment I needed to add ASAP. Thou, Nina Colette Ceceri Quinn, need to get over thy cheating ex.

Tam hung up, muttering about taking chances.

She was a fine one to talk.

Out of everyone, she probably understood best what I was going through. She'd been married only two weeks when she found out she wasn't her husband's only wife. A month later, her bigamist husband was behind bars, her marriage was nullified, and her pregnancy test positive.

All in all, she was coping amazingly well. But I didn't see *her* taking any chances on men. Granted, I wasn't seven months pregnant, but still. That your-heart's-been-ripped-out-and-stomped-on pain tends to linger.

The closing of a car door echoed through the backyard. A second later Kit Pipe, my head landscaping contractor, swaggered into sight.

At six-foot-five and 250 pounds of sheer muscle, it was hard for him to do anything but swagger.

"Yo."

I shaded my eyes against the sun. As the crow's-feet spreading out of the corners of my eyes could tell you, I'd never gotten used to wearing sunglasses.

"You're chipper today." Usually, he didn't say *anything* by way of greeting.

"Daisy's finally gonna let me get a dog."

"No kidding?"

He grinned. Even white teeth gleamed against his bronze skin. His eyes had been tattooed with black ink since before I'd met him five years ago, but it was hardly noticeable as his blue eyes sparkled with happiness.

"What kind?" I asked.

"Not sure yet."

Knowing Kit, he was undoubtedly going to get one of those big scary dogs that sent fear into landscapers' hearts across the globe.

"Maybe," I suggested, "you should get one of those cute little dogs. One she can carry around with her and dress in sweaters. Women love those kinds of dogs—not big slobbery ones that drool."

He looked doubtful. "You think?"

"Absolutely." Landscapers everywhere would thank me for ridding them of a scary would-be pet.

"Hmm. I'll let it simmer."

The sun beat down on the patio, adding a good ten degrees to the already eighty-eight degree temperature. A covered porch was an aspect of my design plans for Maria, and part of me (the hot, sweaty part) wished I'd done that first.

Kit, with furrowed eyebrows and downturned lips, looked like he was in deep doggy contemplation. I supposed I would be too, if I were him. He'd waited a long time for Daisy to give in. "What'd you have to do to convince her, anyway?" I asked.

He winked at me. "You sure you want to know?"

Shaking my head, I fought back a blush. I didn't want to think about anything of that nature at all. My hormones were all up in arms, squawking to their little hearts' content. I'd been separated from my husband Kevin for a little over a month now, and you'd think I'd never been celibate before.

Kit looked around the backyard. "This yard is gonna be a beast."

"I know."

"Everyone on board?"

"As far as I know."

The finalization meeting had taken place nearly a week ago at my office. I'd contracted out the carpentry, masonry, excavating, and irrigation work. This area of southwest Ohio was notoriously dry during the summer, and to up-keep a Japanese theme, sprinklers were necessary.

The sound of a car door closing carried back to us. The neighbors were going to be thrilled when we started work, thanks to the isolated road that served as an echo chamber.

"That's probably Maria. You've never met her, have you?" I asked Kit.

He removed his hat, wiped the skull tattoo on his bald head with the palm of his hand. "Nope."

"Nina?" Maria called out.

"Get ready—you're in for a treat," I said to Kit, barely able to hold in a grin. I yelled to Maria, "Back here!"

Maria came around the corner of the house, her Chanel suit coat slung over her shoulder.

"Holy Moses," Kit mumbled under his breath.

"Think about Daisy," I ordered as I stood up, wiped dust from my rear.

"Daisy?" he said.

I rolled my eyes. "At least wipe the drool away. It doesn't make a good first impression."

Maria's blonde hair shimmered in the sunlight. It hung just below her shoulders, cut just so and colored to perfection. Not that she wasn't a natural blonde—she was. She just liked it a touch lighter than her natural shade.

My mother could often be heard bragging that Maria looked like Grace Kelly. The resemblance was definitely there, lurking underneath Maria's high maintenance. I hadn't seen her without mascara and lipstick since she was thirteen.

That regal, graceful look had probably helped her land a high-paying job as an event planner at Phineus Frye, the most prestigious PR company in the city.

If we weren't family, I think I'd have to hate her.

We were polar opposites, the two of us, especially looks-wise. *My* looks came straight from my dad, who looked like a balding bulldog. I'd inherited his dark hair, dark complexion, and muddy green eyes.

The big blue eyes Maria had inherited from our mother blinked as she took in Kit's gigantic form, and her hand fluttered to her ample chest—also something she'd inherited from our mother.

I'd inherited my Nana Cerceri's figure. Think ironing board.

Unfortunately for Maria, *she* inherited Nana Ceceri's hair-trigger temper, which she'd worked hard through the years to control—not an easy thing, considering how spoiled she was and completely used to getting her way.

"Well, hello," she said to Kit, her long eyelashes fluttering.

"This is Kit Pipe," I told her, "my head landscaping contractor and good friend."

Kit was practically panting. Maria had always had that effect on men.

"Pleasure," she said, holding out her manicured hand.

Kit took it, held it.

"Daisy," I said, elbowing him.

He looked at me out of the corner of his eye. "Shh."

"Think about the dog."

He groaned, let go of Maria's hand.

"Daisy?" she said. "Are you using daisies on the design, Nina? Did we talk about that? And what dog? You know I can't have dogs around. They shed. My clothes would get ruined."

I rolled my eyes. "God forbid you get a lint brush."

Frowning, she carefully tucked a strand of hair behind her ear. A big round sapphire twinkled from her earlobe. Apparently, she'd decided to ignore me. "No sign of Nate yet?"

A former professional baseball pitcher who'd been side-lined after hurting his arm, Nate Biederman, Maria's fi-ancé, was now a junior executive at the Kalypso, a riverboat casino just over the Ohio border in Indiana. He and Maria had met a year ago while working together on some charity shindig or another and had been inseparable ever since.

"Not yet. Maybe he hit traffic?" I said. The Kalypso was a good fifty minutes and two highways away from here.

She wrinkled her nose. "Maybe. I haven't been able to get in touch with him all day. Oh well. I guess we can get started without him."

I grabbed the can of marking paint. Today we were going to draw preliminary pathways on the dirt, so the irrigation work could get started. "Are you happy with the paths on the design board? The ones we already agreed on?" I added for good measure, hoping she wouldn't change her mind. Again.

"Well," she said, and fluttered her lashes at me.

I groaned.

Kit elbowed me out of the way. He looked at Maria with big moon pie eyes. "We can do anything you want," he said, then added, "I'm getting a dog."

Maria's face brightened into a smile and she clapped. She'd been a cheerleader in high school, and even at twenty-five hadn't completely broken old habits. "A dog! How fabulous for *you*," she said to him, flirting up a storm.

I stepped in between the two of them. "A dog, because he wants a baby and his *girlfriend* Daisy doesn't."

Kit growled at me.

So did Maria.

I was beginning to feel unwanted.

The echo chamber produced another slam of a door, quickly followed by a second and third.

"Maybe that's Nate now?" I said.

We all trekked along the back wall to the corner of the house. Coming toward us were a man and two women—one older, one younger. I recognized them immediately, seeing as how I'd just met them a week ago.

Maria stopped short. "Mr. Frye? What are you doing here?" She then turned to me. "Nina, you remember my bosses, Mr. Colin Frye and Mrs. Roz Phineus? And," she nodded to the younger woman, "Mr. Frye's wife, Verona?"

"I remember," I said, holding out my hand. I'd met them at the engagement party they'd thrown for Maria and Nate. I'd been confused as all get-out when I'd first met the bunch until Maria explained that Roz was Verona's mother and that Phineus Frye had been founded by Verona's father. Colin and Roz had taken it over after he died.

Mrs. Phineus waved Maria's introduction away. She had long red fingernails, short spiky silver hair, and sharp eagle eyes. "Call me Roz," she said in a three-pack-a-day voice. Huge princess-cut diamonds sagged on her earlobes.

"This is Kit Pipe," I told them, nudging him forward.

Verona's eyes widened, and Roz smiled brightly. "Oh my," the older woman said with a sigh as she took Kit's hand.

Kit might look scary, but he had a way with women that baffled me.

As Roz released his hand, she smiled, and I noticed her facial muscles barely moved. Obviously, she'd had a little work done.

Maria slipped her suit coat back on. "I—I wasn't aware you were coming . . ."

Colin Frye held his hands up. "Forgive us for just dropping in."

Maria smiled one of her famous charming smiles, and I swear I heard Kit sigh. I passed him the marking paint. "Why don't you go mark . . . something?"

He grinned knowingly at me.

Roz fanned herself as he went.

Verona rolled her eyes. She looked to be a few years older than me—mid-thirties—and was tall, maybe five-ten, with stringy blonde hair and a plain-Jane pale face. She had a pinched look about her, as though she spent a lot of time squinting. With a heavy sigh Verona said, "Roz, please."

I wondered what my mother would do if I called her "Celeste." Possibly she would maim me . . . or worse.

Maria fidgeted. "I'm thrilled you stopped by, Mr. Frye, but I'm not sure why."

On the younger side of forty, Colin Frye had curly golden hair, liquid brown eyes, and a slightly lopsided smile. He folded his arms across his chest, rocked back on his heels.

Verona answered for him. "We were in the area for dinner and thought we'd stop by in hopes of catching Nate. I haven't been able to reach him by phone."

Maria tipped her head, her blonde hair shimmering in the sunlight. "Nate? Why? Oh, something to do with the gala?"

To me, Maria explained, "Phineus Frye and the Kalypso are teaming up again this year to raise money for the Phineus Cancer Foundation. Nate's running things on the Kalypso side."

"And," Verona said, "after what happened to poor Brian Thatcher, Colin has put me in charge of the Phineus Frye side of things."

I looked a question at Maria. Who was Brian Thatcher? She gave a short little "not now" shake of her head.

Ohh-kay.

"She's very qualified," Colin added, as if I had been questioning it.

I hadn't been.

Roz had wandered a few feet away, watching Kit trek

across the backyard to check out the pond. He wasn't marking anything—the design plans were in my backpack.

"Nate has some paperwork I need," Verona said, deftly turning the conversation back to why they were here.

Maria's perfectly shaped eyebrows dipped. "I can check the condo, but he probably has it at work if it concerns the gala."

Nate and Maria lived together in a condo on the other side of town. They were waiting until after the wedding to move in here, their dream house, which was fully finished, furnished, and decorated.

Verona Frye's right hand went to her throat, to a beautiful strand of pearls. "I'm sorry to be a bother, but this is quite important. The caterer . . ."

"I'd call Nate myself," Maria said, "but he's not been reachable today. How soon do you need the paperwork?"

Verona let go of her pearls. "As soon as possible. Tonight would be great. There's been a bit of a snafu. The caterer has a number quite a bit smaller than the one I have. We need to verify, and Nate has the master list."

Maria pressed her lips together. "I'm sorry. I'll ask him about it when he gets home and have him get in touch with you."

Colin Frye's lips curved into a smile. "We'd appreciate it, Maria."

I could tell Maria wasn't entirely comfortable with her boss's presence.

Verona's hand went back to her pearls. "Colin, dear, we should be going if we're to keep our reservations. Roz?" she called out. "We're leaving."

Roz blew a kiss to Kit before accepting Colin's offered arm. They headed toward their car. Maria and I walked with Verona. She watched me out of the corner of her eye, making me a bit uneasy.

"Maybe," I said, "I should go help Kit."

"No!" Verona cried under her breath. She slowed her steps.

"No?"

"I was hoping to get a moment alone with you, without Colin or Roz . . . I've been reading about Taken by Surprise. I'd love for you to come do one of your 'minis' at our house. I think Colin would be tickled. Maybe this coming weekend? He'll be out of town . . ."

A "mini" was a mini makeover. One that took a couple of hours at most and usually focused solely on one trouble area instead of a whole yard.

"I'm sorry," I said. "I couldn't possibly. There's not enough time."

Maria clapped her hands (if she did it one more time, I'd be forced to get out duct tape) and said, "It would be wonderful to surprise Mr. Frye!"

"No. Time."

"If it's cost . . ." Verona said, in a way that screamed dollar signs.

"No, it's not cost. It's time. I don't have any."

"Nina, it's just a mini," Maria said. "How long could it take?"

My jaw dropped.

Maria fluttered her lashes. "He *is* my boss, Nina."

She added the smile.

I sighed. Heavily.

"Think of it as a wedding gift for me."

"Uh . . ." I said, opening my arms toward her backyard. True, I wasn't footing the six-figure bill for the work, but it was my design . . . and my crew who would be implementing the plans.

"An additional gift."

How did I get myself into these situations? "Call my office," I told Verona. "I'll see what I can do."

I thought Maria might do a cartwheel.

"Thanks so much," Verona said to me in a whisper as we reached the car.

Colin helped his wife into the front seat. "Have Nate call us when he gets in, Maria," Colin said. "This is a quite important matter. I don't want any guests going hungry."

"I will."

He turned to me. "Pleasure, Ms. Quinn."

Maria and I watched the car roll down the long winding drive. I turned toward Maria.

"You love me," she said.

"I'm still trying to remember why."

The sounds of "Love Story" filled the air. I groaned. Only Maria would have "Love Story" as a ring tone on her cell phone.

Glancing at the readout, she smiled. Flipping open the phone, she said, "Nate?"

Her smile faded into a grim line. "No, he's not with me," she said after listening for a while. "No, I haven't. I've been trying to reach him myself."

I tried not to eavesdrop, but some things couldn't be helped.

After she said, "I will," and snapped her phone closed, she looked at me, her eyes filled with a bit of panic.

"That was Nate's secretary," she said. "She's worried because Nate went to breakfast early this morning with his boss and has yet to come back."

Two

Despite her three-inch heels, Maria stomped her foot like a petulant two year old. "He's run out on me!"

"You don't know that," I calmly tried to explain. "There could be any number of reasons why he's late. Car trouble, for one."

"And another?" she asked, leveling an icy glare at me.

I said weakly, "Traffic?"

She waved her arms like a whirligig. The sleeves of her Chanel suit coat rode up to her elbows. "He got cold feet!" She stomped some more. "Men just don't know what commitment means."

I tended to agree. I'd been married for seven years to Kevin. Happy years, until I'd found his partner's lipstick on his boxers.

I'd kicked him out, and he'd gone, leaving me the one thing I never realized how much I wanted—his son, Riley.

At fifteen, Riley was as surly as they came, and we continuously butted heads. It wasn't until recently that we both realized just how much we cared about each other. Nevertheless, we were still doing that butting heads thing. Lately it was over his sudden inability to tell time. He'd missed his curfew a handful of times in the last couple of weeks. I still didn't know what to do about it, especially since I was a little time-challenged myself. It's hard to give a teenager a "do as I say, not as I do" lecture.

Dried soil crunched under my Timberlands. "Could be he got a flat tire."

She flipped her hair back. "Claire Battiste has been eyeing him for a while. Maybe he finally gave in."

"Claire Battiste?"

"Nate's boss. You met her."

"I did?"

"At our engagement party. Tall, blonde, early thirties, flirted with every man in the room."

"Oh her. I didn't meet her, but I saw her." It had been hard to miss her. Mini-mini-skirt, mile high legs, and every pair of male eyes watching her.

"Well, she's . . . she's . . ." Maria's chin shot in the air. "I'll just come out and say it."

Lord help us all.

"She's a hussy."

"Maria, I'm sure the CEO of the Kalypso isn't a hussy."

"H-u-s-s-y."

"Okay, okay, she's a ho, but that doesn't mean Nate's cheating on you."

Hands on her hips, Maria mumbled under her breath about tramps and office romances. She paced on her tiptoes, so her heels wouldn't snag on the crusty, chunky sun-baked ground. As she pivoted, she zeroed in on me. "I should have seen this coming. He's not been himself for over a week now. When I asked him about it, he brushed it off." She cleared her throat. "'Don't worry, baby, everything's fine,'" she mimicked, doing quite a good job of imitating Nate's son-of-a-politician's voice. "'I love you, baby; I'd never do anything to jeopardize our relationship.'" She let out a small primal cry. "That lyin', stinkin', rotten, no good, two timin', backstabbin' son of a—"

"Maria!" I grabbed her hands so she wouldn't take a swing at me by mistake.

Her blue eyes widened, focusing on me.

Calmly, I said, "How about we don't get worked up until we know for certain what's going on?"

Footsteps crunched behind us. We turned. Kit came to a dead halt when he saw us. Abruptly, he turned around, walked away. Angry women terrified him, and Maria was fuming.

"There's no need to get upset when we don't know if there's anything to get upset over."

"She's obviously seduced him. Men are weak."

"Look," I said, holding up Maria's left hand. A huge three-carat diamond set in platinum dwarfed her ring finger. "Would Nate give this absolutely gorgeous ring to anyone he wasn't planning happily-ever-after with?"

She held her hand out so the diamond could sparkle in the sunshine. A serene smile came over her face. Crisis averted as she beamed at the ring. "It *is* beautiful, isn't it?"

I sighed. "Stunning."

She obviously missed the mockery in my voice since she said, "Yes, yes it is."

"Why don't you go home?" I suggested. "Take a long bath, do that waxy thing you do to your hands—"

"Paraffin."

She said it as though I was an imbecile.

"*Paraffin* and relax. I'm sure Nate will be calling to check in any minute now."

She pouted. "You think?"

"I know."

"Maybe you're right." She examined her long fingers. "My hands *are* a little dry. The heat, you know."

"Yeah, the heat." I ushered her toward her car, trying to keep my own hands hidden. They were chapped and cracked and rough from years of playing in the dirt.

"Listen," I said, "I've got to get back to the office, then I'm running Riley to work, but after that I can grab Ana and come by, maybe bring a movie with us."

This was a huge sacrifice. Maria loved horror movies—the kind that usually gave me heebies for weeks.

"Don't you have your fitting tonight?" she asked.

Damn. I was hoping she wouldn't remember. "Oh, is that tonight?"

Her stiletto heel punctured the ground as she stomped again. "Nina! The wedding is next Saturday. You must—must!—get your dress fitted. Tonight. Armande is doing us a big favor by keeping the shop open."

Oh yes. Wouldn't want to upset Armande, would I? I bit back a groan and a comment about there not being a wedding if Nate didn't show up. I didn't want her to freak out again. However, I indulged in some mental math: A wedding minus a groom equaled no need for me to get a dress. This could be a prime example of my father's silver lining theory.

"I'll be there," I said.

She batted her long eyelashes. "Then after *that* you can come by with a movie."

A night of torture, that's what this would be.

She cooed as she opened her car door. "You're going to love your dress. It's perfect for you."

"I can just imagine."

As I stepped into my office, I found Tam seated in her huge red rattan chair, hole puncher gripped tightly, and looking more than a bit frazzled.

When I spied the group of men in the waiting area, I knew why. There were seven of them sitting there, each with one leg folded across the other, reading an assortment of magazines—everything from *Home & Garden* to *Highlights for Children* to *Reader's Digest*.

They looked fresh out of a Stepford movie. Almost identical, they appeared to be mid- to late thirties, had buzz cuts, were freshly shaven, and wore colorful variations of oxford shirts and Dockers.

A shiver ran down my spine.

Tam came up behind me. "I told you they were scary," she whispered.

"I see what you mean."

I was desperate for help, what with Maria's yard and all the other jobs I had lined up for the summer. But by the looks of this lot, I needed to keep looking. The whole bunch of them together looked like they weighed less than Kit.

I had to wonder what their arrest records were. Had they all gotten out of hand at a geek convention? Honest to goodness, three of them had pocket protectors.

Tam shifted nervously. "Should I send them all away?"

"No, I'll talk to them. Ana must have had some reason for sending them all here." What it was, I couldn't begin to imagine. April Fool's came to mind, but it was two months too late. "Call the first guy into my office."

"All right," she said reluctantly. "Here, take this." She pushed the hole punch into my hand.

"Why?" I asked.

Her eyebrows jumped up. "For protection, of course."

As I walked into my office, I bit back a laugh because she was perfectly serious.

After six of the seven interviews, I was wondering if Ana was playing a prank on me, April Fool's or not. Seemed most of my interviewees had been arrested for petty theft. The large company they worked for had cracked down on missing office supplies and made an example of these men who had taken home a box of paper clips here, a pen there.

Now they were out of jobs, most with families to feed, bills to pay.

That instinctive maternal side of me wished I could help them all. Realistically, I didn't think I could even help one of them—and I doubted any of them could help me. I didn't have the time to train them or listen to them cry when they got their first blister.

My cell buzzed as I waited for the last man to come in. I fished it out of my backpack, groaning at the caller ID screen.

"Maria?"

Sniffle. "Still no word from him."

"He loves you," I said, trying to reassure.

"Then where is he?"

"Shopping?"

"He doesn't shop."

"Canoeing?"

"Nee-nah!"

At her wail, I immediately felt contrite. "Listen, Maria, I don't know where he is or what he's doing, but he's going to show up. He loves you too much to ever let you go."

A quartet of sniffles echoed across the line. "Do you really think so?"

"I really do."

"Okay, then. I'll give him until midnight; then I get mad."

The echo of her slamming the phone rang in my ear. I hoped Nate got home soon. I didn't know how long Maria could hold her temper in check.

I snapped my phone closed and looked up to find one of the Stepford men standing in the doorway.

"The door was open," he said. "I didn't mean to eavesdrop."

"It's okay. Just my sister."

"Sounded serious." Across from me, a chair groaned as he sat. "Someone's missing?"

I smiled to ease the concern in his gray-green eyes. "Temporarily misplaced." Picking up a pen, I wondered what Nate was doing, where he was. This just wasn't like him, and I couldn't help but worry a little.

I'm a worrier by nature.

I reached across the desk. "I'm Nina Quinn."

His handshake was firm, unlike the other men who had been in.

"Leo Barker."

Little ink spots dotted my blotter as I tapped my pen. "So, Leo, what kind of landscaping experience do you have?"

I steeled myself for the usual, "None."

"I worked for Decker and Sons all through college."

My pen stilled. I sized him up. Truth was, he wasn't as Stepford as the others. There was a little bulk to his arms, his shoulders, underneath the blue button-down he wore. Alleluia! There might be some hope yet.

"What did you do for old man Decker?"

"Grunt work, mostly." He smiled wickedly. "I'm killer with a spade."

I laughed. "Good to know." Flipping through his paperwork, I added, "But college was a long time ago." Fifteen years, if his résumé was up-to-date.

"I've got twenty acres of land in Lebanon. I like to play farmer on weekends. I'm still in shape, if that's what you're wondering."

I could see that now as I took a closer look. Energy surrounded him, and even though he was leaning back in the chair, he looked as though he could pounce at any second.

It would have been unnerving if not for his crinkly I'm-a-friendly-guy smile.

"If you're interested," I said, "and provided your references check out, I'll start you off part-time, see how you fit in. If you fit well, then I'll bump you up to full-time."

"That include benefits?"

"Yep. All the bells and whistles."

After haggling a bit about a starting wage, we shook hands. "Let's plan on you starting tomorrow," I said. "That's assuming, of course, that your references pan out." I'd have Tam check them right away.

He grinned. "Of course. I'll be here."

After he left, Tam scurried in. "I'm glad to see them go. Should I put an ad in the classifieds?"

"I hired that last one—Leo Barker."

"What!?" Her tight curls bounced as she stepped back, hand on her heart. "He was the scariest of them all. He's the *winker*!"

I was surprised by her reaction. "He's qualified."

"He's trouble."

I hesitated at her adamancy. Tam was a good judge of character, where I—well . . . I wasn't. Had she possibly seen something I hadn't?

"He's starting off part-time. Just give him a chance."

She made the sign of the cross. "Call him back and rescind your offer." Picking up the phone on my desk, she added, "I'll dial."

I wrested the receiver from her death grip. "What is it about him you don't like?"

She shuddered. "I don't know. There's just . . . something."

"It'll be fine."

"Oh, Nina. I don't like this at all. Not one bit." She backtracked out of my office, closed the door behind her.

Slumping back in my chair, I flipped through Leo Barker's résumé. Thirty-five. Went to college at the University of Cincinnati. Worked—or used to work—at Procter & Gamble.

I straightened.

P&G? The other Stepford men hadn't worked for them.

Further rummaging through his résumé left me with more questions. He'd never been arrested, according to the box he'd left blank.

Which meant he'd never been on probation.

So, if Ana hadn't sent him . . . who had?

Three

As usual, I was late picking up Riley. I'd never cut it as a professional chauffeur—and was failing miserably as Riley's. Punctuality really wasn't one of my strong points. Something Riley had apparently picked up from me, since he wasn't outside when I pulled up in front of my house.

I honked.

My modest bungalow-style house sat in Freedom, Ohio—a growing suburb wedged between Cincinnati and Dayton. Unlike the booming developments in this area, my neighborhood had been long settled, and was appropriately nicknamed the "Mill." As in "gossip mill." The median age of residents around here averaged sixty-five.

I'd inherited my house from my aunt Chi-Chi right after I met Kevin. I loved living here even though everyone knew everything about everyone.

In my sideview mirror I saw Flash Leonard hobbling across the street, his tattered robe flapping.

Flash, like Nate, used to be a baseball player, but only made it semi-pro. He'd gotten the nickname because batters used to say his fastball went by in a flash. Nowadays, the name fit because, with his robe hanging open, he was always flashing people. I'd yet to figure out if it was intentional or not.

I lowered my window as he got closer.

"Nina," he said to me, once he reached my truck.

"Hey, Flash."

I caught movement in my rearview mirror. Mr. and Mrs. Mustard shuffled up the driveway. Around here, Jacob Mustard was known affectionately as the "Colonel," not because of his WWII decorations, but because no one could resist the reference to Clue, my favorite board game. It was rumored that he and his wife, Margaret, had separate bedrooms—and speculation was high as to why. Right now neighborhood polls favored his snoring over her insomnia.

Mrs. Mustard crowded Flash in my window. She was small, with frizzy gray hair, a sweet smile, and a big heart. "Did Flash tell you?"

"I didn't get the chance," Flash complained.

"What?" I said.

The Colonel nudged his head in. Which wasn't hard. He was taller than both of them, even with the slight bend in his back. His hair was a mousy brown sprinkled with silver. His brown eyes narrowed, the wrinkles surrounding them nearly swallowing them whole. "Mrs. Offel."

I'd always called her "Mrs. Awful." She was a nasty old bat. "What about her?"

"Someone broke into her house last night."

"Another break-in!?" I'd lost count as to how many this made. Definitely double digits.

"He got away," Flash said, smoothing back the lock of salt and pepper (more salt than pepper) hair that always fell onto his forehead. "Again."

Out of the corner of my eye I saw Mrs. Daasch walking her dog, Loofa. Mrs. Carmichael and Miss Maisie flanked her. If I didn't get out of here soon I'd be surrounded.

Thankfully, I saw Riley come around the corner, chatting with my nosy neighbor Mr. Cabrera. When Mr. Cabrera spotted me, he practically sprinted over, elbowing everyone else out of the way, and then shooed them off.

Uh-oh. When Mr. Cabrera shooed, he had something serious on his mind. I called out my good-byes as everyone wandered away.

"Miz Quinn," Mr. Cabrera said. We'd been neighbors for eight years. He'd yet to call me Nina. I doubted he ever would.

I braced myself for a battery of the usual questions. His notorious talent for procuring gossip had earned him the head seat at the Mill's weekly cribbage game. He wanted to keep it. "Mr. Cabrera."

"Fine day," he said.

"Beautiful."

Riley hopped into the passenger seat, buckled his seat belt. No hello, not that I had expected one.

Mr. Cabrera shifted foot to foot. I braced myself for a full-blown interrogation on my separation from Kevin, our divorce plans, and was surprised when he said, "I don't suppose you've heard about Ursula?"

I gasped. "She didn't . . ." My voice dropped. "You know . . ."

With a click of his dentures, Mr. Cabrera's jaw set. "Not that I know of."

"Sorry." I winced. "Bad habit."

I'd played matchmaker for Mr. Cabrera and Ursula Krauss, aka Brickhouse Krauss, a month ago. Once upon a time Mrs. Krauss had been my evil English Lit teacher. I'd recently been reacquainted with her through my job—her daughter had hired TBS to do a mini makeover at her mother's landominium, which was basically a condo with a yard. And I kinda-sorta forgot to mention to Brickhouse that Mr. Cabrera's lady friends had a nasty habit of up and dying while dating him.

His fuzzy white eyebrows dipped. "She broke up with me. It's been two days now."

"She hear the rumors?"

Riley leaned in. "I'm late."

Mr. Cabrera went right on talking. "Let's face it, Miz Quinn, they're not rumors. I'm jinxed. It's just as well my dear sweet Ursula dumped me. I wouldn't want to see anything happen to her."

I was struggling with the usage of "dear" and "sweet" in any context related to Mrs. Krauss. She was as cranky as they came. Still, I felt bad for Mr. Cabrera. He'd really fallen hard for the old battle-axe.

Mr. Cabrera thumped the window frame. "I said, I really miss her."

Cringing as the words slipped out of my mouth, I asked, "Do you want me to call her?"

"Late," Riley singsonged.

"Would you?" Mr. Cabrera's bright blue eyes widened. His whole face lit.

I let out a sigh. "I'm not promising anything, but I'll call."

The seat belt strained as Riley leaned over, held his hand out, palm up. Mr. Cabrera dropped a five dollar bill into it.

My head jerked between the two of them. "What's going on?"

Riley pocketed the money. "I told him you'd do it. He didn't think you would. So we bet on it."

"Mr. Cabrera! How could you?"

His eyebrows danced. "Best money I ever spent."

I looked to Riley. He was smirking. "It was easy money," he said. "You're gullible."

Hmmph.

I shoved the truck into reverse and shot out of the driveway.

We drove in silence for a little bit before I glanced at Riley. "Am I really that gullible?"

"Yes."

There went the kick-ass Rambette image I had of myself.

"When are you going to get a new car?" he asked.

My old Toyota had recently gone to the big junkyard in the sky after a mishap with an oncoming train. Luckily, I'd escaped with just a few scars and a broken pinkie. "My insurance check is due any day now. Why?"

"I can get my permit soon."

Oh, God. Riley on the roads. Maybe I'd hold on to that insurance check for a while.

"How's the job?" I asked, quickly changing the subject. He'd recently gotten a job bagging groceries at a local supermarket.

"Fine."

If it was up to me, he wouldn't be working at all. I'd keep him home, where I could keep an eye on him, keep him safe, which was a laugh since it seemed I had trouble keeping myself safe lately. But his therapist recommended he get a job to occupy his time, to keep his mind off the fact that a couple of weeks ago he'd been willing to shoot someone to protect me. A someone who was certifiable and trying to kill *me* at the time. It didn't matter that he hadn't actually harmed anyone—it was still weighing on his mind.

The doctor also told Kevin and me that Riley needed to work through his problems his own way. But it was hard not to interfere when I could see how much he was hurting.

I met Riley when he was eight. He'd been angry with the world for taking his mom, who had died when he was a toddler in a mysterious boating accident that no one liked to talk about. We've had our ups and downs, but I felt that I was finally getting the hang of this mothering thing. I just hoped I didn't screw it up somehow.

The silence in the car was driving me nuts. I turned on the radio, flipped to the Oldies channel. I was an Oldies junkie.

"Just shoot me," Riley mumbled.

I was just about to launch into the talents of Del Shannon when I realized what Riley had said. *Just shoot me*. And he had been kidding. He must be farther along in his therapy than I imagined if he could joke about shooting anything. I smiled.

"The new job seems to be keeping you out late," I ventured, trying to ease into my, "Where have you been at night?" lecture.

"Have you ever bagged people's groceries?" he asked.

I caught how he'd expertly steered me away from my planned speech. I let it go for now because so rarely did he open up a topic of conversation.

"Uh, no."

"Do you know how often I have to say 'paper or plastic?' "

"Not really."

"Not to mention the little old ladies who want the paper *in* the plastic," he said, groaning. "Besides, nothing exciting ever happens there. I think I need a new job."

He cracked the window and the wind tousled his hair. He'd let it grow and had, thank God above, gotten rid of the dyed black with bleached stripes. Now it was platinum blond. Still bad, but tolerable.

"Excitement is overrated."

"To you maybe," he said, still looking out the window.

"And what's that supposed to mean?"

"It means you're old," he said, a hint of a smile lifting his cheek. "Old people don't like excitement."

Slapping my head, I said, "I must have forgotten. Chalk it up to having a senior moment."

He smiled. Riley actually smiled. Miracle of miracles.

"Oh," he said. "I forgot to tell you that Grandma Cel called."

"And?"

"And she said to tell you that your uncle Giuseppe and aunt Carlotta are flying in early for the wedding."

"And?" I repeated, already dreading what was coming next.

"She's sending them to stay with us, since she doesn't have the room. They'll be here Friday night."

I nearly choked. Just shoot *me*.

"Maria hates me."

My mother's voice floated over the dressing room door. "She most certainly does not."

"She might," my cousin Ana piped in.

I heard a muted *ugh* and figured my mother had elbowed Ana.

I slid the latch on the door and stepped out, heading toward the full-length mirror.

My mother and Ana stepped up behind me, each of our reflections taking up one section of the trifold mirror.

We all wore the same horrified expression.

My mother brought a quavering manicured hand to cover her mouth.

To keep from laughing, Ana was biting her lip so hard tears slipped from the corner of her eyes.

"Ana, *chérie*, this isn't amusing," my mother chastised. My mother called everyone "*chérie*." It was her way of reminding people that she had been born in France and had class.

I blinked at my reflection. Maria was out of her mind.

Plumb crazy. Demented. Loco. Utterly, thoroughly delusional. I closed my eyes trying to come up with more adjectives, but came up empty. Trauma must be setting in.

Opening my eyes, I found my reflection hadn't changed. I turned to Ana. "You could have warned me."

Wiping moisture from the corners of her eyes, she snuffled. "I did."

Reluctantly, I remembered she had.

I turned to my mother for her reaction. It was unlike Celeste Madeline Chambeau Ceceri to keep quiet for so long. She always had something to say, even when I didn't want to hear it—which was often. "Mom?"

She stared into the trifold mirror, mouth agape, her bright blue eyes wide.

I followed her doe-in-the-headlights gaze back to the mirror. Shifting my weight, I hoped to blur the horrifying image. No blurrage, just the billowing of the dress's full skirt—a dizzying palette of shimmery green and toad brown.

My mother finally found her voice. "I think you look . . ." She swallowed audibly. "Interesting."

Oh God. When my mother couldn't find something nice to say, then I knew it was bad. Very, very bad.

"I'm going to need a new dress." I stepped off the platform, simultaneously reaching for the row of lime green pearls that marched down my chest.

Ana leaned against the mirror, wiping away streaks of mascara from her eyes as my mother said, "Out of the question. There's not enough time."

I stood firm. "I am not wearing this . . . this . . ." I couldn't even say the word "dress." It looked more like the result of an ice cream truck crashing into an army fatigue factory. ". . . thing," I finished.

"It's not so bad," Ana said, a twinkle in her dark eyes.

"Hmmph."

My mother's hands flew as she spoke. "The dress, perhaps, needs some tailoring, is all. It's haute couture, you know."

"Don't care. Not wearing it," I said, slamming the dressing room door behind me. I worked the pearl buttons loose. Sliding the dress over my shoulders, I let it puddle around my feet, kicked it into the corner for good measure.

Pulling my T-shirt over my head, I said, "We need to find another dress."

The wedding was next Saturday. There was time. Lots of it. Almost two weeks of it. There had to be something off some rack somewhere that would fit me.

My mother's voice carried over the stall door. "You have no other choice," she said. "Rocks and hard places, Nina. Rocks and hard places."

Groaning, I picked up the balled dress and pulled open the door.

"If you hadn't procrastinated so—" She broke off.

I raised an eyebrow, the one that had the thin six-inch scar above it—one of the results of that run-in with the train. The doctor assured me it was still healing and would fade over time. I was still trying to decide if I believed him.

Ana coughed. She hooked a thumb over her shoulder. "Think I'll go flirt with Armande."

"Coward," I said.

Her dark hair shimmered as she cocked her head. "So?"

As she scampered off, contrition threaded through my mother's blue eyes. "You know what I meant, Nina."

I knew. I *had* procrastinated, but that little matter of me almost being killed hadn't helped my time crunch at all.

I tied the laces on my Keds. "We have time to find a new dress."

She tapped the pointy toe of her strapless shoe. "When?"

I bit my lip. She had a point. I'd never been so swamped at work, and with Riley . . .

My mother gestured with her arms, much like Maria had earlier. "Your sister's counting on you. You must get this dress fitted today."

"It fits," I growled. "But I am not wearing it."

My mother swore under her breath in fluent French. I was blissfully glad I'd never learned the language.

"You must. For Maria."

I wondered if Maria had heard from Nate yet. Something about him going missing was eating at me. It was just so out of character.

My mother looked at me with those eyes. The ones that said, "I am your mother. I gave birth to you. I will guilt you for the rest of your life if you do not do this for me."

I sighed and looked away. I figured if I didn't look directly at her, she had no power.

My mother hung the hideous dress on a hanger. It dangled, taunting me.

I shuddered. My old flannel pillowcase looked better than that thing.

"Nina."

Damn, damn, damn. Now she'd added the Voice. The one that could make the Leaning Tower of Pisa straighten just to please her sense of style.

My mother continued to give me the evil eye. "Listen to Ma-ma . . . it is for one day only."

"The pictures will last a lifetime." And the memories of that dress would undoubtedly give me nightmares for years to come.

As I came out of the dressing area, I noticed that the bridal boutique was empty save my mother, Ana, Armande, and me. Armande was holding both Ana's hands and looking adoringly into her eyes. The man knew how to charm.

Ana spotted us, murmured something, and Armande kissed both her cheeks.

Decorated in nauseatingly frilly tulle and chiffon, the shop was designed to conjure images of joy, of happily-ever-afters.

As if there were such things.

I tried not to be such a cynic. It was true my beliefs in marriage were somewhat tainted, what with the way my Kevin had cheated on me and all, but I supposed true love did exist. Somewhere. Far away.

Again, the thought of skipping town popped into my thoughts. Taking Riley and leaving it all behind—the wedding, work, Kevin.

Hmmm.

"Don't even think about leaving town," my mother warned.

How did she do that? I hated that about her.

"Leaving town?" Ana moseyed over. "You're going somewhere?"

I smiled. "Disney World, maybe."

Color tinged my mother's cheeks.

"When?" Ana asked.

I could sense Ana already mentally packing her bags. "Tomorrow."

"I'd have to call in sick, but I could make it."

The French swearing started again, and Ana's mouth dropped open as she stared at my mother. "Aunt Cel!"

As my mother began rambling about her weak heart (which she didn't have), I rolled my eyes.

I felt a poke in my ribs and looked up into Ana's mischievous eyes. "Did I tell you," she said to me, "that my mother was flying in early for the wedding?"

Color infused my mother's pale complexion. The feud between her and my father's sister Rosetta, Ana's mother, hadn't diminished any since the summer Aunt Rosetta moved her family into our house, sans Uncle Sal, over a decade ago.

My mother knew how to hold a grudge.

Innocently, I asked, "When?"

"Wednesday."

"Wednesday? As in the day after tomorrow? Or next Wednesday?"

Ana smiled wide and bright. The feud between our mothers had become a source of entertainment in our family over the years. "The day after tomorrow."

French cursing filled the air as my mother put her hand over her heart dramatically.

Armande's cheeks pinkened. "Oh my," he murmured.

My mother looked at him. "My dear friend, do you have any whiskey?"

My mother followed Armande into a back room, then came back a second later with three glasses and a bottle of whiskey in her hands. She slumped into an overstuffed floral couch. Looking up at us, she offered up her glass in a silent toast and gulped the whiskey back.

After the day I'd had, I knew the feeling.

Ana poured herself half a glass and offered the bottle to me. I knelt in front of the glass coffee table and filled mine halfway.

The phone rang in the background.

"Mrs. Quinn?" Armande said, his hand covering the mouthpiece.

The look on his face told me that half a glass of whiskey wasn't going to do me any good. I poured it to the rim, took a fortifying sip for good measure. Okay, two sips, but who was counting?

I took the glass with me to pick up the phone.

"There is a very hysterical woman on the phone asking for you," Armande whispered.

I reached for the receiver, not sure what to expect. Who knew I was here? And why wouldn't they call my cell phone? I patted my pocket, suddenly realizing I'd left it in the truck. "Hello?"

Sniffles echoed in the background. "Nina?"

"Maria?" I whispered so my mother wouldn't hear. I glanced over my shoulder at her. She continued to slug courage from her glass. There was no need to worry her about this Nate business if there was no need.

"What's wrong?" I hoped to heaven that fancy wax hadn't burned down her condo.

"I shot him."

My glass slipped from my hand.

I heard my mother murmur something to Ana about me not being able to hold my liquor. I turned so they couldn't read my lips.

"Nate?" I whispered. "You shot Nate?" His name practically stuck in my throat.

"Good God, no." I heard more sniffling and a few hiccups. "The man."

I rolled the phone cord around my finger. "What man?"

"The man who broke into my house."

Longingly, I looked at the whiskey staining the floor. "Call the cops," I said. "I'll be right there."

Four

After dropping off my mother, I drove to Maria's condo, wondering the whole way who it was Maria had shot. I'd taken Ana with me mostly because after I told her what had happened, she'd refused to get out of my car *and* threatened to tell my mother I'd lied to her about why I had to leave the bridal shop in such a hurry.

I pulled into a parking spot in the condo complex and looked around at the cops roaming the common areas; searching for clues, I assumed.

Ana jumped out of my car, her eyes wide as Frisbees. Over the roof, she said, "There's Mike Loney. He's newly single, right?"

I barely heard her. My eyes were glued to the front door of Maria's condo. Kevin was standing under the portico with Ginger Ho, er, Barlow, his partner—and lover.

"I think so," I murmured, not wanting to stare at Kevin but not being able to help it.

Ana followed my gaze. "Oh no."

"It's okay. Really it is. I need to get used to seeing him out and about. It'll get easier once the divorce is final. Right?"

She thumped her chest. "Am I supposed to know? 'Cuz you're looking at me like I'm supposed to know."

I took a tentative step toward Maria's front door. Good, my knees held. "You *are* divorced."

"Does that make me the expert? The Emily Post for screwups?"

I sighed. When she went off on a tangent there was only one way to distract her. "Hottie at five o'clock. No ring."

Ana spun, sashayed away.

Kevin looked up as I approached. Talk about awkward. His eyes filled with a tenderness he had no right to possess since he was sleeping with someone else.

Ginger hooked a thumb over her shoulder. "I'll go, uh—" She disappeared around the side of the building.

"Hey," Kevin said to me.

"Hey."

Scintillating.

"What're you doing here?" he asked.

I was desperately trying to ignore the fact that he could still make my knees weak. I hated that about him. And about me. I should be stronger. I was woman, hear me roar—and all that crap. "Maria called me. Is she okay?"

He shrugged. "Fine. A little rattled. She's hitting the cookie dough."

Uh-oh. Maria had been on a diet for the past month, trying to fit into a wedding dress two sizes too small.

"What about the guy?"

Kevin's steel-toed shoe dragged against the wooden planks. "Gone."

Ack. She'd gone and killed someone. "Maria won't be charged, right? It was clearly self-defense."

Kevin's right eyebrow arched. "I can't imagine the guy will press charges, seeing as how he was the one in her house."

Blue and red flashes lit the side of his face. Stubble covered his strong jaw and shadowed his cheeks. Dark crescent-shaped lines sat under his eyes.

He looked like crap.

It did my heart good.

"Press charges?" I repeated after his words sunk in. I tipped my head, thoroughly confused. "How can he press charges if he's de—"

"Nina!" Maria, clad in a silk robe, launched herself at me. "Oh, it was horrible, just horrible."

Kevin hid a smile behind his hand. "Awful," he murmured.

Maria stomped her foot. She stomped better than anyone I knew. "This isn't funny."

Kevin's sparkling green eyes sobered, but his smile was still cemented to his lips.

"Really, Kevin, a man was shot." I took Maria's hand. "It's okay. It was self-defense."

"He was going through my things," Maria explained. "What was I supposed to do?"

"I know. Now shut up. Don't say anything more. We'll get you an attorney. It was self-defense, pure and simple. When did you get a gun?"

"What gun?" Maria asked, her pale eyebrows dipping.

A chuckle escaped Kevin's tightly pressed lips.

I looked between the two of them, feeling like I was missing something. "What? What's so funny?"

Hands held up and palms out, Kevin said, "Nothing. Nothing at all."

Maria pouted in his direction. "I never did like you."

My radar went off. Maria adored Kevin. "What am I missing?"

Kevin straightened to his full six-foot-three-inch frame. "There was no gun involved, Nina."

"What? I thought there was a shooting? What is going on!?" I was not amused. Not at all.

Maria smiled. "There was a shooting. Technically. I do have the best aim around."

Kevin wore a cocky half smile. He nudged Maria. "Tell her what you shot the guy with."

Maria's bottom lip puckered out.

"Maria!"

She murmured something under her breath.

"What? What was that?"

"Hair spray, okay? I shot him with hair spray."

I closed my eyes, leaned back against a column. This wasn't happening. "Hair spray?"

Maria managed to whimper and look beautiful at the same time. "It was all I had."

I looked at Kevin. "And by 'gone,' I assume you literally mean gone, as in he ran?"

"Faster than Maria from a tag sale."

"Hey!" she said, stomping again.

"Did you recognize him?" I asked her.

"No. He had a mask on, one of those horrible ones that mat your hair and leave little creases on your face."

"A ski mask," Kevin put in.

Glancing at him, I found he was smiling wide. I shot him a this-is-not-funny glare, but it had no effect whatsoever.

I turned my focus back to Maria and asked, "He take anything?"

"My peace of mind. I was this close," she held up two fingers, "to forgetting that Nate had run out on me!"

Kevin's dark eyebrows shot up. "Nate bailed?"

I hedged. "We don't know that for sure."

"Well, he's not back, is he?" Maria paced the small landing. "Where was he when a crazy madman came in and attacked me?"

"I thought you weren't hurt."

"Physically no, but emotionally, I'm a wreck. I've been mentally abused." She flipped her hair back over her shoulder and checked her reflection on the front door's glass pane.

"Yeah, I can tell."

This was ridiculous. I'd practically had a stroke when she told me she'd shot someone. I'd rushed over here, breaking several traffic ordinances, and above all I'd lied to my mother about why I was in such a rush to drop her off. And it was just a matter of time before she figured it out and punished me in that way only mothers could.

One of the uniformed officers called Kevin away. I watched him go for a second. I tried to ignore that ache in my chest. Despite my hectic schedule, I was actually grateful I was too busy to dwell on the end of my marriage.

"He *could* have attacked me," Maria was saying, running her hands over her body as if checking for injuries, and looking like she enjoyed it.

I held a pissy comment in check. She was right—she could have been hurt . . . or worse. Letting that thought simmer, I felt my anger slowly fade. Besides, it was impossible to stay mad at Maria. She had that way about her.

"Why don't you pack a bag?" I suggested. "I can bring you over to your new house. You can't stay here tonight."

She pouted. "All right."

Inside, her condo looked like it was moving day. All the furniture had already been moved to the other house, and boxes, both full and empty, filled the living and dining rooms in neat stacks. Nothing looked disturbed. One of the French doors leading onto the back patio was ajar, the wood around the handle splintered. "Is that how he got in?" I asked.

Maria nodded. "Kevin said it looked like he used a crowbar. I need to get someone to come fix it before I leave." She laughed, and there was a slightly hysterical edge to the sound. "Don't want anyone to break in."

A yawn threatened to escape, and I clamped my lips closed. "You go pack. I'll call Kit and see if he can help us out."

Tears brimmed along her eyelashes. "Thanks, Nina."

"Hey, everything will be okay." I shook fake pom-poms. "Rah. Rah."

There was a reason I never made Saint Valentine's cheerleading squad.

She smiled at me, wiped her eyes, and headed for the stairs, looking a little lost and forlorn. I wasn't used to having our roles reversed. She'd always been the cheery one.

Using my cell, I called Kit, who promised to be over in no time after a quick stop at the local home supply store.

I poked around Maria's place as I called to check on Riley. He should have gotten home over an hour ago, and with his late night disappearing acts, I wanted to make sure he was where he was supposed to be.

He answered on the third ring, sounding a little breathless. "H'lo?"

"Ry? You just getting in?"

"Uh, yeah. Stopped at McDonald's after work."

At least he'd eaten. My dinner with Ana had gone right out the window, and my stomach was starting to yell at me.

"I'm going to be a little late," I told him.

He didn't ask for details, and I didn't fill him in.

"I'll probably be in bed, so keep it down," he said, a hint of teasing in his deepening voice.

Squatting, I looked closer at Maria's damaged door. It was a little scary to think that a simple crowbar could make locks so useless. "Don't forget to lock the doors—use the dead bolts too—and set the alarm."

Our neighborhood burglar hadn't been caught yet, and as I glanced around Maria's place, I wondered if maybe he was marking other territories.

I said good-night to Riley and began snooping around. Cardboard boxes of various sizes lined the walls of her dining and living rooms. All but a few things remained in her kitchen cupboards and drawers. Just the basic necessities to get through life for the few days before the wedding.

I moseyed my way into Nate and Maria's study, absently wondering what was taking her so long. How much could she possibly need for one night?

I stopped short just inside the study's door. Boxes marked OFFICE had been sliced open and dumped onto the floor. Papers, file folders, pens, and other desk clutter covered the gleaming hardwood.

I bent down, scooped up a pile of papers and leafed through them. Pages and pages of Maria's Phineus Frye letterhead were mixed in with Nate's Kalypso memos and reports.

"He was looking for something," a voice said.

I let out a small "eek" and jumped, my breath sharply lodging somewhere between my ribs and my collarbone.

Kevin leaned against the doorway, arms folded, his triceps straining against his T-shirt. His gun holster was nestled next to his ribs under his left arm, and his badge was clipped to the waistband of his jeans.

I rounded up my breath and willed my brain not to notice how good he looked despite the circles under his eyes.

"Did he find it?" I asked.

"Maria says nothing was taken. Her computer, laptop, the expensive hideous sculpture . . . it's all here still, and the guy's arms were empty when he fled the house after Maria doused him."

"He could have stuffed something like this in his pants," I said, holding up a file.

"True. Maria said she won't know if anything's missing from the files until she goes through them, but I don't think she'll find anything gone."

"Why not?"

He pushed away from the door, taking a step toward me. Mentally, I restrained the feeling to go to him, to wrap my arms around him, feel him, touch him . . .

Ginger, I reminded myself.

My head snapped up. He was gazing at me, a softness in his eyes. Or that could have been my imagination because when he blinked the emotion was gone, replaced with the mask he slipped on when he worked.

"He comes in," Kevin said, "comes straight to the office. Doesn't stop and poke around the boxes in the other room marked 'crystal' or 'silver.' He knows what he's looking for. Knows where to find it. Or thinks he does. But it's not here in the office, so he goes for her briefcase."

This was the most he'd talked to me in weeks.

"But that's not here either," he continued. "Which forces him to go upstairs. He knows Maria is up there—her car is parked in the driveway, the lights are on, and music is playing. I'm guessing this wasn't part of the plan, but he's willing to take the risk."

"Why?"

Kevin shrugged. "Don't know. And Maria doesn't either. So it's kind of hard to put together."

For some reason, I thought of Verona and Colin Frye . . . and the missing guest list.

Even though it was utterly ridiculous to think that the Fryes would break in to Maria and Nate's condo to look for a guest list, I found myself asking, "Do we know for sure if it was a man?"

Kevin shook his head. "No. Too dark. But it took some

strength to get that door open. I'd put good money on a man."

"Women can be strong," I said.

"She'd have to be really strong," Kevin said. "That door was dead-bolted."

"Women can be *really* strong," I said, feeling like arguing.

"Nina . . ." He sighed.

"What?"

"Do I need to remind you about the bathroom window?"

Once—once!—I couldn't lift the bathroom window. Okay, maybe twice. And I was fairly strong.

"Okay," I said, giving in, "let's just say it's a man."

"Whoever it was," Kevin said, a smile twitching his lips, "certainly didn't expect Maria to confront him with a bottle of Aqua Net."

I grinned. Maria, who wore six hundred dollar shoes and bought designer perfume and makeup, still faithfully used the same hair spray she did in junior high when she teased her hair to impossible heights. She'd never been able to break her Aqua Net addiction.

Although I hated to think about it, I had to know. "Do you think she's in any danger?" She annoyed me, but she was my baby sister, and it would kill me to see anything happen to her.

"My gut instinct?"

I nodded.

"No. If she were, he'd have gone to her first."

"But he didn't get her briefcase. Won't he try for it again?"

"Maybe."

I stuffed the papers back into a box. "Thanks for the reassurances."

Absently I wondered if Ana was having any luck outside.

Kevin nudged an overturned box with his toe. "Maria's not staying here tonight, is she?"

Shaking my head, I said, "Going to the new place. It has an alarm system."

"Good."

I heard sharp clip-claps on the wooden stairs. Apparently, Maria had felt the need to put on heels.

"I'll be leaving now." Kevin turned to go.

"Hey," I said.

He looked back at me, a question in his eyes.

I forced the word out. "Thanks." Damn. That was harder than I thought. "For coming, I mean."

He nodded and walked away.

Ack. My knees were knocking. I hated thanking Kevin for anything these days. I copped a spot on the floor. For weeks now, I'd managed to keep my feelings for him at bay. Denial worked miracles, but soon I'd have to deal with things. But not here. And not now.

Too many witnesses.

"You two should never have broken up."

I jumped. "Jeez! Why is everyone sneaking around tonight?"

Maria had put on a hot pink silk tank and a clingy black skirt. She'd redone her makeup and pulled her hair back into a fancy twist. Pink-tipped toes peeped out from a pair of expensive looking slides.

She leaned against the door, holding a large black tote bag in her hands. A huge rolling suitcase rested near her feet.

Fanning herself with one hand, she said, "The way he looks at you . . ."

I got up. "Let's not talk about this," I said.

"Nina—"

"I have one word for you. Ginger."

That quieted Maria—for two seconds. "Ginger is a phase."

I shot her a look that said "shut up" loud and clear.

She snapped her mouth closed and looked out the window. "Is that Ana?"

On tiptoes, I peered over her shoulder. The front lights clearly illuminated Ana and Officer Hottie invading each other's personal spaces. "Yep."

"Oh. She's really desperate, huh?"

"Yep. You ready?" I said.

Delicate lines creased her eyes and lips as she frowned. "Nina, what if Nate doesn't come home?"

I paused for a second, thinking about it. What if? I shrugged, looked at my baby sister. "We'll just have to hunt him down and kill him."

A smile lit her face and she clapped happily. "Deal."

Five

The alarm beeped as I unlocked and pushed open the front door. With a few button punches, it silenced. I slipped off my Keds, padded into the kitchen.

Out of habit, I checked the locks on the windows and the dead bolt on the back door in the laundry room. I groaned loudly when I found it unlocked.

Riley. I didn't know how many times I had to remind him to keep the back door locked—and leave it locked.

I flipped the bolt, headed back into the kitchen. My stomach cried for attention. Unfortunately the fridge was nearly empty.

Leftover mashed potatoes? Raspberry yogurt? Pudding cup?

After a half a second of deliberation, I bypassed the potatoes and yogurt, grabbed the pudding.

Snatching a spoon from the drawer next to the sink, I popped the top off the pudding. I licked the aluminum cover clean and then tossed it into the trash.

My pudding and I headed upstairs to check on Riley. I tapped lightly on his door with the end of my spoon.

"Ry?"

Silence. I slowly opened his door. A wave of teenage boy

smell nearly knocked me over, a musky mix of sweat and dirty socks. Holding my breath, I whispered, "Ry?"

The motionless lump cocooned under the covers didn't move. To the right of his headboard stood a glass fish tank. I didn't look in it. Xena lived in there. Xena was Riley's snake. Xena and I had come to a live-and-let-live agreement, but I still got the heebies whenever I saw her.

Quietly, I backtracked from the room.

As I headed downstairs, I thought about Maria and Nate and couldn't help worrying.

Was Nate really cheating with his boss?

Who had broken into Maria's house, and why?

Could the two be connected somehow?

I was giving myself a headache, so I let it go for now.

Switching on the news, I turned up the volume for the weather forecast. The weatherman was predicting passing showers, and I couldn't help but groan.

Rain was the last thing I needed. It would muck up my work schedule beyond repair.

As the sportscaster teased about the latest Reds game, I tossed the empty pudding cup, set the spoon in the dishwasher, and sat down to lose myself in the tail end of a *Seinfeld* repeat.

The phone rang, and I jumped up to answer it before it woke up Riley. Maria's cell number glowed on my caller ID screen.

"I hear noises outside," she said when I answered. "Someone's out there. I'm sure of it."

"How do you know?"

"Something squeaked."

"It's pretty windy out. Could be the soffets. Or one of the neighbors. You know how that place echoes."

There was a pause before Maria said, "It was too loud to

be wind. Do you think the person who broke into my condo earlier followed me here? Maybe he's so taken with my looks that he can't leave me alone. He did see me in my nightie, after all. Has he come back for me?"

I sat on a kitchen stool, unsure how to answer. Okay, I knew how. "No."

"You're just jealous."

I laughed. "Of what?"

"That I have a stalker," she said, but I could hear the smile in her voice.

"You're nuts. You get that from Mom."

"I know." There was a slight pause before she said, "Seriously, though. I heard something."

"Did you look out there?"

"No."

"Do you think maybe you should?"

"Okay."

After a second, she said, "I don't see anything moving, but it's raining. Oh no! Is that going to put my yard behind schedule?"

"No, no," I lied. She had enough to worry about without adding landscaping troubles.

"Good."

"Is your alarm set?"

"Turned it on as soon as I closed the door."

"You should be fine, Maria. If you're worried, though, I can give you Kevin's number."

Oh, how I was hoping she'd say yes. There was nothing I'd like better than to get Kevin out of bed and make him traipse around in the dark and rain looking for someone who'd probably never been there in the first place.

"No, it's late."

Damn. "You sure?"

"Yeah. I'll be okay. I've got my hair spray."

I wrapped the phone cord around my finger. "Any word from Nate?"

"No."

"Oh." Not much else to say to that.

"I'm thinking about ways to kill him so he dies slowly. Painfully."

Ah, okay. "Just make sure you brush up on not leaving evidence behind."

"Gotcha."

I said good-night and went back to the couch. My eyes drifted closed as I thought more about Maria. I couldn't help but think that if Nate really had run off, then the wedding would be off, and then I wouldn't have to wear that horrible gown . . .

I jumped when the doorbell rang.

Squinting at the clock through sleepy eyes, I saw that it was almost midnight. I must have dozed off.

Rubbing my eyes as I pulled open the door, I blinked at the bright lights outside. Red and blue strobe lights arced across my lawn. Police cars were lined up in front of Mrs. Warnicke's house across the street.

Uh-oh.

Mr. Cabrera stood on my front porch. His white hair dripped steadily and his red button-down shirt with yellow pineapples on it was soaked. Rain fell in a solid sheet. So much for passing showers. Lousy forecasters.

"What's going on?" I asked, stepping onto the porch.

"It's happened again. Another burglary. This time at Mrs. Warnicke's."

"Is she okay?"

Mr. Cabrera shook his head. Rain droplets went flying. "Went and had herself a heart attack when she found the guy standing over her. The rat ran when she woke up, and she managed to call 911."

"Oh no!"

"They took her over to Mercy. Mrs. Mustard went with her."

The poor old lady! Mrs. Warnicke was a sweet thing, barely five feet tall if an inch, with light purple permed hair and a pair of the most beautiful blue eyes you'd ever seen. She tended to smell like mothballs, but people overlooked her scent because she made the best fudge in Ohio.

The rain had brought a chill to the air, and I motioned Mr. Cabrera inside. "Come in. I'll make you some cocoa."

His blue eyes lit up. "With marshmallows?"

"Of course."

I ran upstairs, grabbed a towel from the linen closet. Back in the kitchen, I handed it to Mr. Cabrera. He heaved himself up on a stool and leaned across the kitchen's island to pluck a grape from the bowl on the counter.

I filled the teakettle with water from the tap and set it on the stove. "Did Mrs. Warnicke say anything before they took her away? Was she conscious?"

"She can't see much without her glasses."

I pulled two mugs from the cupboard and thought about the burglaries in the Mill. There had been at least a dozen, if not more, during the past couple of months. All seemingly random except they took place in the Mill and the creep only took one or two things.

Stupid things too. Like an umbrella from Mr. and Mrs. Krayloc and a paperback romance from Mrs. Ansel's. Nothing of any value. The guy had even passed right over Mrs. Sieback's diamond ring.

It didn't make sense.

I ripped open two packages of Swiss Miss's finest and

dumped them into the mugs. "Did the guy take anything from Mrs. Warnicke?"

Raindrops dripped onto the floor as Mr. Cabrera towel-dried his hair. His bushy white eyebrows rose. A grin slipped across his face, his smile so wide his dentures looked ready to pop out. "Her skivvies."

"What?!" The teakettle nearly slipped right out of my hand. I carefully set it down.

"Her skivvies. You know, her granny panties. You'd think this guy would at least break in a young gal's place and steal those thong-y thingies they wear now."

I rubbed my temples, not sure where to go with this conversation. I tried not to picture Mr. Cabrera thinking about women in thongs, but the image just wouldn't go away.

Ew!

Cringing, I said, "How do you know?"

"Word is, the police found the panties on the floor. Guy must've dropped them on his way out."

What kind of loon watched women sleep while holding their panties? I shuddered. Then an idea hit that turned my stomach. What if the Mill's burglar wasn't breaking in to steal things so much as to watch women sleep? While holding their skivvies . . .

I let that stew for a minute while I filled the mugs. I dropped a handful of mini-marshmallows into Mr. Cabrera's and slid it across the island to him.

Mr. Cabrera said, "Got a spoon?"

I opened the silverware drawer, pulled one out. He dipped it into his cocoa, scooped up some soggy marshmallows, and slurped them down.

It was like watching a three-year-old, I swear.

From the fridge, I grabbed a can of whipped cream, loaded my cocoa with it, sipped. *Mmm.* "All the break-ins . . . Did women live in every house?"

His forehead crunched as he thought, the many wrinkles blending into one thick line. "Yeah. Some were married, though. Like Mrs. Voehlke."

Yeah, but *Mr.* Voehlke wore two hearing aids, and probably not to bed. All the burglaries just so happened at night.

"And Mrs. Rheindstat."

Again, a deaf husband.

Now that I thought about it, every one of the houses broken into were owned by women who were either single (one way or another) or had a husband who was deaf or near to it.

"What're you thinkin'?" Mr. Cabrera asked.

My whipped cream had melted into a foamy white puddle. "I'm thinking that maybe these so-called burglaries are just a cover-up for some sicko who likes to watch women sleep." I blinked. "Actually, I wonder if this guy is taking panties! No one would notice if a pair went missing." I set my mug down. "Maybe he just wants the panties and takes other things to cover it so everyone will think that's why he went in."

Mr. Cabrera nodded like a bobble head. "I can see this."

"Yeah?"

He looked at me like I'd grown two heads. "No."

I sighed. "Why not?"

"Who wants old women's panties? That's gross."

Rolling my eyes, I said, "Around here, there are only old women to choose from."

"Well, there's you," he said with a wicked teasing gleam in his eye.

Yeah, but I had a husband who wasn't deaf.

Oh.

Right.

That husband thing wasn't happening for me anymore.

Great.

Aha! I had Riley. That had to count for something. Except the boy slept like the dead. I wonder if our neighbor-hood burglar knew that?

I was now convinced it *was* someone local. Very local. He knew these people, knew them well.

And it reinforced my earlier thought that Maria's burglar and the one from the Mill were not the same. For a second I let myself think about why someone would break into Maria's place. What had he been looking for?

Shaking my head, I pushed those thoughts out.

"I just can't see it, Miz Quinn. Who'd want a bunch of granny panties?" Mr. Cabrera said in between sips.

The spoon clanked against my mug as I set it in the sink. "I think it's something we should mention to the cops."

Absently, I wondered if Kevin had been keeping up with the burglaries in the area, if he cared.

A lump of something that felt suspiciously like self-pity built in my stomach, making me feel slightly sick. I needed to stop thinking about Kevin. Denial was a good thing. Ig-norance and bliss and all. I groaned, catching myself sound-ing like my mother again.

Mr. Cabrera levered himself off the kitchen stool. His blue eyes shimmered under his whitened lashes. "Yeah, yeah. Like they'll listen to us."

Before I could argue that point, he said, "What we need to do is organize us a neighborhood watch. We can set up twenty-four-hour patrols in shifts. Keep tabs on everyone."

I closed my eyes as he rambled on. For years Mr. Cabrera had been trying to get a neighborhood watch together. For years the Mill had been loath to do so. Around here, a watch wasn't needed. Everyone knew everyone, and everything about everyone. No one had wanted to give Mr. Cabrera permission to snoop. He did well enough on his own.

But that had been before this string of burglaries that

proved the Mill wasn't quite as close-knit as everyone thought.

No, we weren't immune at all. And with the news tonight about Mrs. Warnicke, I had to admit I was a little nervous about some wacko breaking in here and pawing through my undie drawer.

I shuddered. "Maybe you ought to talk to people tomorrow, see what they think."

He smiled a mischievous kind of smile that had me thinking this wasn't such a good idea. "Yeah. I'll do that." Then he looked up at me with hopeful eyes. "You didn't talk to Ursula yet, did you?"

Oh, the guilt! I reached out and patted his liver-spotted wrinkled hand. "Not yet."

In the silence that hung in the air after that, I heard a scratching noise coming from the laundry room.

"Did you hear that?" I asked, my nerves jumping to full alert.

"*I'm* not deaf, thank you very much." He shot me a cranky look that I suspected had more to do with me not talking to Mrs. Krauss than with any unintentional insult to his hearing.

This time a definite rattling came from the laundry room—someone was trying to get in the back door.

I grabbed the can of whipped topping, and Mr. Cabrera grabbed the dish towel hanging on the oven handle.

Together, like we were joined at the hip, we ambled toward the back door, nearly toppling when Mr. Cabrera missed the step down into the laundry room. I grabbed hold of his damp shirt and righted him.

Through the sheer curtain, I could see the dim outline of someone on the other side of the door. The outdoor sconce highlighted his every move as he tried to get in.

Mr. Cabrera motioned to throw the dead bolt. I nodded, and he flipped the lock and yanked open the door in one smooth move.

I sprang forward, spraying whipped cream into the intruder's face while wishing I had Maria's Aqua Net. Mr. Cabrera started whacking him in the head with the towel.

"Stop!" the intruder yelled. "Nina! Stop!"

He sounded suspiciously like Kevin, but the height was all wrong. I dropped my can. "Riley?!"

Rain poured down on us. Mr. Cabrera used the towel to wipe away whipped cream. He *tsked* as Riley's petulant face was slowly uncovered, his tongue swiping the corner of his lips.

I pulled him inside. Mr. Cabrera closed the door. We all dripped on the floor.

White cream flecks dotted Riley's dark lashes. I checked the rest of him. Jeans, sneaks, hoodie—all soaked. The ends of his platinum hair dripped onto his shoulders.

I tapped my soggy foot. "Explain."

Mr. Cabrera tapped his foot too. "It better be good."

I looked at Mr. Cabrera. "Don't you think it's time you go home now?"

A limp white eyebrow arched. "No."

"Look, I heard the commotion outside," Riley said. "The sirens woke me up."

Hmmph. I'd managed to sleep right through them.

Riley continued, his hands gesturing here, there, and everywhere. "I went to see what it was." He rocked, heel to heel, little squishy sounds echoing through the small room. "Poor Mrs. Warnicke, huh?"

"Why didn't you wake me up?" I asked.

His eyes widened and a high-wattage smile formed. "But, Nina, you looked so peaceful . . . on the sofa?" he ventured, all angelic-like.

Crap! Too late, I realized Riley hadn't known I was asleep! Why? Because he'd probably been out all night! The bugger. I could have kicked myself. "Go," I ordered, mad at myself more now than at him. You'd think after eight years I'd be better at this mother thing. "Go clean up. And then go . . . to . . . bed."

With a devilish grin on his face, he scampered off, his shoes squeaking on the kitchen floor.

Mr. Cabrera took a step back, eyed me with disdain. "How do you expect to catch a panty thief with such poor interrogation skills? You practically spelled out that you were asleep on the couch and didn't know what was goin' on!"

I pointed toward the door. "Out. You go to bed too."

Hinges squeaked as he pulled open the back door. "I'll find you tomorrow, Miz Quinn. Fill you in on the latest happenings." He stepped out into the rain, turned back to me. "You want to be in on the neighborhood watch? Maybe Tuesday nights?"

"Think I'll pass."

"Fine. But when that thief comes a'calling, don't come cry—"

I slammed the door closed, took a deep breath, and went to take inventory of my undies.

Six

Early the next morning, I barreled into my office, trying to escape the rain. Luckily, Tam had already arrived, and I hadn't had to fight with the door's dead bolt.

The idea of a portico out front popped into my head, and I stored it away to think about later. Time. There just wasn't enough of it these days. Not with everything going on.

A skivvy stealer, Riley's late night activities, and most importantly, Maria and Nate.

Though the cow bell above the door jangled loudly, Tam didn't look up. She stood motionless, staring at her desk, hands on hips. The maternity blouse she wore clung to her curves, exaggerating her belly.

By the expression on her face, something was wrong. Terribly wrong.

"Tam?" Sloshing over, I waved my hand in front of her face. She jumped back in surprise.

"Nina! I didn't hear you."

"What's wrong?" I asked, setting my damp backpack down.

She walked around her desk, pulled out her huge red rattan chair. Her throne, as I liked to call it. Gingerly, she sat.

Her eyebrows snapped together into devil-like points. "Someone went through my desk."

My eyes widened. Her desk looked perfectly normal. "How can you tell?"

"Do you doubt me?" she asked in that regal tone of hers.

I wasn't about to argue with a paranoid pregnant woman. "Nope."

"This," she said, pointing to a small ceramic jar that held pens and pencils, "is in the wrong spot." She slid it an inch to the right.

I pressed my lips together. I wouldn't have noticed if my pencil cup was missing, never mind having been moved a fraction of an inch. "Is it?" I asked.

She either missed my sarcasm or had decided to ignore it. "It is."

With an irritated tone, she went on to list things that had been moved, misplaced, or rifled through. When she finished, she folded her arms on top of her belly. Anger clouded her blue eyes. "The Winker."

"Leo? What about him?"

She glared at me. "He did this. I knew he was bad news. His references may have come back okay, but he is bad, bad, news." While muttering under her breath about pretty boys and not being able to trust them, she dragged a tote bag onto her lap.

"How could Leo have done it?" I asked. "You were the last one out last night and the first one in this morning . . ."

"Oh," she said, her voice full of contempt, "he has his wicked ways, I'm sure."

Her vehement tone reminded me that I had my own reservations about Leo Barker. Ana hadn't sent him to me, and I still didn't know who had. I added finding out who did to my growing to-do list.

Tam unpacked her tote, unloading a stapler, the infamous

hole punch, several small knickknacks that usually dotted her desk, and even a small potted African violet.

At my astonished glance, she explained. "I had a feeling this would happen, so I took a few things home with me last night."

"You think he'd break in here to steal your African violet?"

"It's award-winning. And her name is Sassy."

Holding in a smile, I remembered that she was part of a local African violet club and took it *very* seriously.

I gathered up my backpack, thinking that pregnancy was making her a little bit nutso.

Not trusting myself not to say something that would make her cranky, I beat a hasty retreat. "I'll be in my office should you find any more evidence."

Her right eyebrow dipped. "Are you mocking me?"

I gasped and teased, "Never."

The sign on my door read NINA QUINN, PRESIDENT. I hated that sign. "President" sounded so hoity-toity. I kept it only because Tam had insisted, I still wasn't clear why. Something about being in charge and showing it.

Nina Quinn. Quinn. Hmmph. I still needed to decide if I was keeping that last name too. I hated to admit it, but I'd kind of grown fond of it. And going back to being a Ceceri seemed like a step back into full-blown dysfunction.

Still, it was *his* name and he was persona non grata these days. However, next to Riley, Kevin's name might be the only other good thing I'd gotten out of my marriage.

Rain beat against the windowpane inside my office, and I groaned. My schedule had taken a backseat to Mother Nature. Not that there weren't things to do, there were. Bills, invoices to double and triple check, design plans to create, presentations to complete . . .

I had six employees all together, three part-time, three full-time. Tam, Kit, and Deanna Parks worked full-time;

Marty Johnson, Coby Fowler, and Jean-Claude Reaux worked part-time, except for summers, when Marty and Coby, full-time students, worked more than forty-hour weeks. No one was quite sure what Jean-Claude did in his free time. No one wanted to know.

Since all my employees came to me through Ana, they'd all been on the wrong side of the law at one time or another. We all suspected Jean-Claude was *still* on the wrong side, but what he did on his own time was his own business. Until it affected his work, I'd stay out of it.

The phone rang and I heard Tam pick it up.

I booted my computer, and waited for it to clear out the cobwebs. I thought about the Fryes and how I'd agreed to do a mini for them.

The things I do for my sister.

I hadn't heard from Maria yet that morning, but I knew it was just a matter of time. I hoped she'd call with good news.

Forcefully, I pushed thoughts of Maria and Nate away. Work. I needed to get some work done.

"Nina, call on one," Tam called through my open door.

Picking up the phone, I said, "Nina Quinn."

"Hi there."

My stomach did a happy little flip. He didn't need to say who it was—with my body's reaction, it could only be one person. Robert MacKenna.

"Hi," I said.

"You haven't returned my calls. I was worried your stash of Almond Joys had run out and you'd fainted somewhere."

I told my stomach to knock off its happy dance. Nothing good could come of this *friendship* MacKenna and I shared. Nothing. He was married. Off limits. I was on the rebound. It was a disaster waiting to happen. Still, I didn't want to let him go. So I compromised. "Robert, I can't talk right now. Lots of work to do."

"Liar!" Tam shouted from the other room.

"I'll talk to you later," I said, while giving Tam the Ceceri evil eye through the wall.

"Wait!" MacKenna said. "You've been avoiding me, Nina. Why?"

"I . . . It's complicated."

"Is it because I'm Riley's vice principal?"

Oh jeez. I hadn't even thought of that.

"I've got to go," I repeated.

"Liar, liar," Tam yelled.

I was seriously thinking about wringing her neck.

"I thought we had . . . something," MacKenna said.

"We . . . did." I swallowed. "We do."

"Then why?"

Taking a deep breath, I let all my misgivings hang out in a big rush of words. "I can't be the other woman, Robert. I can't. Not after what Kevin did to me, and even if he hadn't. It's just not in me to be a home wrecker. You're married, and I won't cross those lines."

"But Nina, I—"

I hung up before he said something to make me change my mind and question my morals.

Almost immediately the phone rang again. I sprinted to Tam's desk. "Don't answer it!"

Her hand inched toward the receiver.

"Don't!" I warned.

"You're being chicken," she said.

Another ring.

I grabbed Sassy off her desk. "If you answer that phone, Sassy's gonna be nothing but a stem," I said, holding a leaf between two fingers.

The phone rang again.

Tam gasped. "You wouldn't!"

I tugged.

"No!" she shouted, eyes all wide. "Fine! I won't answer. Just put her down."

The phone kicked over to voice mail. "And if he calls again, you're going to say what?"

"You're busy," Tam mumbled, not taking her eyes off her prized African violet.

Carefully, I set Sassy back on the desk and backtracked into my office before Tam hole-punched me.

Back at my desk, I opened my bottom drawer and stared at the stack of Almond Joys. Robert had been sending me them once a week since the day I'd almost passed out in his office from hunger.

I plucked one out of the drawer, tore open the wrapper, and tried really hard to get Robert MacKenna off my mind.

Work. I needed to focus on work.

Verona Frye wanted a mini. Leaning back in my chair, I could just imagine what she considered mini. I seriously needed to learn how to tell my baby sister no.

Part of me wanted to pawn this project off onto Deanna, an up and coming designer, but I had the feeling Maria wouldn't stand for anyone other than me doing the job.

As I wondered how to get out of doing the mini, I double-clicked to check my e-mail. It took a few minutes to delete spam. Served me right for not checking my mail for a few days.

One e-mail in particular caught my attention: nbiederman@kalypso.com. It wasn't unusual for Nate to e-mail me. We'd been sending backyard plans back and forth for a while now.

This e-mail, however, had come in yesterday, which made me hurry to double-click it open.

First off, I checked the time: 8:45 A.M. My gaze then jumped to the text.

> Nina, no time to explain—my boss is waiting for me. I've messengered a package to you. Could you bring it with you this afternoon when you meet Maria and me at the house? Whatever you do, don't open it, and don't tell Maria about it. Thanks much. Nate.

Two things struck me. One, that Nate had fully intended to meet with Maria and me yesterday. Second—I looked around my office—I hadn't received any package.

I found Tam, clipboard in hand, pencil between her teeth, taking stock of the fridge in the lounge area.

There didn't seem to be any lingering hard feelings about Sassy as she looked up, removed the pencil. "There's a Mountain Dew missing."

I didn't even want to know how she knew that.

"I bet *he* drinks Mountain Dew."

Oh. We were back to being paranoid about Leo Barker. "I drink it too, once in a while."

Her gaze narrowed. "Maybe, but I'd know if *you* drank it."

I didn't want to know how she'd know that either. I think maybe I was too predictable. "Tam," I said, "did I happen to get any packages yesterday? Something by messenger?"

"Lyle."

"Who's Lyle?"

"The messenger."

"Oh."

"Do you know what happened to the package Lyle brought?"

Her eyes widened. "With those men here yesterday, I forgot to give it to you. Then you left and I didn't want to leave it here overnight, because if it was special enough to be messengered, then well, it must be important, right? I didn't want Leo to put his sticky fingers on it." She stood up slowly, wobbled slightly. "Now look! Look what he's done! He's making me incompetent at my job!"

I'd never seen her so angry. It was the first time she hadn't sounded like Queen Elizabeth in the three years I'd known her. "Tam," I soothed. "It's okay. It's not important at all. Just something from Nate."

She walked over to her desk, rifled through her tote. "I forgot I had it."

Which said a lot. Tam never forgot anything.

Ever.

Whatever animosity she held toward Leo was taking its toll on her. That, and maybe the six pounds of baby and twenty-five pounds of water she was carting around.

She handed me a small five-by-seven manila envelope. "You've got to get rid of him, Nina."

There was no need to specify who the "him" was. Since she felt so strongly about it, I considered it, but the thought of unlawful termination lawsuits flitted through my head.

"Let me think about it, Tam," I said to appease her. "In the meantime, why don't you run a more thorough background check on him?" All Leo's references had panned out, but maybe Tam, with her notorious computer skills, could dig deeper. If nothing else, it would keep her busy.

Her chin dropped down, and she fiddled with one of the buttons on her blouse.

"Tam?"

"I already did."

I should have been shocked, but I wasn't. "And?"

She looked up. "Clean," she grumbled.

"And?" I knew Tam wouldn't stop there.

"I'm still digging. I've got feelers out."

"Just don't get arrested," I said, turning.

"Oh, don't worry about me," she said regally. "Him. It's him you need to worry about."

Envelope in hand, I ducked into my office and closed the door.

To open or not to open.

My inner voice begged me to take my letter opener to that manila. However, Nate had specifically asked me not to open it.

But, that voice argued, Nate had gone missing, and what was in that envelope might help him.

Oh, the decisions.

I shook, squeezed, and held the package to the light. Whatever it was had a square shape and was flexible.

Nate was missing, I told myself as I reached for the letter opener . . .

Or was he?

I still hadn't heard from Maria this morning. It was entirely possible that Nate had shown up in the middle of the night full of excuses and apologies.

I jumped at the knock on my door. Kit poked his head in. "Found the new guy lurking in the parking lot." He shoved Leo into the room.

"Didn't want to be too early," Leo said, all wide eyes and innocence. "I was taking a look around, trying to familiarize myself with the grounds."

"Hah!" I heard Tam cry out from the other room.

Kit folded meaty arms across his chest and gave Leo a look that should have had him shaking in his Docs.

His explanation had made perfect sense, but with Tam's feelings about him, and my own questions about how he'd learned about this job in the first place . . . I doubted him.

Sue me.

I tucked Nate's envelope into my backpack. "Actually, Leo, I wanted to ask you about some—"

The buzz of my cell phone cut me off. *Maria.*

Leo would have to wait.

As I flipped open my phone, I thanked Kit again for his help the night before with Maria's door and asked him to show Leo around. In other words, babysit.

"Maria?"

"Ever heard of ricin?"

I sighed. "Do you really want to poison him?"

"Yes," she said.

"So, he still hasn't shown up?"

"Nope."

"No calls?"

"Nope."

I really didn't like what I was hearing.

"Well, not from him. I did get a call from Nate's secretary this morning. She just wanted me to know that Nate's boss came back yesterday afternoon and told everyone she was resigning. Said she'd be back today to clean out her office. When Nate's secretary asked her about Nate, she got the brush-off."

A horn blared in the background.

"What was that?"

"Idiot driver didn't want me to pass him."

More likely, she cut him off.

I held the phone away from my ear as she yelled, "Dammit, bimbo, the gas is on the right! The right!"

Horns shrieked and tires squealed.

"*Where* are you?" I asked.

"Coming to get you."

"Me!?"

"I'm going to the Kalypso. I made an appointment to meet with Claire Battiste. If she knows what's good for her, she better tell me where Nate is. If she doesn't know what's good for her, I need you there to back up my claims of self-defense."

Could it be deemed self-defense if it was premeditated? "Maybe this isn't such a good idea."

"I'll go alone—"

"No!" Jeez, with her temper, there was no telling what she would do. "I'll go. I'll call Ana too." I might need her help to restrain Maria if it came to that.

"Fine. I'll be there in ten minutes."

I hung up and called Ana.

"Ana Bertoli, probation officer extraordinaire," she said dryly.

"Hi," I said. "Listen, I don't think you're feeling well."

"Huh?"

"Cough."

Ana hacked. "Why? What's up?"

"You need to go home sick."

She coughed some more. Added a sniffle and a moan. "What're we up to?" she whispered.

"Going on a field trip."

She coughed some more, added a wheeze. "How sad is it that that excites me? I really need a man, Nina."

"Maybe you'll find one at the Kalypso."

"The Kalypso? *You're* going to the Kalyspo? Are you out of your mind?"

Her voice sounded so hoarse I almost believed she was ill. "No, I'm not."

She coughed some more. "Do I need to remind you—"

I cut her off. "No, you don't."

"Oh, we'll see about that."

"Can you be at my house in twenty minutes? Maria and I will meet you there."

"Yeah, but I really don't think you should—"

" 'Bye!" I hung up before she could launch into an inventory of my past sins that involved casinos and too much liquor.

I left Kit in charge of the office. With the rain, there wasn't much anyone could do. Catch up on paperwork, tend to the tools, clean the storage barn . . .

Dragging my backpack up onto my lap, I pulled out the envelope Nate had sent.

I tucked it into the front pouch and pulled the zipper closed.

I'd wait to see what we'd learn at the Kalypso before I opened it.

Seven

Out the front window, I saw Maria's Mercedes fishtail into TBS's parking lot, the windshield wipers on high. I looked back at Tam. She was holding her hole punch with a speculative gleam in her eye.

"Behave," I called to her before pulling the door closed. I thought I heard an insane laugh float out.

Great. I made a mental note to make sure Leo was still alive when I got back.

Maria honked. Through the windshield, I saw her throw her hands up in a what's-taking-so-long motion.

She was never one for patience.

I opened the door and choked as a haze of Chanel No. 5 engulfed me like a bear hug.

As I got in, I said, "Jeez, Maria, you have enough perfume on?"

"No," she said, backing out. She sniffed. "And it wouldn't hurt for you to wear some. That, and," she said, eyeing me critically, "a little makeup wouldn't kill you either."

I checked my reflection in the window. A thin red scar arched above my left eye. My dark green eyes looked nearly brown in the dismal light, and the bags that hung beneath them didn't help my self-esteem any.

"What about some highlights? Some gold to sass things up a little?" she asked. "My stylist could probably fit you in later today."

"I don't need highlights. My hair's fine."

"It's brown," she said, hitting the brakes as she took a corner a bit too sharply.

I reached behind me and buckled my seat belt.

"What's wrong with brown? Lots of people have brown hair."

She looked over at me, her nose scrunched in distaste. "You need texture. Nuances," she said, accentuating each syllable. "Men can get away with having brown hair. Women cannot."

I ignored her. It was either that or strangle her, and I really didn't think my mother would forgive me. "Ana's meeting us at my house. I need to leave Riley a note and change."

She grimaced. "Yes, you do. Khaki, Nina? Really?"

I held my tongue only because her fiancé was missing.

She turned onto Jaybird, heading toward my house. No blinker, no warning. Just a jerking of the steering wheel and irritated honks from the car behind us.

Taking her eyes off the road, she looked at me. "I'm beginning to get worried, Nina. What if something has happened to him?"

"Maria! The road!"

She quickly turned her head. We were thisclose to rear-ending a Grizzly Bear water truck. She jerked the wheel hard right. The car bounced up on the berm. The tires spit gravel. Clear of the truck, she got back in her lane and stepped on the gas.

I wished I had another seat belt to put on. Maybe a helmet too.

"It's just not like him," she said as though our conversation hadn't been halted by two tons of delivery truck.

"I'm sure he's fine," I lied. I wasn't sure at all. Everything about his disappearance didn't make sense. Nate was habitual. Shredded wheat for breakfast. Light lunch at his desk. Home by seven o'clock. "We'll nose around today and see what we can find out."

She looked over at me. "Do you think Claire will talk to us?"

"Please, Maria, keep your eyes on the road. I don't know if she will, but just promise me you'll be on your best behavior."

Her mouth thinned and dipped into a frown. "We'll see," she said as she hurtled into my driveway and slammed on the brakes. "We'll just see."

Inside, I hurried to change. I scribbled a note to Riley that I might be late, and I was wrestling my Keds onto my feet when my cell phone buzzed.

Could be Kevin, my inner voice crooned.

Why I would automatically think that, I wasn't sure.

It couldn't be because I wanted him to call, because I wanted to hear his voice.

Nope. Not me. Not Nina Colette I'm-so-over-him Ceceri Quinn.

The phone buzzed again.

I hopped toward my backpack and tripped on a shoelace.

It could be my mother letting me know about Uncle Giuseppe and Aunt Carlotta's travel plans. I definitely didn't want to pick up the phone to that. Maybe if I pretended I wasn't home, she wouldn't send them here to stay with me. Hadn't my relatives ever heard of Motel 6?

The phone buzzed a third time as I rooted around in my backpack. *It could be Robert again*, my inner voice trilled.

Definitely didn't want to answer that. Because if he was calling it was either because Riley was in trouble, or he was calling to talk to about that chemistry between us. I just couldn't deal with that right now.

Finally, I found the phone and pressed the Talk button before it switched over to voice mail.

"Hello?"

Static echoed across the line.

"Hello?" I said again. Really, I needed to actually check the caller ID screen *before* answering the phone. What was I paying Cincinnati Bell all that money for anyway?

"Don't," a voice said.

"What?"

"Don't open it."

It was a man's voice. He sounded out of breath and spoke quietly, like he didn't want anyone to hear him.

"Open what? Who is this?"

"Nina, don't open it."

A bell of some sort sounded in the background as silence stretched across the line.

It struck me like a knock to the head who I was talking to. "Nate?"

"Be careful," he said.

The phone went dead.

I had a major case of the heebie-jeebies as I scrolled back through the caller ID readout. *Out of Area. *000-000-0000.* Damn.

Don't open it, he'd said. The package.

A rock of uncertainty sank to the bottom of my stomach.

Nate certainly hadn't sounded like a man on a romantic getaway. He'd sounded . . . scared.

Ack.

What do I do now? Should I tell someone about the package? Tell Maria about the call? I ixnayed that idea immediately. It would just freak her out. I didn't have any real information at all to tell her. Actually, I didn't even know for one hundred percent certainty that it had been Nate I was talking to.

Just gut instinct.

And that voice in my head telling me it was.

One thing I did know for sure: I wasn't letting that package out of my sight. I double-checked to make sure it was secure in my backpack and pulled open my front door.

Ana and Maria had been cornered by Mr. Cabrera on my front porch. They stared at me accusingly.

"You really need to talk to Brickhouse, Nina," Maria insisted as I closed the door behind me, making sure it was locked. "I have such fond memories of her class."

I shot a look at Mr. Cabrera. The tattletale.

He nodded to me. "Came over to let you know Mrs. Warnicke didn't make it."

I dropped my backpack. "What!?"

"Who's Mrs. Warnicke?" Ana asked.

Maria clutched her chest. "Oh no, not Mrs. Warnicke!"

I shot her a look. She didn't even know Mrs. Warnicke.

Mr. Cabrera, always the flirt, scooted closer to Ana. "She's the sweet old lady who lives across the street. Lived." He shook his head sadly. Today he wore a Hawaiian print shirt and khaki cargo pants. I wondered if Maria had given him the khaki lecture.

Ana had recently developed a morbid curiosity where death was concerned. "What happened to her?"

Rain splashed off the porch roof as Mr. Cabrera's eyes widened. "The granny panty thief killed her."

Please, Lord, let her leave it at that.

But Ana perked right up. "Details!"

He explained about the rash of burglaries in the neighborhood, and how Mrs. Warnicke had woken up to find the thief in her bedroom.

"That's horrible," Maria murmured. "Just horrible."

Mr. Cabrera's bony chest puffed out. "I'm setting up a neighborhood watch."

"We better go," I said before he roped the two of them into helping.

As we made our way to the car, Mr. Cabrera said, "Tell Ursula I miss her! You will see her today, right?"

Just stick a knife in me and be done with it already.

"You know," Maria said as she slid into the driver's seat, "we're really not in that much of a rush."

Oh no.

"Seat belt," I told Ana. "Trust me."

"The Kalypso isn't going anywhere," Ana added from the backseat. "He really loves her."

"No."

Ana persisted. "He really does."

Maria backed out of my driveway, bumping over the curb. She put the car into drive and stepped on the gas.

"No, I mean, no, I don't want to go to Mrs. Krauss's."

Maria slammed on the brakes. Ana and I flew forward, our seat belts keeping us from taking a header out the windshield.

Maria glared at me. "That poor old man!"

Colonel Mustard came out his front door, stared at us like we might jump out and raid his wife's underwear drawer.

"Oh, all right!" I said. "We'll go."

Beyond the screen door, Brickhouse Krauss's cucumber-colored front door was open wide, allowing in rain-cooled air. I knocked softly at first, then more loudly.

No one answered. I turned to the car and shrugged.

Maria and Ana frowned at me and pointed toward the house in a "keep trying" motion.

Mrs. Krauss's car was in the driveway, the front door was

open, and I apparently wasn't going anywhere until I spoke with her.

Great.

"Mrs. Krauss?" I called through the screen. Silence.

I stepped down off the front landing. Well, I'd tried.

Ana's window powered down. "You're not giving up already!"

"She's not answering."

Maria's window slid down. "She's got to be home! Maybe she's out back. Go check."

My jaw dropped open. "You go check!"

"You're already wet." Her window slid back up. So did Ana's.

Grrr.

Sighing, I pulled the hood of my spring coat over my head and trudged around to the back of the house.

I should really be at work, I told myself. Here I was, trying to be a good sister by helping Maria track down Nate, and somehow—somehow!—I'd ended up at Ursula Krauss's landominium. How did these things happen?

Nate. God. Had it been him on the phone? What was going on? I hadn't been able to stop thinking about that phone call or what was in that package. And how scared he'd sounded.

Ursula was sitting on the stone bench in the small garden I'd designed for her not too long ago. An umbrella protected her crisp white bob as she stared into the small goldfish pond.

Looking up, she frowned, wrinkles pulling the corners of her blue eyes downward. She clucked at me. "He shouldn't have asked you to come."

I swear she had powers like my mother. Always knowing. The two of them should open a fortune-telling shop. I could see them now in twin turbans.

I didn't bother denying it. "He misses you."

She offered me a seat on the drenched bench. I pulled the hem of my coat down over my rear end and, reluctantly, sat.

Brickhouse Krauss. Once upon a time she'd been my tenth grade English teacher. She'd made my life miserable, her animosity toward me quite clear. The feeling had been mutual.

Still was.

Once I'd finished her job, I'd (for some reason I'm still not clear about) volunteered to set Brickhouse up with Mr. Cabrera . . . and was living to regret it.

"I know he misses me," she said. "I'm a hard woman to get over."

I fought back a snort.

She was short, squat, a German powerhouse, a true force to reckon with. I didn't want to be here, reckoning at all. But I felt slightly guilty for Mr. Cabrera's broken heart.

"Any chance of reconciliation?"

She clucked.

Bright colored goldfish swam in the small pond, blips of gold flashing under green and fuchsia water lilies. Raindrops splashed and spread in rings in the water.

I looked around, pleased with the growth of the garden. The varying pinks of the flowers surrounding us looked amazing. Mr. Cabrera had done a great job helping the garden grow. Not a deadhead to be seen.

"I don't know," she said finally. "I do care for Donatelli."

Hearing Mr. Cabrera's first name always took me aback. For as long as I'd lived in the Mill, he'd always been Mr. Cabrera to me, and I was Miz Quinn to him.

"But," Mrs. Krauss continued, "I want to live to see my grandchildren grow."

That would be a long wait considering she didn't have any grandchildren.

"Those are rumors," I said. For the most part. Okay, so Mr. Cabrera's lady friends had been known to, er, up and die on him. All of natural causes, of course.

"He's jinxed."

I really couldn't argue with that.

The impatient blast of a car horn rang out. I rolled my eyes. Maria's empathy for Mr. Cabrera apparently only stretched to five minutes.

I rose. "I need to get going, Mrs. Krauss. My sister's waiting for me."

She clucked, looked so sad. I almost felt sorry for her.

Almost.

"I go nowhere," she said, "now that Don and I are no more."

Ah, jeez. Okay, so I felt a little sorry. Eensy. Barely even enough to mention. "Call him."

She rose, looking every bit like her nickname. Put a head, feet, and arms on a brick, give it a hostile attitude and a slight German accent, and it was Ursula Krauss. A white eyebrow arched. "Where are *you* going?"

"The Kalypso," I said, realizing too late she'd been fishing. Her face lit. "Oh?"

I cringed. "Business, really. Maria's fiancé . . ."

"I'll go with you, play some craps." She turned toward the house.

I followed her. "Really, Mrs. Krauss, I don't think that's a good idea." Not good at all. I'd be much too tempted to push her off the boat into the river.

"Ach. Nonsense." She waddled away. "I'll get my purse."

Eight

You didn't know fear until you'd driven on a rural highway with my baby sister. Unfortunately for Ana, Brickhouse, and me, the Kalypso was located in southeast Indiana, less than an hour under normal driving conditions. Thirty minutes if you drove with Maria. And that counted being pulled over once by a state trooper.

Brickhouse, looking decidedly green around the edges, quickly excused herself to find a restroom. "Go on ahead. I'll catch up," she squeaked.

Ana didn't look so good herself. Her dark complexion had faded three shades to a deathly mushroom color.

"Ana's right, you know," I said to my sister. "Your driving is terrible. You can stop that pouting and just own up to it."

Maria frowned. "It wasn't so bad!"

Ana wrapped her arms around her stomach. "Your license should be taken away."

Maria stomped her foot. "A few minor, *minor*," she repeated for emphasis, "mishaps and you all get bent out of shape."

Ana ran a hand over her dark hair, smoothing stray strands. "Well, excuse me if I don't like getting an up close and personal view of the guardrail."

I tuned out their bickering. My thoughts of casinos, even in this day and age, conjured images of Vegas-style mobsters, money laundering, racketeering . . . murder.

I wouldn't go there where Nate was concerned, even though my overactive imagination wanted to.

But something was certainly going on. He'd sounded terrified on the phone. Add that to someone breaking into his and Maria's condo and the mysterious package he'd sent me . . . and my mind was jumping to mafia-style conclusions.

The package Nate sent was burning a hole in my backpack. What in the world was in it? Had he turned up evidence of wrongdoing onboard the Kalypso? Was he the one doing the wrong?

Oh, the questions.

To get to the Kalypso we had to take a monorail from the Odyssey, a luxurious hotel a good mile away from the boat. The Odyssey was a huge affair, six stories of cold glass and hard steel, air-conditioned to the point of me having goose bumps.

Maria was still pouting when we took our place behind the throng of people waiting for the monorail. Mid-morning and the place was packed—mostly, I noticed, with senior citizens. I looked around for any of my neighbors, but didn't see anyone I knew.

"I'm going to go find out when the next train is coming," Maria said, and stalked away.

I felt a tug on my sleeve and turned around.

"Are you a virgin?" a little old lady asked me.

I ignored Ana's sudden burst of unrestrained laughter and turned to face the woman who spoke to me.

"Sorry?" I said. I couldn't have possibly heard right.

The woman looked to be about sixty-five, my size, with cotton-candy-like blue hair. Her slightly wrinkled eyes were lined with cobalt blue liner, and small sparkling diamonds dotted the corners of her lids. Fake lashes were weighted with a slightly darker shade of blue than her liner and were in need of being reglued. Her cheeks were somewhat sunken, the hollows colored candy apple red. And her mouth—her mouth was decorated in orange lipstick. Orange. I shook my head.

The blue-haired woman placed her hands on her hips. For the first time I noticed that she wore a kimono. A chartreuse green kimono. Completing the outfit were Nikes protecting her big feet. I blinked, thinking maybe I was hallucinating.

I wasn't.

With all the colors she wore, she looked like the snow cones I used to get at Coney Island as a kid.

"I asked," she said, "if you were a virgin."

Her statement started Ana laughing all over again. Really, it wasn't that funny. I shifted, stepping on her toe.

"Ow!" she cried, pulling her foot away.

"Why don't you go see where Maria went?" I said to her.

"Snippy," Ana accused, wagging a finger, her voice cracking with giggles.

"A virgin?" I repeated.

"You know," she said, her voice reaching octaves that would make an opera singer envious, "a riverboat virgin? Is this your first time?"

I laughed. "Yes, this is my first time onboard."

"You're gonna love it!"

"I am?"

"Three floors of gambling. A thousand slots. It's heaven. And the food . . . The buffet is gorgeous."

I didn't think I'd ever heard a buffet described as gorgeous, but I took her word for it.

I scrunched my nose, charming-like. "I'm not really here for the gambling." Unfortunately.

I looked over her blue hair to see if I could spot Maria or Ana . . . or even Mrs. Krauss. They had disappeared. When I turned my attention back to the woman, she was looking at me as though I had just proclaimed that Don Ho lip-synched "Tiny Bubbles."

"Not here for the gambling?" she asked.

"I'm kind of looking for someone."

She poked me in my ribs with her elbow and made a tsk-ing noise. "Here for the men, are ya?"

"Uh, yeah. Looking for men," I agreed so I didn't have to explain about Nate.

"I'm Stella Zamora, by the way."

Shifting my backpack, I held out my hand. "Nina Quinn."

"Five more minutes!" I heard someone complain loudly.

I knew that someone. I turned and saw Maria stomping toward me.

Ana followed closely on her heels. Ruined mascara circled her eyes, making her look like a raccoon. Served her right for laughing at my expense.

"But look what I found in the gift shop," Maria said, holding up a small container.

"Dramamine?"

Maria put her hands on her hips. "You know how I get on boats, Nina."

Ew. I definitely knew.

"Who's the princess?" Stella asked me.

Uh-oh.

"Princess?" Maria asked, her chin up, her voice as cold as an Antarctic wind.

"Think I'll check on Mrs. Krauss," Ana said, retreating. Coward.

"This is my sister, Maria," I said, making introductions. "Maria, this is Stella."

"Yeah 'princess.' Just look at you," Stella said to her.

Maria's eyes narrowed.

I thought I heard a cat mewl somewhere behind me.

"What about me?" Maria said in a staccato burst.

"Chanel from head to toe," Stella said, shaking her head. "Chanel's the best."

"Hah!"

"Um," I said, breaking in. "What kind of food do they serve in the buffet?"

Maria balled her fists. "And just what's wrong with Chanel?"

"Do they have chicken here? I like chicken." Both of them ignored me. It was as if I had suddenly disappeared.

"Listen here, girly. Expensive shmensive. It's not for you. You need something with pattern."

Maria's mouth dropped open. Telling Maria she needed to wear patterns was like telling a nun to wear a skimpy bikini.

"I'd never!" she exclaimed.

"Well," I said, interrupting. "There was that time when you were six and made a tie-dyed T-shirt at day camp."

"Only because the counselor made me," Maria retorted.

Oh, yeah. Now I remembered the hissy fit she'd thrown over it. It hadn't been a pretty sight, and I was afraid that it might be repeated if Stella continued goading her.

"Well, you should," Stella said. "It will zazz up your life."

Zazz? Was that really a word?

"I don't need any zazzing," Maria said.

"Whatever you say, Princess."

Maria put her hands on her hips. Her chin jutted forward. The temper she'd inherited from our Nana Ceceri was on a short fuse. From experience, I backed away. On rare occasions Maria's fiery temper had instigated a fight or two. Or three. I learned the hard way to keep out of the line of fire.

However, despite the steam practically coming out Maria's ears, she kept quiet. I did see that she was giving Stella the Ceceri evil eye. Apparently it had no effect on blue-haired, kimono-wearing old women.

A series of chimes pealed and a tinned voice came over the PA, announcing that the monorail would be arriving in less than a minute and to move away from the edge of the platform.

"Well, then," I said, stepping between the two. I faced Maria. "Be nice," I whispered. "Say good-bye."

Maria hmmphed.

I turned back to Stella. "It was nice meeting you."

"Same here, sweet thing," she said to me. She focused on Maria. "Princess." Swiveling, she hitched her shoulder bag, which was more sack than bag, and turned to go.

I heard a loud *CLUCK* and spun in time to see Brickhouse Krauss knock Stella Zamora onto her wrinkled behind with her purse. Once down, Brickhouse sat on Stella.

Shock rooted me to the floor. Maria clapped. I expected a "two-four-six-eight" from her any second now.

I found my voice. "Mrs. Krauss!"

"Ach! Shame! Shame!" Mrs. Krauss continued to hit Stella repeatedly with her purse.

She continued on in rapid German. I didn't understand a word of it, but by the look of fury in Mrs. Krauss's blue eyes, it spelled trouble.

The monorail, smoothly and rather quietly, slid up to the platform and slowed to a stop. Stella Zamora tried to slither away, but Mrs. Krauss sat tight, clucking. She looked like a hen sitting on a blue-haired egg.

People circled around us and got onto the monorail without even looking twice.

Stella was yelling about not being able to breathe, and

Mrs. Krauss was spouting German as she rooted through Stella's giant sack.

"Aha!" Mrs. Krauss held up a package.

My package! The one Nate had sent me.

My mouth dropped open as I stared at Stella. She'd pick-pocketed me! I couldn't believe it!

A security guard rushed over. He tried not to smile at the image in front of him, but I saw the quirk of his lips.

Mrs. Krauss heaved to her feet. Stella gasped for air.

"Ma'am?" he said to Maria, who probably looked like the only sane one around—little did he know. "Is there a problem?"

Horror resonated in her eyes. "Yes! Do I look like a 'ma'am' to you?"

"Princess," Stella ground out.

I held Maria back before she could take over where Brickhouse had left off.

"Er, *miss*? Is there a problem?"

Maria leveled a high and mighty stare at him. "That woman!" She pointed to . . . nothing.

Stella Zamora was nowhere to be seen.

Mrs. Krauss let out a string of very recognizable words—in any language. The young security guard blushed.

In a rush, Brickhouse explained how she'd seen Stella steal the package from my backpack.

"We'll look around for her, ma'am," he said to me.

I felt a prickle at the term too. *Hmmph.*

He took my name and phone number and sauntered away.

The chimes sounded again, and the monorail's doors closed. It slid away without us onboard.

"Of all the nerve," Maria whined. "Calling *me* ma'am. Now, you . . . Perfectly justifiable."

What was justifiable would be me murdering her if she continued razzing me.

Ana caught up with us. I noticed she'd washed her face. She must have seen her raccoon eyes in the mirror and decided that no makeup was better than looking like something that knocked over trash cans to forage for food.

She looked around. "Did I miss anything interesting?"

Nine

Sirens whooped to my left, and I turned in time to see a woman sitting in front of a slot scoop handfuls of quarters into a bucket.

Brickhouse veered off, muttering about craps tables and good luck.

Unable to help myself, I took a step toward the slot machines.

Ana grabbed my arm. "Uh-uh. And get that look off your face."

"What look?" I asked, still gazing at the slots.

"What look?" Maria echoed.

Ana stepped in front of me, forcing me to look her in the eye. "The kid in the candy shop look, the kid on Christmas morning look, the *newlywed* look."

I feigned innocence. "Newlywed look?"

She narrowed her eyes. "Don't play dumb with me. Chapel of Forever After remind you of anything?"

Ugh. I really didn't need the reminding.

"The chapel of what?" Maria asked.

"Nothing," I said quickly.

Ana smiled. "So you do remember."

How could I forget? How *did* I forget? The Chapel of

Forever After was in Vegas. It's also where Kevin and I married. Which Ana was delicately trying to remind me was after a long night of gambling and watered-down gin and tonics.

Looking over Ana's shoulders, I spied a blackjack table. I gazed at it longingly. "Just one hand?"

"No," Ana said.

"Come on." Maria tugged on my arm. "We've got to find Claire Battiste. How do we get upstairs?"

"Maybe there?" Ana said, pointing to a door camouflaged into the wall by a large fake ficus tree. A keypad glowed bright. Closer inspection revealed that the door could be opened only by a key card. I tried the knob anyway, hoping luck was on our side. *Locked. Damn.*

"May I help you?"

I jumped up, pressing my back against the door.

He was tall, thick. Not in a fat way, but in a cop way. Although he wore no uniform, his stance, his eyes, his polished shoes, and his up-close inspection screamed security. Okay, I confess, he had a credit card badge attached to his Dockers pocket that said SECURITY. S. Larue was his name.

He took hold of my elbow and pulled me away from the door. "This area is authorized access only."

"I have an ap—"

Ana's coughing cut Maria off. She waved her hand in front of her face. "Doesn't this place have vents?"

The cigarette smoke hanging in the air was becoming thicker by the minute. But, for as long as I'd known Ana, she'd never had a problem with smoke.

Ana coughed again. And again. "My asthma," she said. "I didn't bring my puffer."

Now I knew something was up. Ana didn't have asthma. She was the healthiest person I knew. I narrowed my gaze on her face, trying to figure out what she was doing.

As I watched, she held her breath and kept coughing. She honestly looked like she was having an asthma attack. And not only that, but she had positioned herself so that when she slumped over, Security Man would be in the perfect position to catch her.

Maria gasped as Ana went down, but I simply watched in stunned amazement.

S. Larue scooped Ana into his arms.

"Air. I need fresh air," she choked.

"I'll take her to the balcony and then to the first aid office," he said, all business now.

He turned with Ana in his arms, and I saw that behind his back Ana held his credit card badge in her hand.

As I reached out to take it, S. Larue dropped Ana. She landed on her hind side, her "Owww!" echoing.

S. Larue snatched his card back, clipped it back onto his pants pocket. "Nice try," he said to Ana, picking her up and tossing her over his shoulder in a fireman's hold. "But I usually tend to notice when a woman's hand is in my pocket."

"Oh," Ana murmured.

He looked at us. Maria and I took a step back. Maria said, "*We* didn't steal it!"

Over her shoulder, Ana glared at Maria. "I believe 'borrowed' is the preferred term." She cleared her throat. "Look at that. I'm feeling much better. You can put me down now."

He smiled at us, a wicked, lazy smile.

Uh-oh.

"I don't think so." He nodded to us. "You two can come with us."

Maria stood firm. "I have an appointment with Claire Battiste. I'm Nate Biederman's fiancée, Maria Ceceri."

"Why didn't you say so?" S. Larue said. He motioned to

a corner of the room where a set of double glass doors blended into the decor. "Sign in *there*." He pivoted and walked away, Ana hanging over his shoulder.

I could hear her protesting her innocence as he disappeared into the maze of slots.

Funny, she didn't look too distressed. Now that I thought about it, S. Larue had been kind of cute.

"Come on." Maria tugged on my arm.

So much for cousinly concern. "Where do you think he's taking her?"

Maria shrugged. "She knows where the car is."

We checked in with the receptionist behind the double doors, who buzzed us through another set of doors. We followed a long hallway before coming to the executive offices.

At the end of a long hallway was a large reception area ringed with offices. Smack-dab in the middle sat an empty desk.

A phone rang in an inner office. And kept ringing.

"Hello?" Maria called out.

After a second a woman came hurrying out. She was around fifty or so, with a wobbly bun. "Maria! I'm so glad you're here."

Maria rushed introductions. The older woman turned out to be Nate's secretary, Missy.

"It's been chaos," Missy said. "With Nate's sudden disappearance, and then Claire's . . ."

I blinked. "What? Claire's disappeared?" I asked. "I thought she came back yesterday."

Missy looked like she needed a Valium. She threw her hands in the air. "She's here, she's gone. No one knows anything. No one's seen either of them. The junior executives are trying to cover and not doing a very good job of it."

"So Claire's not here?" Maria asked.

Missy huffed. "No. She came in yesterday afternoon, re-

signed, said she'd be back this morning for her things. She
never showed. She's not answering any of her phones and
the doorman at her apartment building hasn't seen her since
yesterday morning."

Very strange. Very, very strange.

Missy pointed us in the direction of Nate's office. "Feel
free to look around," she said, and excused herself, leaving
us alone.

Dragging Maria along, I found Nate's door and opened it
slowly. As soon as we entered, Maria turned her pout on full
wattage.

"He's sleeping with Claire," she said.

"We don't know that."

She glared. "Oh, it's so coincidental that they both up
and disappear the same day."

Now would probably be a good time to mention Nate's
phone call. But I really didn't want to worry Maria. I struggled with something to say. "Nate is not cheating on you.
He loves you."

Maria sniffed.

"He does. I don't know what's going on, but I'm sure
Nate has a good explanation for whatever it is he's doing."

She crossed her arms over her chest. By the look on her
face, I could tell she wasn't buying my cheerleading.

"Well, help me look around," I said.

"For what?"

"Anything. A date book. A calendar."

I rifled through his desk. An eight-by-ten picture of him
and Maria sat on top. Nate, with his sandy blond hair, blue
eyes, and charming smile gazed adoringly at Maria.

Nope, no way he was cheating.

What, exactly, he *was* doing, I hadn't a clue.

In his top drawer I found a small leather-bound calendar.
Most of the dates were filled in with everyday duties that

had to do with his job. I flipped back to the day he disappeared. One of the tasks listed was *Double-check PCF guest list*.

Guest list? The one Verona and Colin Frye had been looking for? For the gala?

"What does P-C-F stand for again?" I asked.

Maria pouted. "Phony Claire Friends?"

I gave her my version of the evil eye.

"All right. It's Phineus Cancer Foundation."

"How did Nate become involved with the gala? Did you recommend him?"

"I don't have any say in that sort of thing. Brian Thatcher brought him into the mix on Claire's recommendation. Nate had been in accounting until Claire handpicked him as her right hand man here in public relations earlier this year."

"Brian Thatcher? How do I know that name?"

Maria shrugged. My mother would have pitched a fit. Grace Kelly did not shrug. "Maybe you heard it on the news. He died. Got carjacked about two months ago, was shot to death. He was my supervisor at Phineus Frye and was the go-to man for the gala."

Brian Thatcher. Suddenly, I remembered. I hadn't heard his name from the news . . . I'd heard it from Verona Frye. Yesterday. She'd taken over his job planning the gala for Phineus Frye. I'd forgotten. "Carjacked? Really?"

Maria leveled an icy glare at me. "No, I'm making it up."

Those kinds of things just didn't happen in Cincinnati. Scary. "Who's in charge of the gala now?"

"On this end, Claire and Nate. On our end, Roz asked Verona to take over the planning after Brian died."

Roz Phineus didn't strike me as the business type. It was hard to imagine her, with her foot-long fingernails, as a CEO of anything. And I said so.

Maria shrugged again. "She set herself up at Phineus

Frye after her husband died. She does a good job, as far as I can tell. She founded PCF—in memory of her husband Alfred. He died of cancer a couple years ago. PCF sponsors children with cancer. They pay their bills, send them to camp, etcetera."

Nate had told me to be careful.

Of what?

Of who?

After searching through the trash can and flipping through a few files, and finding nothing of any interest, I said, "I think we can leave."

Missy ran up to us on our way out, held out a small card. "We'd appreciate a call if Nate turns up." She led us to the door.

Something was bugging me. "Missy, did you send any packages out for Nate yesterday?" I was hoping she could shed some light, any light, on that package.

She bit her bottom lip. "No. Just some regular mail. Why?"

"Just wondering. Thanks."

Downstairs in the main gaming room, Maria and I searched for Mrs. Krauss. I found her standing by a game called the Big Bang. People were standing in line, waiting their turn for a five-dollar pull on a giant slot machine that stood floor to ceiling. If you were lucky enough, three cars would match up and a brand new red BMW Z3 convertible would be yours, free and clear.

Fighting the pull to play myself, I tapped her on the shoulder to get her attention. "Time to go."

"Ach!" She pouted just like Maria.

We found Ana in the Odyssey's bar. "How's the asthma?" I asked.

"Cured. It's amazing what a little fresh air and—" She held up a martini glass. "—a little gin will do." She looked

over my shoulder at Maria. Who was, surprise surprise,
pouting.

"Didn't go too well?"

I shook my head.

As we searched for Maria's Mercedes in the parking lot,
I looked back at the boat. Amazingly, my first time onboard
had been a lot like the time I lost my virginity.

Disappointing.

Ten

All was fairly quiet on the way home from the Kalypso. I'd taken over driving duties from Maria, who sat next to me staring out the window sullenly.

Mrs. Krauss and Ana were in the backseat discussing the pros and cons of dating.

They were having trouble finding any pros.

I heard a cluck just before Brickhouse said, "And the way they fuss over every hair like it's their last?"

Ana laughed. "I once caught a guy I was dating trying on one of my wigs."

My mouth dropped open. I caught her eye in the rearview mirror. "You have wigs? Plural?"

"I'm surprised you know plural, Miss Nina Ceceri, for all the talking you did in class," Mrs. Krauss cut in.

I wondered if there was a way to crash the car so that only her seat was affected.

"I have some," Ana murmured, a grin turning up the corners of her lips.

"Do I dare ask why?"

She waggled her eyebrows. "Halloween?"

Mrs. Krauss said, "Ha!"

Maria lifted her head. Her gaze lingered on each of us

before she looked at me and said, "You should borrow one. Anything's better than what you've got."

This led us into a conversation on hair coloring that lasted until after I dropped Mrs. Krauss off at her lando. She'd promised to rethink her decision about Mr. Cabrera, at least.

Ana begged off on hanging around for dinner, saying she needed to get the house clean. Her mother, my aunt Rosetta, was flying in early the next morning.

I groaned thinking about my aunt Carlotta and uncle Giuseppe. I really needed to call my mother about them. I didn't have time for houseguests.

Not to mention that I didn't have *anywhere* to put houseguests. My house was a modest two-story bungalow, with two bedrooms and two baths. Sure, the couch folded out, but it tended to sag in the middle. Uncle Giuseppe was a big man. I didn't want to see Aunt Carlotta smothered when they both rolled into the dip.

I supposed we ought to fill my mother in on Nate's, er, misplacement too.

Or maybe not. If Celeste Chambeau Ceceri heard there might not be a wedding . . .

I shuddered.

After dropping Ana off at her condo, I drove Maria home.

"What do you think has happened to him?" Maria blinked her big blue eyes at me. "Honestly."

Honestly, I had no idea. It would be easy to speculate that he'd run off with Claire Battiste, but then there was that envelope and that phone call and that funny feeling in my chest that told me something wasn't quite right.

I pulled into Maria's long driveway—she had decided to stay at the new house permanently. "I don't know."

Maria pouted. Her mood was getting seriously depressing. And annoying.

"Let's go in," I said. "Maybe he's called."

The rain had let up, but left its damage. I cringed at the puddles in Maria's yard and the acre of muck. It would take days for things to dry out. Days I didn't have. Unless the wedding was off.

Inwardly, I groaned. I hadn't thought of the repercussions of a canceled wedding. Nate's dad was footing the TBS bill. What would happen if there was no wedding? Would he back out? What would I do with all the materials? All the off-site work that had already been done?

My contractors would have to be paid in full for the work they'd completed, wedding or not. Trees, shrubs, and plants had already been bought and paid for and were sitting in TBS's fenced-in backyard just waiting to be planted.

Ugh.

Suddenly feeling sick, I followed Maria inside. She hurried to the phone and frowned after checking her messages.

"Nothing," she said, kicking off her heels and sinking into a sleek curved chair. It baffled me how she didn't slide right off.

She sighed heavily. I didn't know what to say, so I left her there and wandered over to the bank of tinted windows overlooking the backyard.

How much did Maria have in the bank? Probably not enough to swallow the cost of the yard. The completed job would be in low six figures. My parents lived on a fixed income—my father's retirement money from forty years of teaching at the University of Cincinnati. They'd planned well and had extra, but not that much extra.

If worse came to worse, TBS could swallow the debts, but *worse* would put a serious dent into my bottom line.

I didn't want to think about it; I wanted to focus on Nate. But as owner of TBS, I *had* to think about it. I had responsibilities. I had a giant load of topsoil being delivered on Saturday. I needed to know whether or not to cancel it.

Maybe Nate would show up with some ludicrous story of temporary amnesia and everything would be all right.

There was that delusion thing again.

The envelope he'd sent me was once again tucked safely in my backpack. Had it been a coincidence that Stella Zamora had tried to steal it? As much as I wanted to believe that, I just didn't. To do so would break a cardinal commandment about coincidences.

Maria sighed again, heavier this time.

My mind whirled, skipping to and from ridiculous theories. The packet had been snapped and zippered into my backpack, and true enough, it would have been the easiest thing for a thief to grab.

Of course, I thought, staring out at the rivers of mud in the backyard, Stella had completely bypassed my wallet, which only fed my suspicions.

Why would a pickpocket choose a manila envelope over a wallet . . . ? Unless it had been the envelope she was after?

If that were true, how had Stella Zamora known *I* had the envelope? Had Nate told her? He was the only one who knew.

Maria sighed again.

I gritted my teeth. She had every right to sigh, I suppose. Once. But she tended to wallow for attention's sake.

"What am I supposed to with all the wedding gifts? The caterer? The florist?" She gasped. "Mom!"

Ugh! Enough! I couldn't take any more today.

"What's that?" I said, pointing outside, squinting, and acting up a storm. My mother always said I had a face for the movies. She just never specified what kind of face . . . or what kind of movies.

"What?" she said, getting up in one smooth glide.

"That," I said. I gestured toward the horizon. Inwardly, I smiled in glee.

"I don't see anything. Really, Nina." Again the pout. "I was comfy."

If I'd had any reservations about what I was going to do, they scurried off in a flash. I pulled open the back door. Grabbing her arm, I shoved her out.

"Shoes!" she shrieked.

Before she could turn around, I nudged her farther out, down the step, off the patio. "Mud's good for the skin, right?"

"Eee!" She jumped around, mud squishing between her toes. She threw a dangerous glare my way, her eyebrows dipping low. "Neeee-naaah!"

I laughed.

"Argh!" Maria yelled.

I looked up just in time to see the fistful of mud heading my way, but not in enough time to avoid it. It landed on my right thigh and oozed down my leg.

"Serves you right," she said smugly.

"Oh yeah?" Bending down, I scooped a handful of Ohio's finest sloppy, goopy gray-brown clay and heaved.

Maria's mouth dropped open as she took in the Pollock-like affect on her suit. "This is Chanel! Chanel!" She kicked, sending mud flying in my direction.

I ducked, but it splattered my face, my hair. I wiped a hunk from my eye. Out of which I saw Maria smile in self-satisfaction.

That's it! This was war!

Two-handed, I scooped and hurled. Maria pivoted and mud splattered her backside.

She looked over her shoulder with a wicked gleam in her eye. Mud landed square on her mouth. I yelled, "Now you won't have to get a facial this week!"

She sputtered, bent, and scooped. "Neither . . . will . . . you!" She laughed, a hysterical-sounding chuckle.

I turned but not quick enough. Thick mud hit like a slap on my cheek.

We both dropped to our knees and started tossing mud pies.

"That's . . . that's for being so—so pouty!" I shouted.

"Pouty!? I am not pouty!"

I sighed dramatically, mocking her. Mud flew, hitting my ear and the top of my head. "Poor me," I mimicked. "The gifts. The flowers!"

"Ooooh!"

"You're not the only one with problems, you know! The world doesn't revolve around you!" I tossed, and mud oozed down her cleavage. "Other people have problems too!"

"Like you?" Sarcasm dripped from her words.

"Yes! Like me!"

"Aww." Mud hit me on my chest. Unfortunately there was no cleavage for it to slide into.

"Riley? He's sneaking out again."

"Boo-hoo!"

I shoveled and tossed. Mud darkened Maria's hair. "And there's a panty thief in the neighborhood."

"You poor thing. Has he not hit your house yet? Is that why you're in an uproar?"

I sent her my best evil sister smile and rose to my feet. Maria scrambled up. I chased her, my fists full of mud.

"My fiancé is missing!" she called back to me over her shoulder.

"Uh, hello? I found Ginger Barlow's lipstick on Kevin's boxers!"

"Yeah, but why would Nate cheat on *me*?!"

She must have been reading my homicidal thoughts, because she scampered away, mud splashing back at me as she ran.

She was fast, I'd give her that. As I chased her, I wondered at this weird competitiveness. This my-life-is-worse-than-yours thing we had going on. It was utterly stupid, yet . . .

I wanted to win.

I *had* to win.

Maria stopped short to avoid falling into the freshly dug pond, arms flailing. She lost her balance as she rocked, going down on her rear. Quickly, she scrambled away from the edge.

I dove for her ankles before she could escape.

"I have dozens of relatives flying in!" she cried out. She kicked her foot out of my grasp, slithered sideways.

"Yeah—all who seem to be staying with *me*!"

I grabbed her other foot, and she rolled onto her belly and tried to crawl away.

On hands and knees, I went after her. Abruptly she stopped, turned toward me, slightly pale.

Ah! Victory. "And," I said, slightly out of breath, "I have to make nicey-nice with Brickhouse Krauss!"

Take that, I silently added.

Maria swiped a muddy lock of hair off her face, narrowed her eyes as she adopted her Grace Kelly look. "Well, *I* have a dead body in my pond."

It took a second for her words to register. I was too busy thinking ahead to the next miserable aspect of my life.

Carefully, I edged toward the pond, hoping this wasn't a ploy to push me in.

I peered. Sure enough, there was a woman facedown, dressed all in black, in the shallow murky water, her hair floating around her head like a blonde halo.

Slowly, I looked back at Maria, who was looking rather smug. "You win."

Eleven

Best the medical examiner could tell without a full autopsy, Claire Battiste had been dead less than a day.

I wasn't impressed. By now, two hours after Maria and I had found her body, everyone knew Claire had been seen at her office yesterday afternoon.

Kevin and Ginger Ho, er, Barlow had been questioning us since they'd arrived at Maria's. I cursed my luck that there weren't any other homicide detectives on duty.

I pulled a blanket tighter around my muddy shoulders as two burly medical personnel carried the stretcher with Claire's body on it, zipped inside what looked like a Gor-Tex cocoon.

I shuddered.

Kevin rubbed his chin. "Tell me again why you two were out in the mud?"

Maria looked up at him, arched a muddy eyebrow. "We were dumping a dead body in the pond."

I gave her a sharp jab with my elbow.

Her high-pitched voice scraped my eardrums raw. "What? They've asked us the same questions over and over."

I glanced up at Kevin, gave him my best please-help-me face. It wasn't hard considering I looked the way I did.

"Detective Barlow, why don't you walk Ms. Ceceri through the events."

Out of the corner of my eye I saw Maria's lips press into a thin, tight line. Her control over her temper was being sorely tested.

As they walked away, toward the pond, Kevin picked up a lock of my mud-covered hair. It crunched between his fingers. "Mud's good for the skin, right? Same for hair?"

I was in no mood. "Can we go now?"

We'd been through everything that had happened in the last two days—from Nate's disappearance to our trip to the Kalypso that morning.

"Not yet."

I sat on the concrete step leading from the back door to the patio. "Maria called me last night," I said. "She'd thought she heard something back here . . . I thought she was just being paranoid after the break-in at the condo."

"Did she come out and look around?"

I shook my head. Mud crackled and fell to the ground. "No, but she did look out the window. She didn't see anything."

"Is there any chance Nate was sleeping with Claire?"

I looked him straight in the eye. "I don't think so. Nate's not that kind of guy. Of course, I didn't think you were that kind of guy either."

The muscle in his jaw pulsed. "Was Maria jealous of Claire?"

I jumped to my feet. "Oh no! No, you don't. Maria has nothing to do with any of this."

He shrugged. "She's a suspect. The victim was found in her yard."

I swallowed hard. He was just trying to upset me.

Or prepare me, my inner voice said.

I told it to shut up.

One of the crime scene guys carried a Ziploc bag with a ski mask in it past us. I blinked.

A ski mask. Dressed all in black . . . bulky black too. A huge sweatshirt and baggy sweatpants.

Jaw dropped, I looked up at Kevin.

"Yeah, I noticed that too," he said. "We'll see what the autopsy says about her eyes."

"She had to be the person who broke into Maria's!"

"We can't assume anything. And I wouldn't share that theory with anyone until we know for sure."

With anyone . . . Like Maria. She did have a big mouth.

I thought he was probably just being stubborn because he didn't want to admit a woman could have gotten through a dead bolt. "All right."

"We'll put out an APB on Nate and his car and continue to investigate all angles."

I wasn't above assumption. Claire had to be the one who'd broken into Maria's condo. It was too coincidental. What had Claire been looking for? The package Nate sent me?

I opened my mouth to tell Kevin about the phone call I'd gotten and that package. After a second's hesitation I closed it again.

Kevin was a good detective. He'd learn soon enough of the courier who'd brought the package to me. Until then, I wanted to get it home and get a good look at what was inside.

"What?" he said.

"What, what?"

"You were about to say something."

I took off the blanket, folded it and put it on the concrete step. "I'm just worried, is all."

"About Maria?"

I nodded. "Nate too."

His bright green eyes darkened as he dipped down to

look me in the eye. "I'm worried about you," he said, nudging up my chin.

I backed away. "Don't. I can take care of myself."

Ha! Take that.

"Like you did when you got involved with the Sandowskis?"

Oh. Nothing like taking me down a notch. He was referring to the murder investigation I'd stuck my nose into a few weeks ago. The one that almost killed me.

I decided to ignore him. "Can we go now?"

"Yeah." He wagged a finger at me. "But stay out of this."

I saluted him. "Yes, sir!"

Maria and Ginger were walking back to us. I looked at Ginger with a critical eye. What did she have that I didn't? Okay, sure. The long legs, long gorgeous auburn hair, the big boobs . . .

But I had *personality.*

That had to count for something, right?

I shot a murderous look at Kevin. He apparently had the ability to read my mind because he took one look at me and turned away, his eyes filled with guilt.

Good.

Maria sighed loudly. I could tell by the expression on her face that her patience was threadbare.

"And why, again, were you having a mud fight?" Ginger said.

Maria's perfectly plucked eyebrows dipped dangerously low and her lips were curled in a snarl.

Uh-oh. I saw a dry cleaner in Ginger's future. Inwardly I cheered Maria on.

"Ms. Ceceri?" Ginger prompted when Maria didn't answer.

As if in slow motion, I saw Maria's bare foot snake out to trip her.

Ginger's arms flew out to grab Maria for balance, but Maria slyly backed away. Ginger fell head first into the mud. It covered her from forehead to toes.

Maria squatted and said in a fake beauty queen voice, "Oh, I'm so sorry! I don't know what happened. I must have slipped!"

I held in a laugh as Kevin shot me a dirty look.

"What? I didn't do it."

"No, but you wanted to."

I smiled as innocently as I could. "Never!"

"Hmmph."

He turned to walk over to help Ginger up. That little inner voice in me egged me on. Really, I didn't need all that much encouragement. My muddy foot darted out.

Kevin stumbled and fell forward like a giant sequoia.

He shook mud from his hands as he looked over his shoulder at me, narrowing his eyes.

I shrugged. "Oops."

A little after three, I parked Maria's Mercedes in my driveway and jumped out. I hurried up my front walk before I was swarmed by nosy neighbors.

I'd dropped Maria off at my mother's and promised to get her car back to her as soon as possible.

I was thinking next week. It was a seriously nice car.

A long hot bath sounded heavenly, but I would settle for a shower.

I caught sight of Riley next door, his head bent close to Mr. Cabrera's. What were they up to? My stomach filled with dread.

I snuck in the back door, hoping I wouldn't get waylaid by Mr. Cabrera. I was in no mood to play his game of twenty questions as to why I looked the way I did. Or get into another conversation about Brickhouse Krauss. I'd done all I could on that front. My conscience was officially clear.

I threw my Keds, jeans, and T-shirt into the washing machine, and grabbed a clean towel from the dryer. I wrapped it around me as I ran through the kitchen and up the stairs.

Rivers of muddy water swirled down the drain as I showered.

Claire Battiste, dead.

I didn't for a second believe Nate was behind it, despite what Kevin thought. Nate was much too kindhearted, and his voice on the phone earlier still sent chills down my spine.

He *had* been scared. Of what? Did he know who was behind Claire's death? Was that why he was on the run?

As I shampooed for a second time, I realized that supposition didn't make sense.

Last time *Nate* had been seen was *with* Claire at lunchtime. *Claire* had last been seen *without* Nate in late afternoon.

If Nate hadn't called me this morning, I'd be phoning the morgues. As it stood now, I still might.

What was in that package?

Don't open it.

I shut off the water, the pipes squeaking, and reached for a towel. I know he'd told me not to open it, but I had to.

With Claire dead and Nate missing, there might be something in there to give us all a clue.

I slipped on a pair of faded denim shorts, pulled a tank top over my head.

As much as I wanted to, I couldn't forget that somebody had also tried to steal the envelope from me—so someone, maybe Nate, maybe the person who'd killed Claire, knew I had it.

The sooner I learned the contents and handed it over to Kevin, the better.

Quickly, I blow-dried my hair and went in search of my backpack. At the top of the stairs, I stopped short at the sound of voices rising and falling.

I crept down the stairs, peered over the banister.

Blinked.

Mr. Cabrera spotted me. "Miz Quinn! You're just in time!"

I took the rest of the steps slowly, hoping I was imagining things. There weren't twenty-odd old people crowding my living room.

I rubbed my eyes, blinked.

Oh Lord. There *were*!

I opened my mouth to ask them what they were doing here, how they got in, and how soon could they leave, when Riley came in the room, carrying a pitcher of lemonade and a stack of paper cups. I blinked, wondering when he'd taken hostess lessons from my mother.

He spotted me, grinned. "Hope you don't mind I volunteered to have the neighborhood watch meeting here."

"Me? Mind? Haha." I gritted my teeth. "Don't be silly."

I supposed mine *was* the only house in the neighborhood with enough room to fit everyone . . . Just before she'd died, my aunt Chi-Chi had renovated the whole house, adding more room upstairs for a master bath, and downstairs, a bigger eat-in kitchen and a laundry room. She'd also knocked out the wall separating the living room from the unused dining room, making one big great room, which was where everyone was now seated.

Still, it had turned into a beautiful day. Couldn't they just pull up lawn chairs and do this outside?

Flash Leonard rose on shaky legs. "Here, Nina. Take my seat."

I averted my gaze as his robe slipped open. But not before I saw boxers covered in heart shapes.

Waaaayyy too much information.

"Go ahead and sit," I told him, copping a spot on the arm of his chair.

He smiled at me and winked. "Were I but ten years younger," he said, patting my leg.

By my calculations, ten years younger would put him at eighty. Still, I'd heard rumors about him at eighty that would put most randy teenagers to shame. I smiled and covered his wrinkly hand with mine. "If I were but ten years older."

He winked again.

I smiled. Between him and Vice Principal MacKenna, my ego was slowly gluing itself back together. Just because Kevin didn't want me, didn't mean no one else did.

All right, so one was married, and the other was old enough to be my great-grandfather. But still. It felt nice.

Mr. Cabrera called the meeting to order by clearing his throat repeatedly. After it was determined he wasn't choking, and he had everyone's attention, he got right to the point. "Miz Quinn thinks our burglar is a pervert."

Twenty geriatric heads turned my way. I rolled my eyes and wished I'd stayed in the shower.

"I never said pervert," I defended.

"What else would you call someone who goes around stealing gra—" He cleared his throat. "Ladies' panties?"

I bit back a smile at him not saying "granny." Probably didn't want to ruffle any feathers since most of the women in the room constituted the Mill's dating pool.

"He has a point," Mrs. Daasch said.

"How do we know for certain that's what the burglar's doing?" Mrs. Mustard asked, crossing her legs as if the panty thief might be in the room at that moment and thinking about stealing her JCPenney briefs right out from under her polyester skirt.

Actually, if my theory *was* right, the panty thief might very well be in the room.

I glanced from face to face as the debate about burglars and panties grew heated.

Colonel Mustard sat next to his wife on the love seat. He was a decorated World War II hero, and I really couldn't see him getting his jollies from a bunch of stretched out underwear.

Mr. Cabrera? I ruled him out immediately. Not that I didn't think he could get his jollies from old ladies' underwear—I think he could. And has. But he'd be more likely to come out and ask for them.

My gaze landed on Riley, who stood in a corner, listening intently. I allowed myself to think about him being involved with this—but only for a few seconds. I could see him doing this only as a prank. Once. Not numerous times, and not to the point where it would cause someone a heart attack.

I ruled him out. Mostly because I refused to believe it.

Denial was sometimes a good thing.

Flash? I looked down at his crown of white hair. It was thinning on top, but was white as down. It was true his days of being a player were over, both on the field and in the bedroom, but would he resort to panty stealing?

Mr. Weatherbee? I looked over to where he sat on the hearth. He was a mean old man, the kind who kept your ball if it went into his yard. He'd been divorced nearly thirty years ago, and now lived with his mother, who was pushing one hundred. He never dated, as far as anyone knew—and in the Mill we'd know—and received *Playboy* in the mail.

He looked up, caught me staring. He scowled and turned away.

Well, so much for my healing ego.

The Molari brothers? I doubted it. One never went anywhere without the other, and there was no evidence about there being two burglars.

Really, I couldn't see any of them being involved. Well, maybe Mr. Weatherbee, but that was just because I didn't like him.

The meeting dragged on for an hour. I kept eyeing my backpack sitting by the front door and wishing everyone would leave.

As much as the panty thief was a problem, what was happening with Nate was bigger.

Riley looked at his watch. "All right, everyone! Meeting's over! I need to get to work."

Bones creaked and knees popped as people rose. I helped Flash to his feet when he had trouble getting out of the double wide chair.

As people filed out, Mr. Cabrera shook Riley's hand. He turned to me and said, "Good boy you got there."

"Sometimes," I said.

Riley rolled his eyes. "I'm gonna be late," he said as Mr. Cabrera shuffled out the door.

"And whose fault is that?" I asked. "What was this all about anyway?"

"What?"

"The meeting? Here?"

"I didn't think you'd mind."

"I don't." All right, I did, but he didn't have to know that. "How'd you get involved in this?"

"Oh. Mr. C asked if I wanted to be his partner. Said he needed a young pair of eyes, ears, and legs."

Partner? "Partner in what?"

Riley beamed. "Crime solving."

"What!?"

"It's gonna be so cool. I'll be just like Dad," he said, oblivious to me freaking out in front of him.

"Riley . . ."

He ran up the stairs. "I'll be ready in a minute."

I slumped into the chair Flash Leonard had just vacated, dropped my head into my hands.

Twelve

I dropped Riley off at Kroger and got him to promise he'd come straight home after work.

I wasn't holding my breath.

Out of the corner of my eye I checked my backpack for the hundredth time to make sure Nate's package hadn't upped and disappeared.

It hadn't.

I'd successfully evaded all temptation to open it at every stoplight. I needed space to spread out whatever was in there.

And if it was especially shocking, I didn't want to be behind the wheel of Maria's Mercedes if I crashed.

Maria. I'd dropped her off at my mother's after finding Claire's body. She'd promised to tell my mother everything that had happened, from Nate's misplacement to finding Claire's body. I still hadn't heard from her, and I was holding onto that no news, good news saying.

Ugh. Again with sounding like my mother! Tam would pitch a fit.

Ugh. Tam. I wondered if Leo Barker was still alive.

I thought about calling the office to check on things and decided to let it be. However, I couldn't stop thinking about all the preparation going into Maria's backyard. I needed to find out ASAP if I should continue as planned. Which meant contacting Nate's dad. I wondered if Maria had already called him about Nate. Someone needed to.

I frowned in confusion as I pulled into my driveway. Kit's TBS truck was parked at the curb, and he was sitting on my porch swing.

I hoped the bolts held.

"What are you doing here?" I asked, hopping out of the car.

"Sweet ride. New?"

"Maria's."

"That explains it."

I took the porch steps two at a time. "Tam didn't kill Leo Barker, did she?"

I didn't really think she had. Okay, so I was a little worried. All right, I was a lot worried.

"Not yet."

I noticed he wasn't smiling. Kit was almost always smiling. "What's wrong?"

"This." He pulled a small animal carrier out from under the swing. I hadn't even seen it there behind his tree trunk legs.

"What's that?"

"That's Gracie," he said.

I swallowed, not liking his dark tone. "Who's Gracie?"

His thick eyebrows rose. "Your new dog."

"What?!"

He mimicked my voice. " 'Get a small dog, something cute. Girls don't like big slobbery dogs.' " He narrowed his lined eyes at me. "I should have told you that Daisy isn't like most girls."

I took a step back. "Uh, she didn't like the dog?"

A dark eyebrow slashed upward. "You think?"

"Um. Well. Why don't you take it back, get a refund?"

"No takesies-back where I got this dog," he said in a way that made "takesies" sound menacing and not cute.

Gulp. I didn't even want to know.

"There's got to be a shelter that'll take him?" I asked meekly.

"Her. It's a her. And Daisy won't hear of it. Wants her to go to a good home."

I shifted my backpack. "Your home is a good home."

He rose. "The dog's certifiable. She needs to be with someone equally crazy." He shoved the carrier at me.

Reluctantly, I took it.

He went down the steps. "Have a nice day," he called out without looking back.

I watched him drive away. Peering into the carrier, I wondered how bad it could be. Something so small should be cute and cuddly, right?

I unlocked the front door and set my backpack and the carrier on the floor.

It took me a full minute to get the cage door open and another five to coax Gracie out, her yipping and growling the whole time.

Gracie was a Chihuahua. All black, with white fur on her feet that looked like little bobby socks. She was adorable, with big black ears, a pointy nose, and huge dark eyes.

She shook in my arms. I set her down. "Well, Gracie, looks like you'll be staying here for a while."

This wasn't going to be so bad. I don't know what Kit was talking about. She was a sweet little thing.

She looked up at me, tucked her tail between her legs and peed on my carpet.

An hour later I was trying my best to persuade Gracie to come out from under the couch.

Every time I actually got her out, another puddle appeared, and she'd zip back under.

I wondered about her bladder size and realized that maybe Kit hadn't been exaggerating crazy.

I didn't know what to do. I couldn't just leave her under there. Not to mention that the rug needed to be cleaned. But she just wouldn't come out—and stay out.

I nudged the couch with my foot. It slid an inch backward and Gracie came darting out, ears back, tail tucked, and ran into the wall behind me.

She bounced back, turned, and zipped past me. She bumped into the coffee table leg, yipped, and dove back under the couch.

Ohhhkay. I'd leave her be for now.

I grabbed my backpack, pulled out Nate's package, set it on the table.

Guilt tugged at my conscience. He'd told me not to open it. But that was before Claire was found dead. All bets were now off.

Taking a deep breath, I ripped the top off the package Band-Aid-style, quick and fast.

I squeezed the envelope so it billowed out and peeked inside. I saw several folds of cream-colored paper protecting a smaller wrapped bundle.

Swallowing hard, I put the envelope on the table.

Did I really want to be doing this? Hadn't I learned my lesson about snooping into other people's lives?

My inner voice nagged that this wasn't *people*. This was Nate, and consequentially, Maria. My baby sister.

Usually, I didn't listen to that voice. I likened it to the angel and devil that sat on cartoon characters' shoulders . . . Over the years I recognized that my inner voice tended to run more hot than halo—which meant that I probably shouldn't be doing what I was about to do.

I reached in and grabbed hold of the paper. Slowly, I slid it out, and dropped the whole thing on the floor when someone thumped on my door.

My heart lodged in my throat, beat there wildly while I gathered up the envelope, the papers, and shoved them back into my backpack.

"Neee-nah!"

Maria. "Oh crap," I muttered under my breath. "I'm coming!"

Gracie shot out from under the couch, started running in circles, yipping and yapping.

A cab was pulling away from the curb as I pulled open the door. Maria was on the porch, a Louis Vuitton garment bag draped over her arm. Her huge rolling suitcase at her feet. Her gaze narrowed on Gracie.

"Eeee!" she squealed. She pulled me in front of her as a shield. "Is that a rat?" she asked.

I ducked out of her grasp and quickly closed the door before Gracie darted outside in a manic haze.

"Yeah. Rats bark."

Maria's lashes fluttered. "Are you mocking?"

I ignored her. Squatting, I said, "Come here, Gracie."

More yips and yaps. I scooted closer to where she was still running in circles. She tucked her tail between her legs and peed on the floor.

Maria stepped back. "Ewww!"

I closed my eyes. I was going to kill Kit. Turning, I looked at Maria. "What are you doing here?"

"What do you mean?"

"You. Here. Why?" Any patience I'd had seeped into the rug with psycho Chihuahua pee.

"I'm moving in, of course."

Of course. How silly of me. "Why?"

"I can't possibly stay at either of my places. Everything's

tainted. By the stalker at my condo, and then with Claire's body being in my backyard . . ." She set her garment bag on the chair.

Gracie dove back under the couch. I heard a thud and hoped she hadn't knocked herself out.

I sat on the floor, crossed my legs and looked up, wondering when lightning was going to strike me, because apparently I'd done something so horrible that I was being punished.

"I mean, really," Maria said, kicking off her shoes. After looking at Gracie's puddle, she put them back on. "Claire's body couldn't have been dumped somewhere else? It had to be *my* yard?"

I really didn't think it was a coincidence Claire's body was found in Maria's yard. Was someone trying to frame Maria or Nate? Or was it left there as a message of some sort?

I felt a sisterly duty to warn Maria about living here. Maybe then she'd leave. "You do know a teenage boy lives here, right?"

"I love Riley."

"He has a snake."

Maria shuddered. "I'm not planning to play with it."

"And it looks like I have a new dog. You don't like dogs, remember? Maybe you should stay at Mom and Dad's."

She arched pale eyebrows. "Are you trying to get rid of me?"

Yes. "No, not at all."

"Kevin thinks Nate might have done it. Killed Claire, I mean," Maria said, changing the subject. Looked like I had a houseguest.

Gracie poked her pointy nose out, sniffed Maria's leg. "Are you sure that's really a dog?"

"Yes."

"Is it really yours?"

"No. Yes. Maybe."

She arched an eyebrow at that. Gracie ventured out and sniffed Maria's leg. Miraculously, Maria didn't seem to mind. Apparently she'd forgotten she had dog issues.

"Nate would never leave a body in his own backyard," she said as if we hadn't been sidetracked by a five-pound dog with bladder problems. "He's not that stupid."

In the blink of an eye Gracie lunged forward and bit Maria's ankle. "Ow!" She pulled her leg up on the couch.

Gracie darted back under the couch.

"She bit me," Maria whined.

"She's little—it couldn't have hurt that much. Maybe that's the way she kisses. It was a love bite."

Maria narrowed her eyes. "Has she had her shots?"

I shrugged.

"Nee-nah!"

"Don't panic. I'll ask Kit when I see him."

"Kit?" She smiled dreamily.

Rolling my eyes, I got to my feet. "Could we get back to Nate?"

She rubbed the spot Gracie had bitten. "He's not dumb, Nina. I know professional athletes have that kind of reputation, but he's not. He's got a master's in business, for goodness' sake. I think he could figure out not to dump a body in his own yard."

"Unless he knows people will think that he's too smart to do something like that, then when he does do it, he doesn't look guilty."

Maria rubbed her temples. "You're giving me a headache. Nate didn't kill Claire. He wouldn't."

I tended to agree, but it begged the question, Where was

Nate? And why was Claire's body dumped in his and Maria's backyard? And what was in that package? It had to be what Claire was looking for at Maria's condo.

My gaze dropped to my backpack, at the papers I'd shoved in there.

Gracie ventured out from under the couch. She hopped up next to Maria, stared at her with big black eyes.

"You bit me," Maria accused.

Gracie tipped her head, her big ears trembling.

"Don't do it again."

I watched in amazement as Gracie climbed onto Maria's lap, turned three circles, and plopped down.

Maria looked up at me. "What do I do now?"

I grabbed my backpack. "Dog-sit?"

"What? Where are you going?"

"I need to go out for a while. Riley should be home around eight."

I hedged toward the door. Maria looked like she wanted to chase after me but didn't want to disturb the dog on her lap.

I didn't blame her. I'd seen what Gracie had done to Berber. I can only imagine what she'd do to Donna Karan.

Thirteen

Twenty minutes later I was nestled on Ana's overstuffed sofa, clinging to my backpack.

Ana was still laughing about Gracie. "And you left her with Maria?"

"They seem to get along."

"You're not worried she'll make the dog into a purse or something?"

I probably should have thought of that. I bit my lip.

"What's wrong?" she asked me. "I can tell you have more on your mind than a crazy dog and a crazier sister."

Fresh vacuum marks lined the rug. I needed to confide in someone, to get a fresh opinion. "Claire Battiste is dead."

Ana's cocoa-colored eyes widened as I told her about finding Nate's boss.

"Was Claire all bloated, like in the movies?"

I sighed. Maybe coming here wasn't a good idea.

"And," I continued, ignoring her, "I got a call from Nate this morning."

Ana leaned so far forward I thought she was going to topple right out of her lounge chair. "Oh my God! You did?"

I told her about the call, and how I didn't know for sure if it was him. Then I told her about the package and how I thought that Claire was the one who broke into Maria's place, probably looking for it.

"Well, what's in it?"

"I don't know."

"Do you have it? You brought it, didn't you? 'Cuz you can't leave me hanging like this!"

I pulled it out of my backpack.

Ana stared at it, shivered. "Aren't you going to open it?"

"I don't know! Nate had the package and he's missing. Claire wanted it and now she's dead! I don't know what to do. Should I call Kevin? Tell Maria? Close up the package and pretend I never got it?"

"Don't talk crazy! You need to open it. It's your sisterly duty to know what's in there."

More like *she* wanted to know what was in there. Still, I couldn't really argue with her reasoning. I'd had similar thoughts when I opened the package in the first place.

"Go ahead," Ana urged.

I unfolded the packet of cream-colored paper first. Opening it, I stared at a list of names.

"Well?" Ana scrambled out of her chair and sank down next to me. My cushion dipped.

"It's a list."

"Of what?"

I skimmed the three pages. Names. A ton of names. At least five hundred. At first glance the names didn't mean much, but then I saw the names of the mayor, local celebrities, the governor of Kentucky, Cincinnati city council members.

Next to the names were a series of columns labeled in a shorthand I didn't understand. Most names had several checks next to them. A guest list, I realized. The gala guest list—the one Verona and Colin Frye had been looking for?

Attached to the paper was an invitation to the event. On fancy vellum paper, it read:

Phineus Cancer Foundation Annual Gala
June 30ᵗʰ
The Kalypso
Black tie
Tickets $5000.00

"Five thousand dollars?" Ana gasped. "A plate?"

"I'm not sure."

"If it were, that would be ten thousand a couple."

I looked at her. "I can add."

She stared back. "Who has that kind of money?"

I flipped back through the pages. "Lots of people, obviously."

"There are five hundred names on the list. At five thousand a plate? How much is that?"

Okay, maybe I couldn't add all that well. I shrugged.

Ana scurried off and came back with a calculator. "That's two point five million!" She gasped. "Five million if everyone brings a date."

"It *is* a charity event."

Ana blinked and shook her head, her sleek sable ponytail swaying. "Wow."

I couldn't imagine what this all had to do with Nate's disappearance, but it was obvious that Nate had thought it important for some reason.

Ana picked up the envelope and dumped the small bundle inside it onto the table.

I reached for it, resigned. Any voice that might have warned me to stop, that I was in over my head, was drowned out by my inner voice chanting, *Do it, do it, do it.*

Pulling on the flap, I automatically cringed, preparing myself for what might be inside.

Nate hadn't wanted me to open the package, had sounded terrified. Why? Not over a guest list, certainly.

I blew out a deep breath as Ana leaned in. I emptied the packet onto my lap.

Polaroids. At least ten of them.

On top of the stack was a picture of a man from chest up, sitting in a chair. Late twenties, early thirties. Dark brown hair, five o'clock shadow, and a grim set to his jaw. The chair was Windsor style, with thin spindles and a bowed back. Behind him was a set of built-in bookshelves that were too far away to make out any details.

"Who's that?" Ana asked.

"Don't know."

"Do you think Nate has a boyfriend?" she asked.

I turned to look at her, blinked.

"What? It's possible."

It *was* possible. Anything was possible.

"Come on," Ana urged, grabbing the stack of pictures off my lap. She flipped to the next one, her breath catching.

"What? What?" I leaned in, felt my breath catch too. "That's Claire Battiste."

"You recognize her even though you only saw her when she was all bloated?"

"I saw her at Maria and Nate's engagement party."

"Oh. So she wasn't all bloated?"

"Ana!"

"Fine. Fine. That's a Smith & Wesson pistol in her hand. Nine millimeter, black polymer grip, three—no, four—inch barrel."

I gaped. "How do you know that?"

"It's a gift."

The picture showed Claire holding the gun by her side.

Her eyes seemed empty as she looked into the camera. No fear, no excitement. Just a dead calm.

I noticed too that the man's hands were pulled behind him, probably tied.

I swallowed. My pulse had kicked up a notch and perspiration dampened my palms. What had Nate gotten himself into? At this point, I almost wished he had a gay lover.

Ana flipped to the next picture. The gun was now pointed at the man's head.

Ana gasped. "Do you think these are real?"

"I'd say no, but a dead, bloated Claire Battiste was in Maria's backyard."

"So she *was* bloated!"

"Ana!"

"All right!"

Ana flipped to the next shot. Claire had moved back and pointed the gun cop-style at the man's temple.

My stomach knotted, afraid of what the next picture would show.

Claire's eyes were shut, I noticed, when she fired. The man's head was a blur as he slumped sideways, still held in place by the ropes holding him to the chair.

Ana and I looked at each other. Neither of us could find words.

The last pictures were of Claire cleaning up the mess.

Ana dropped the stack on the table.

I flipped them facedown.

My stomach twisted and turned.

Ana reached over and grabbed my hand, and we sat there a long time.

"Okay," Ana said. "I can kinda see why Claire might have wanted these pictures back. I'd have broken into Maria's for them too."

I was feeling kind of numb. "What now?" I asked.

"I wish I knew, Nina."

"This is surreal."

"No idea who the guy is?"

"I've never seen him before."

"What about Maria? Would she know?"

Maria. Ugh. Just how did I explain this to her? "She might," I said. "I don't know."

"You need to call Kevin."

I thought the same thing. I'd learned my lesson about homicide investigations. I wanted no part of this. None. Zero.

Still . . .

"Who do you think the woman who tried to steal these pictures was?" I asked.

"The blue-haired lady?"

"Yeah."

"A pickpocket?"

"Who bypassed my wallet to get this package? I don't think so."

"Creepy."

"Very."

Her eyes brightened.

"What?"

"Let me have the prints run."

"Huh?"

"The prints on the envelope. The lady had to have touched it, right?"

"So did I, and Brickhouse, and Tam and Lyle—"

"Lyle?"

"The messenger."

"Is he single?"

"Don't know."

"Oh." It took a millisecond for her to leave Lyle in the dust. "Come on," she pleaded. "Let me get the prints run. I never get to do anything fun. I can take the envelope to a friend of mine at the police department, ask a favor. What can it hurt?"

I ran through this in my mind. If Ana took the envelope and had the prints run, then we might know who the blue-haired lady really was. And if we knew who she was, we might be able to figure out who she worked for, and that might lead us to Claire's murderer.

No, no, no, I told myself. I was not getting involved.

But . . . wasn't I already involved?

Besides, what could it hurt to know? It wasn't like I was going to do anything with the information. And once Kevin got the package, I'd probably never hear another word about it again.

My curiosity needed closure.

"All right," I said, already planning. Should I tell Kevin I threw the envelope away? Or wait until Ana was done with it and then pass everything on to him?

"What does fingerprinting do to an envelope? Would Kevin know we'd done it?"

"Yeah, he'd probably know," she said.

All-righty, then. I'd tell him I lost the envelope. If we turned up anything, then we'd take it to him and plead ignorance.

I put the pictures into the folds of the guest list and fished around in my backpack for a rubber band.

I was going to stop at the drugstore on the way home and have copies of the pictures made on one of those Kodak machines. I'd also have the guest list photocopied.

Hey, it couldn't hurt to have a set of duplicates, I told myself, breaking a cardinal commandment. Thou Shalt Not Delude Thyself.

I'd suffer the consequences later, I was sure.

I packed everything up, gave Ana a hug.

"Everything's going to be all right," she said.

"Promise?"

She half shrugged and smiled. "You know how I am about commitment, Nina."

I had to smile too. "Well, *I'm* holding you to it."

"Seriously, you okay?"

I had to think about it. It was true my life was a stressed-out mess right now, but overall . . . "Yeah."

"Good. Because my mother wants to get together for supper tomorrow night."

I smiled. I loved my aunt Rosetta. She was crazier than Ana and me put together. "That'll certainly take my mind off things."

Ana bit her lip.

"What?"

"She wants your parents to come too. I kinda need you to invite them. She wants to end this feud once and for all."

Oh no. What she really meant was that I needed to trick them into coming. Because that was the only way my mother would be there.

Ana smiled wide. "And I kinda volunteered you to cook."

"What?!"

"No need to get snippy. I'll bring the wine."

I sighed. I wasn't going to need wine. I was going to need a defibrillator when my mother saw Aunt Rosa.

"Oh, and Nina?" she said as I pulled open the door.

"Yeah?"

She nodded toward my backpack. "Who do you think it was who took those pictures?"

Oh my God. I hadn't even thought of that. I could only think of one person—the person who sent them to me.

Nate.

Fourteen

Early the next morning, I stumbled, bleary-eyed, into TBS. Between the crazy dog and Maria's moaning and groaning every time she turned on the sleeper sofa—not to mention those awful, awful pictures—I'd barely gotten any sleep.

The cowbell above the door rang out, and Tam looked up from her computer screen. Dark circles rimmed her eyes. "You're early."

I opened my mouth to explain about Maria and the dog, but closed it again. I didn't have the energy.

"So are you," I said.

She grumbled something under her breath. I thought I heard "winker" and "intuition."

I plopped into the chair in front of her desk. "You okay?"

Curled and sprayed into submission, her hair didn't move when she shook her head. "No."

"Is this still about Leo?"

Drawing her bottom lip into her mouth, she bit it. "He's made it personal. He asked me out."

Maybe Leo had a death wish. "And?"

"How does he know I'm not married?"

I suggested the obvious. "No ring?"

"Pregnant women often take their rings off. Swelling," she said, as if I didn't have a clue.

She was right, but still. "But you're not married. Or dating. So, maybe he was hoping?"

Her blue eyes narrowed. "He's . . ."

"Cute?"

"Weasel-y. He's like that Eddie Haskell character." She growled at her computer as if it had let her down. "I can't find anything on him. He's squeaky clean!"

"I'd think that was a good thing. What?" I said when she looked at me, eyebrows furrowed, a frown tugging on her thin lips. "Not good?"

"Not good at all."

"Well, I hope you let him down gently." I didn't want him to quit over this. TBS was in desperate need of help for the next few months.

She rubbed a finger over one of Sassy's leaves. "I said yes."

I blinked, wondering if I was still in bed, dreaming. "What? Yes? As in, yes you'll go out with him?"

"It's time to fight fire with fire."

Rising, I held up a hand to stop her from saying anything else. "I don't want to know." The less I knew, the less the police could get out of me.

I passed the coffeemaker, almost tempted. But I despised the bitter taste, so I made a beeline for the small fridge and pulled out a Dr Pepper. I needed caffeine in a bad way.

I held it up to Tam so she could check it off on her inventory list and ambled into my office, closing the door behind me.

The Dr Pepper hissed as I popped the top. I rooted around the bottom drawer of my desk and came up with an Almond Joy.

My mother would have a fit if she knew what I was eating.

I groaned. My mother.

I still needed to call her about dinner.

Swiveling in my chair, I looked out the window. It had finally stopped raining. My gaze settled on the gardens behind the office. There were six separate ones, ranging from cottage style to contemporary, water to xeric. My glance lingered on a copper water feature with a lustrous green patina.

Kevin was supposed to be stopping by later to pick up the package. I hadn't told him *what* he was picking up, only that I had something important to the Claire Battiste investigation.

I'd say.

Was Nate really involved? To what extent? Maria had finally called Nate's dad, who was frantic. He'd put the pressure on the Cincinnati cops, the Freedom cops, and even called the FBI. I supposed a former governor had that kind of pull.

I was expecting a visit from someone with a badge any second now, as soon as they found out Nate had sent a package to me the day he disappeared.

Hopefully, the contents of that package wouldn't be in my possession when they showed up.

For what seemed like the thousandth time, I wondered if Nate had really taken those pictures. If he had stood by and watched a man get murdered.

I shuddered.

It was hard to imagine Nate being involved in something like that. But I couldn't explain those pictures otherwise. My only other thought was that he found them, but it was highly unlikely that Claire—or anyone else—would leave something like that lying around.

I set my cell phone on my desk in hopes that Nate would call again. For the time being I'd try to stay focused on work.

Glancing up at the clock, I wondered when Leo would be in. I still had questions about him that needed answers. And the fact that he was cozying up with Tam only added fuel to my fire. If he had ulterior motives for getting a job here, then Tam was putting herself—and her baby—in danger.

I checked my day-planner, groaned when all it said was *Maria*.

Not good.

Everything to do with that job needed to be put on hold. I couldn't risk spending thousands of dollars on materials without knowing if the wedding was off. I'd already used up the deposit Nate Sr. had given me. Thankfully, that was nonrefundable.

Which left me doing something I really didn't want to do.

I'd spent most of my sleepless night debating and finally figured I had no choice. Picking up my phone, I dialed Verona Frye.

Desperate times and all.

I had employees to pay, bills due, and an overhead to keep up. With Maria's job on hold, and nothing on the schedule for another three weeks . . . these *were* desperate times.

All right, so there was also a part of me that wanted to ask Verona Frye a few questions. Questions about the PCF gala. I was still trying to figure out why Nate had included a guest list in that packet.

Verona was involved in planning the gala. She'd have known Claire and Nate. Maybe I could get some insight from someone on the inside.

Verona Frye answered on the fifth ring. "Oh, I'm so glad your schedule opened up," she said after I reintroduced myself and told her why I was calling.

I wondered if she'd heard about Claire yet. By her joyful tone, I didn't think she had. "I'd like to schedule a consultation, Mrs. Frye. I'll need to sit down with you to get a feel for what you're looking for, and also take some measurements and pictures of the space. Of course, if this is a surprise for Mr. Frye, I suggest he not be home."

I was continually amazed at how often people forgot that one tiny detail.

She laughed. "Verona, please. And Colin never seems to be home this time of year, with the gala preparations. A lot of thought goes into the event."

"Oh?" I said, prying. "Like what?"

"Everything from gift baskets to lighting."

"Aren't details like that handled by the Kalypso staff?"

"Yes," she said, something cold in her voice. "Colin and Claire work closely together to make sure everything is perfect." Her tone softened a bit. "Of course, my mother gets final say, and she can be picky."

My stomach twisted at the sound of Claire's name, but I pried on. "What about you?" I asked. "Don't you get a say?"

She laughed, a brittle titter. "Not usually. Just this year since they were in desperate need of my help. Even still, I'm mostly implementing *their* plans."

"Why just this year?" I asked. "You are a Phineus."

"PCF is Roz's baby."

I wanted to keep questioning her, but I didn't want to arouse her suspicion. "Oh. Well, is there a good time for us to meet?"

I heard papers rustling. "I have two o'clock today open. Is that good for you?" she asked.

"Perfect." Hopefully, I'd get lost on my way home or caught up in work and forget that I had to make dinner tonight. I shuddered when I thought of my mother and Aunt Rosa in the same room. It was bound to be ugly.

I took down Verona's address, which was in the swanky town of Indian Hills, jotted directions, and hung up.

While my computer loaded, I sipped my Dr Pepper, nibbled my Almond Joy. First things first. I wanted to Google the Phineus Cancer Foundation. After that I'd tackle Nate, see if I found anything that would explain what he was doing with pictures that showed someone being killed.

Really, I ought to get Tam to do this search for me. She was a whiz with computers—which is how she ended up working for me. She'd been caught computer hacking back in college. Luckily, she'd gotten off with probation and had been on a straight and narrow path ever since. Okay, maybe once in a while she took a wayward fork in the road, but I didn't hold it against her. Especially since I was usually the one navigating.

I decided to leave her out of this. She had enough on her mind right now.

Hunting and pecking, I typed in "Phineus Cancer Foundation" on Google's search page, and a whole list of sites spewed onto my screen. Luckily, PCF's official site was near the top.

I scanned as I scrolled, looking for anything and everything. I wasn't sure why I was even bothering, except for the guest list that had been in Nate's little care package.

I shuddered.

I clicked on various testimonials from families, local charities, even research facilities that had benefited from Phineus Cancer Foundation's generosity.

By the end of my search, I almost wanted to donate to PCF myself. Except the image of a man being killed by Claire Battiste held me back.

Try as I might, I couldn't figure out how it all tied together. There were too many questions. Why had Nate put the PCF guest list in the package with those pictures? Who was the man Claire had killed? How did the blue-haired lady know *I* had the package? And how did she fit in? Because I didn't believe for a second that her pickpocketing was coincidental.

If the pictures in the package were real (and they definitely looked real), Claire had killed a man. Then someone had killed Claire.

And Nate was missing.

Glancing at the phone, I wished he would call me again. If not to out and out confess to something, then to reassure me that he wasn't some serial killer.

I back-clicked to Google's main page and typed in "Nate Biederman." After thirty minutes of wading through pages and pages of mind-numbing info, I finally signed off.

There hadn't been anything I didn't already know about Nate. He was, according to the Internet, the epitome of the all-American boy next door living a perfect life.

But as I pulled out the copies I made of the pictures Nate sent me, I knew that just wasn't true.

Fifteen

Indian Hill was a bit of a hike from the office. I took I-75 south, then jumped onto I-275 east. Once off the highway, I tried not to drool as I drove through the neighborhoods of Cincinnati's elite. This is where the best of the best lived.

Behind large stone walls and iron gates, mansions sat proudly. Lawns were meticulous, the landscaping incredible. I thought about slipping some business cards into mailboxes on my way home, but decided against it. I liked to play hard to get.

Hopefully, the mini at the Fryes would get my name into this social register. Where I hoped it would stay for a long, long time.

Unfortunately, as I drove along, I recognized there was little need for my services. Every mansion was landscaped to perfection.

As I drove, I also kept glancing at my backpack. I hated toting those pictures around. Kevin hadn't made it to the office before I'd had to leave. I called and left a message asking him to stop by the house later to pick up the package I had for him. I'd almost wanted to say "the package with the pictures of Claire shooting some guy," but I didn't know who'd be in hearing distance when he played his messages.

Approaching the Frye's house, I slowed. As I drove up the single lane driveway, I took it all in.

The grounds were immaculate, every blade of grass cut with precision. The gardener had gone with a red theme. Red begonias shared a winding bed alongside the walkway with red petunias. Bright crimson spikes of salvia and feathery astilbe complemented the theme and added height and texture to the mix. By the end of summer it would be breathtaking.

It was already beautiful. And I had to wonder why I was here.

The driveway widened into a courtyard. I parked in front of a pristine carriage house that looked like it had been converted to a guest home. I oohed over window boxes stuffed full of scarlet primroses with bold yellow centers and cascading vinca vines.

I looped the strap of my Polaroid over my shoulder, grabbed my drawing pad and measuring wheel and hopped out of my truck.

Verona Frye strode down the walkway. She wore moss green silk lounging pants and a cream-colored tank top. A strand of pearls hung on her neck and pearl studs decorated her ears. Her long blonde hair was pulled back, secured with two long sticks that made me wonder how it all stayed put.

On anyone else—even Maria—the outfit would look ridiculous. Somehow Verona Frye pulled it off.

Instead of shaking my hand, she grasped my elbows lightly and brushed a kiss on each of my cheeks. "I'm so glad you came. Colin will be thrilled with this surprise. Just thrilled. We're both so busy right now that he'll never suspect a thing."

"Beautiful place," I said.

"Thanks." Her nose scrunched up. "It's a little ostentatious for my tastes, but Colin likes it. And so does my mother."

"Roz?"

Verona motioned with her head to the carriage house. "This is her place."

I shuddered at the thought of my mother living so close to me. Verona must have been reading my mind.

"It does get a tad," she pursed her coral bottom lip, "*cozy* sometimes, but overall it works well." She looked around as if seeing it for the first time. "It's hard to believe my father was the son of a poor barkeep."

Her father. Alfred Phineus. "How long has he been gone?" I asked, hoping I didn't sound too nosy.

"Three years now." She scrunched her nose again. "He'd hate this."

"This?"

"The house, the cars . . . all the show."

"Really?" I'd assumed with his millions that he'd lived a similar lifestyle.

"Until he died, he and Roz lived in a small split level in Avondale. Daddy didn't believe in material things. It was the way he was brought up, I guess. Which is why I'm not completely comfortable here, I suppose."

"What about your mother?" I asked. Curiosity was one of my weaker traits. I just couldn't help myself. I couldn't imagine Roz, with her platinum hair and red talons, living in a split level anywhere, never mind Avondale, which wasn't known for its high society.

Verona's hand plucked the pearls at her neck. "Roz tolerated well," she said. "She was never lacking for anything, but she wasn't spoiled."

Not like now, I thought, remembering the multicarat princess-cut diamonds she wore the other day.

"Why don't you show me the area that needs a make-over?" I asked.

How did I work in questions about Nate? About Claire? Would Verona even know anything about them?

As we walked, she said, "I'm so glad your schedule opened up, Nina."

I didn't mention why it had opened up, so I hedged, feeling her out. "I am too. It's always nice to help out a friend of the family. Maria has had nothing but nice things to say about Phineus Frye."

"She's an asset, that's for certain. Colin raves about her work, and is as proud as can be for setting her up with Nate."

"Do you know Nate well?"

Again the cloud crossed her face. I wondered at it, but when she spoke, there was nothing somber in her tone. "Not very." Suddenly, she laughed. "I actually remember worrying about him."

I hoped my eyes didn't pop out of my head. "Why?"

She stopped walking and again her hand went to her pearls. "It seems silly now, but he was so trusting, so open. I worried about him working at the Kalypso with Claire, though it all seems to have worked out."

I stared at my mud-covered Timberlands. If she only knew.

This was probably a good time to sneak Claire into the conversation. "Claire has taken good care of him."

Her lips thinned. "Yes. Well."

All right-y. Obviously Claire was a sore spot. I decided to press my luck. "You said Claire works closely with Colin? Just on the gala? Do they get along?"

She twisted the pearls so tightly I thought they were going to pop loose or choke her.

"I'll say this for Claire: She knows how to get what she wants."

I winced at the venom in her voice. I wanted to pry, but her tone warned me to back off.

Part of me wanted to tell her that Claire was dead, but then Verona might start questioning me, and that wouldn't do.

I shifted to a droll conversation about the weather. As we talked, she led me around to the back of the house. A three-foot-high stacked stone wall lined the perimeter of the backyard. She opened a rusty iron gate and led me down a curving brick path. I stopped dead in my tracks when we rounded the corner. "Whoa."

She beamed. I hadn't thought her pretty. Not really. Her nose was too long, her face too narrow. Average blue eyes were set too close together, and her lips were wafer thin. But when she smiled . . . it transformed her whole face.

"It's gorgeous," I said, taking in the informal English garden.

The path meandered through beds of gorgeous annuals and mature perennials and shrubs. Sunbeams highlighted the vibrant colors of tea roses, hydrangeas, columbine, lavender, peonies, and delphiniums. Spirea, lady's mantle, foxglove, hollyhock, and lamb's ear accented the bold hues. Closer to the ground, bellflowers, daisies, yarrow, phlox, and pink coreopsis added a stunning depth to the garden.

It should all be too much, but it wasn't. It worked. Which was the beauty of a cottage garden.

I turned to her. "Why am I here, Verona? It's obvious you don't need any help from me."

"Nonsense," she said, starting down the brick path. With outstretched arms she said, "All this was done by the previous owners. I admit it's why *I* fell in love with the place.

And why I pay a small fortune to my gardener to keep it looking this good."

We veered left off the path, toward a hidden corner of the lot.

"This," Verona said, "is why you're here."

I looked around at this little corner nook and wondered What Went Wrong. Something obviously had.

"Colin loves this spot, especially in the spring," she said.

Behind the stacked stone wall, someone had planted a lilac hedge. I could just imagine the amazing scent when the shrubs were in bloom. I'd love it here too.

Looking around, I took everything in. Behind the hedge, dense woods blocked any view of neighbors, though I did notice a horse trail cutting through the trees. A lone wooden Adirondack chair sat in the Corner That Had Seen Better Days.

"I tried to pretty this up, but nothing seems to work. The perennial garden withered and died. I tried a vegetable garden here last year. Nothing grew. Just two days ago, I dug out a bed of three dozen impatiens. They'd all wilted and withered."

Bending over, I frowned. Bits of limp green stems had been left behind. Pink petals littered the area. The soil was damp, but it was good soil, rich and dark, and it looked to have good drainage.

I brushed my fingers against my jeans. There were a number of reasons Verona had no luck planting here. She could have a black thumb, for one. Overwatered. Underwatered. Overfed.

"Colin has always wanted to use this space as an outdoor getaway. Somewhere to be alone with nature. Our anniversary is coming up and I'd love to surprise him. Do you think you can help me?"

"I know I can help," I reassured her. "It's just a matter of coming up with something."

Her blue eyes sparkled in the sunlight. "Do you have any ideas?"

I bit my lip, looked around. After a few minutes I said, "Maybe we could put a small arbor here with a hidden bench, and plant vines that will cover it by the end of summer. Something elegant that will blend in with the rest of the garden."

Verona nodded, and I kept on talking. "Or, we could try to work with the soil and create a raised grassy terrace, a natural patio where you could have a cozy seating area . . . but—"

"What?"

"It's a lot of work. Too much for a mini."

"Oh. Do you have any other ideas?"

Usually it took me days to come up with even one idea. I'd pore over photographs of an area and draw several rough drafts of a design before I found one that worked. But today I knew what I wanted right from the moment I saw the area. I'd been saving the best for last.

"What I'd really like to do is work with the beautiful stone wall. I'd love to build a water feature—a small pond with a tumbled fieldstone waterfall that will look like it has always been here." As with every job I did, I felt the excitement building. "Around its base, we'll put in a small flagstone patio—just large enough to fit a chaise lounge to lie back on and enjoy the sights and sounds, and a small table to put your drink on."

Verona played with her pearls. "It's perfect! It's serene, yet masculine with all the stone. Colin will love it. When do you think you could have a design for me?"

Realistically, I'd need a week at least to come up with

something. However, realistically didn't pay the bills. If I worked late into the night on it, I could probably have a decent draft done by tomorrow afternoon.

Verona beamed when I told her. "That's fantastic! When do you think construction could begin?"

Unfortunately my schedule was wide open. "Did you have a day in mind?"

"Colin is out of town on Friday. He and Roz are meeting with their New York attorneys. They're leaving late Thursday night and will be back on Friday night. I could surprise both of them with it! How wonderful."

Already I was compiling a mental shopping list. The supplies for the water garden were fairly common, and I didn't think I'd have any problem getting what I wanted in such a short amount of time.

I took a few snapshots of the area and measured it out. Roughly, I sketched my vision on my notepad, already loving the way it looked. The curves and informal structure of the pond would complement the existing garden perfectly.

As Verona walked me back to my truck, she asked, "Would you care to come in, have some lemonade?"

"I really can't. I have so much—"

"I have fresh sugar cookies too. I just baked them this morning. Haven't even frosted them yet."

I think I drooled. "Frosting?"

"Vanilla."

No doubt about it: I was a certified cookie addict. "Sounds great," I said.

After dumping my stuff in the truck, I locked the doors out of habit and followed Verona into the Frye manse. I'd been in nice houses before, but this looked like something out of *Architectural Digest*. High ceilings, polished marble floors, dark woods, and subtle lighting. A curved marble staircase rose up two stories, and my gaze followed it straight to the round stained-glass skylight above.

I blinked as I looked back at Verona. "Wow."

"It *is* something," she said. "Sometimes I feel like I shouldn't be wearing shoes in here, and that I should whisper."

Her voice echoed slightly through the cavernous room and up to the vaulted, beamed ceiling. I knew what she meant. The place had an air of a museum—or church. I didn't know which was worse. It made my little bungalow seem downright cozy.

Sure enough, in the kitchen a big plate of cookies sat on the counter. Verona pulled a bowl of homemade frosting from the fridge. My stomach leapt with joy.

I sat on a stool at the breakfast bar. Verona stuck a knife in the frosting bowl and pushed it, and the plate of cookies, toward me.

"Please help yourself." She took a cookie and dipped it in the frosting, her smile falling, her face suddenly looking sad.

I spread frosting on a cookie. "If you hate it here, why don't you move?" I asked, the cookie high making me brave.

"Things aren't always that easy, unfortunately. This is where Colin wants to be. And I want to be with Colin. I'll get used to it. Eventually."

My nosiness reared. "Have you been married long?"

"Five years."

Out of the newlywed stage but hadn't hit the seven-year itch yet. "He seems like a nice guy."

She reached over for another cookie. "He is," she said. "But I'd rather him be home more. He's always working."

I opened my mouth to tell her that she needed to let him know how she felt, but snapped it closed again. In light of my impending divorce, I didn't think I was one to offer any kind of marital advice.

I took another bite of cookie. *Ahhhh*. It was so buttery and soft. "Had Colin worked at your dad's company long? Before he met you, I mean?"

"A couple of years."

"He made partner fast."

Her cheeks colored. "I think that had more to do with me than anything. The partnership was a wedding present, but Colin deserved it. He works hard and brings in a lot of lucrative accounts."

I was on my fourth cookie. "What about your mother? Has she always been interested in public relations?"

"My mother? Oh!" Her face lit. "She's just—"

A shrill beeping cut her off. She winced. "What's that?"

I was already on my feet. "My truck's alarm."

Hurrying out the front door, all I could think of was those pictures in my backpack. The backpack in my truck.

Outside, a white Lexus was parked next to my truck. Roz Phineus had her hands over her ears.

With the remote on my key chain, I silenced the alarm.

"Roz?" Verona's voice sounded slightly off-key and guilty.

I went into my Pinocchio mode. Verona had said she'd wanted to surprise her mother with the makeover as well. I needed an excuse as to why I was here—and fast.

"What're you doing here?" Verona asked her mother.

Roz placed her manicured hands on her hips. "I *live* here."

"Uh," Verona mumbled. "You're just . . . early."

"I have to get my nails done. I broke one," she said, frowning. Well, at least I thought she was frowning. It was hard to tell because of all the Botox.

She looked at me, narrowed her eyes. "Nina Quinn, right?" she said in that scratchy voice of hers.

I nodded.

"How is Maria?"

How was she? She was a neurotic mess. But I kept that to myself and went along with Maria's phony illness. She'd been calling in sick these past couple of days. "She's getting better."

"And Nate?"

My nose was growing by the minute. "Nate's, um, good."

Verona's eyes narrowed again. "Does he have the same flu as Maria? Because I heard he hasn't been into work either. With the gala coming up, it's terrible timing."

"I'm sure they'll both be better soon." I shifted foot to foot. "I, um . . . Why was my truck alarm going off?"

"Oh, that!" Roz laughed. "I was curious who was here. I peeked in the window and the buzzer went off."

It was my turn to narrow my eyes. "Really?"

She tipped her silver head as if daring me to call her on it. "Yes."

Interesting, since my alarm only went off if the door handles were engaged. Why was she lying?

"What are you doing here, Mrs. Quinn?" she asked.

Verona looked at me helplessly. Great. Seems she was a lousy liar. Fortunately, I'd had many years of practice.

"Verona mentioned her beautiful gardens to me the other day, and asked if I'd like to stop by sometime to see them. I'm always looking for inspiration for my work." Just keep shoveling, I told myself. "Everything here is gorgeous. Just perfect." I cleared my throat. "I wouldn't change a single thing."

Roz stared at me. Verona smiled and said, "We were just having cookies. Would you like some?"

"Cookies? How trite." Tight skin strained as if she was trying to frown.

Verona's smile fell. "Oh."

"Actually, they were quite good," I said. "Much better than the ones I had at Congressman Chanson's house."

All right, so I never had a cookie at the congressman's house. But I'd been there. That had to count for something. Verona's chin hitched up and she shot me a grateful look.

Roz continued to stare and it was making me uncomfortable. "Well, I need to go," I said. "I've got company coming." With the remote, I unlocked the truck's doors. "Thanks for having me over, Verona."

She nodded. "Any time."

"Roz," I said.

Roz nodded stiffly.

Climbing into my truck, I shuddered. Something cold had blown through, and I wasn't sure why.

I reversed down the driveway and had to stomp on the brakes when I spotted a car rolling to a stop behind me, blocking me in.

And I nearly lost the cookies I'd just been eating when I saw who it was.

Kevin.

Sixteen

Kevin tapped on my door.

Oh great. I'd kinda-sorta hoped he wouldn't notice I was here.

Sucking in a deep breath, I pushed open the door, climbed out. "What now?"

Roz came around the hood, stepped in close to Kevin and purred like a cat in heat. "You know this fine man?" she asked me.

I smiled through clenched teeth. "He's my husband," I told her.

Her eyes lit like I'd just issued a challenge. "Lucky you."

"Yeah. Lucky. That's me."

I pulled Kevin aside. "I told you I'd meet up with you later," I said in a tight whisper. "What're you doing here?"

His bright green eyes zeroed on my face. "What are *you* doing here, is more like it."

"Working," I said under my breath.

"So am I." He pulled a hand over his face and I noticed the dark circles under his eyes.

Slightly confused (okay, a lot confused), I said, "Huh?"

He grasped my arm, and I tried to ignore how his touch sizzled along my skin.

Need. To. Get. Over. Him.

It was easy enough to tell myself that, but really, really hard to convince my heart of it. It was somewhat attached to him—even after finding Ginger's gaudy lipstick on his boxers.

It'd only been a month, I told myself. A month.

Seemed like a lifetime.

Maybe I did need to start dating again. Not MacKenna, because he was married and I refused to cross those lines, but someone else. Flash Leonard was starting to look good.

"Are you Verona Frye?" he asked, turning his gaze to her.

Eyes wide, Verona said, "Yes. Did you come here to see me, Mr. Quinn?"

Kevin reached for his badge. "*Detective* Quinn."

Roz purred again.

I wanted to kick her. Kevin must have sensed it, because he stepped in between us.

"Detective?" Verona folded her arms across her chest. "I don't understand."

I didn't either. What on earth would bring him *here*?

He looked at me. "Maybe you should go."

"You're blocking me in."

"Why aren't you two wearing rings?"

I peered around Kevin at Roz. She was buff, I'd give her that. But I had a month's worth of tension in me and probably fifteen pounds on her. She didn't stand a chance.

I smiled sweetly. "We don't believe in material things to show our love." I looped my arm around him. "Do we, *honey*?"

When he looked down at me, I saw that his eyes clouded with something that looked suspiciously like desire.

Gulp!

I stood frozen as he tipped my chin up. "Not at all, *sweetheart*." Then he kissed me.

Kissed. Me.

Not just any old "Hey, how ya doin'" kiss. It was a want-to-swallow-you-whole kind of kiss.

And go back for seconds.

I quickly came to my senses. All right, all right. It took me a minute or two. So sue me.

I pinched him and he pulled away, smiling.

Oooh!

I pinched him again for sheer pleasure.

He looked at me like he was going to kiss me again. I took two steps away.

"I'm sorry," he said to Roz and Verona. "That wasn't very professional."

Roz sniffed. "I should say not."

Verona smiled. "I think it's rather romantic."

I wanted to wipe my lips off. More than that, I *really* wanted to take a cold shower. Damn, I hated the effect he had on me!

Kevin lowered his dark lashes. "Mrs. Frye, I'm afraid I have bad news."

I straightened. Bad news?

"It's about your sister," he said to Verona.

Roz sucked in a breath.

Sister? Sister? What sister?

"I'm sorry to tell you this," Kevin said, "but Claire Battiste is dead."

"Nee-nah, make it stop!" Maria whined.

My parents were due any minute. Ana and Aunt Rosa too. I was busy putting the finishing touches on supper. "Make what stop?"

"The rat!"

"Her name is Gracie." Ears lowered, Gracie wagged her tiny black tail.

"She follows me everywhere."

I set a plate of dog food on the floor, and Gracie gobbled it down in two seconds flat. I'd never seen a dog eat as much as she did, and I'd yet to find something she wouldn't eat. "She likes you," I said.

Maria tipped her head to the side and studied Gracie. "She *is* kind of cute in an ugly ratlike way."

I opened my mouth to argue, but snapped it closed. Maria had a point.

Maria settled onto a stool, leaving Gracie on the floor whining. I wondered if the dog had somehow picked that up from her.

My stomach twisted. I still needed to tell Maria about my afternoon, but I hadn't been able to digest it yet.

Claire and Verona were sisters. But Roz wasn't Claire's mother. From the pieces I picked out of Kevin's questioning, I learned that Claire was Alfred Phineus's love child. But he hadn't learned of his oldest daughter until right before his death.

On his deathbed, Alfred had made Verona promise to take care of Claire by giving her a job at the Kalypso, which, it turns out, had been partly owned by Alfred Phineus.

Kevin also confirmed to me—privately—that it apparently *had* been Claire who broke into Maria's condo. The autopsy confirmed the damage done by the hair spray.

As I looked at Maria, I debated telling her that Claire was the one who'd broken in. She hadn't put it together yet, and I definitely didn't want her to know about those pictures Nate had sent me.

After a minute of deliberation, I decided I'd wait and let Kevin do my dirty work. Unfortunately, in my hurry to leave the Fryes' house that afternoon I hadn't given the package to Kevin. I'd have to track him down and hand it over to him after dinner. I didn't want anything to do with it anymore.

Maria sniffed the air. "Is something burning?"

I checked the pot of rice I'd made and found that most of it had stuck to the bottom of the pot. I groaned. Never in my life had I been able to make a decent pot of rice.

"There's something I need to tell you," she said, not looking me in the eye. She scrunched her nose.

Rolling my eyes, I braced myself. Maria only scrunched her nose when she was trying to look cute so I wouldn't be mad at her.

"I kinda-sorta didn't have a chance to tell Mom and Dad about Nate," she said.

"What?!"

She shrugged. "It didn't come up."

"How can it *not* come up?"

She scrunched again. "I kinda-sorta didn't want to tell them."

"You have to tell them."

"And what do I say? He's gone but I don't know where? That I thought he'd run off with his boss, but she was found dead in my backyard?"

I bit my lip. My mother would freak if she knew all that. It might actually give her the heart attack she's been faking all these years. "You have to tell them something. Something to explain why he hasn't been around. And the news is bound to pick up on Claire's death sooner or later."

Maria sighed. "I'll think of something."

"Soon. I think they'll be wondering where your groom is on your wedding day."

"I think maybe Nate and I should elope," she said, completely ignorant to the fact that there might not be a wedding.

Rummaging in the freezer, I pulled out my emergency bottle of vodka. I'm not a big drinker, but this was definitely an emergency in my opinion. I twisted the cap off and chugged from the bottle.

I shuddered as the ice cold liquid slid down my throat. Almost immediately, I felt a little woozy. Alcohol and I didn't get along.

After wiping my mouth with my hand, I put the bottle back in the freezer and turned to Maria. She said, "You don't think eloping is a good idea?"

I smiled through clenched teeth and said, "It's a fabulous idea. I highly recommend it."

Maria clapped, oblivious to my sarcasm. "I'm so glad you think so."

When the doorbell rang, she bounded out of the room, Gracie at her heels.

I hung my head, wishing there was a noose around it.

"Eeee!" I heard from the living room, followed by my mother screeching, "Is that a rat!?"

My gaze jumped to the laundry room. Did I have enough time to sneak out the backdoor?

My father poked his head in the arched doorway. "Nina?"

Sighing, I pushed escaping out of my mind. "Hi, Daddy." I kissed his cheek.

"Did you know on this day in 1755 Nathan Hale was born?"

"Uh-uh." I didn't want to mention to him that I had no idea who Nathan Hale was. If I did, I'd get a two-hour lecture.

"Or that in 1971 this was the day the last *Ed Sullivan Show* aired?"

I shook my head. "Nope." Dad was a former history professor and a Trivial Pursuit guru. We all humored him for the most part. "But that's good to know."

"Smells good in here," he said, poking at the stir-fry with the spatula.

"Thanks."

"Where's Riley?"

"Work. He should be home soon."

Since my father rarely came into the kitchen other than to eat, I knew he was definitely fishing. He looked like a balding bulldog, all olive-colored wrinkled skin and big bulging eyes. He looked worried too, like he knew there was something up.

My mother's voice drifted into the kitchen. "Are you sure it's not a rat?" she asked Maria.

Dad sidled up to me. "So what's this dinner all about?"

"Eating?" I suggested hopefully.

"You don't say." His dark green eyes crinkled. "You're being awfully evasive."

That's me. Nina Colette Evasive Ceceri Quinn.

"Really? You think so?"

"Out with it, kid."

I sighed. "Aunt Rosa's coming."

He didn't say anything, but he crossed over to the butcher block and started removing knives and putting them into drawers. I helped him.

My mother came into the kitchen. Dad and I froze.

"Nina, *chérie*. Aren't you going to say hello?"

"Hi Mom." Behind my back, I slid a drawer closed.

I went over to her, and she kissed both my cheeks. "When did you get a dog?"

"Yesterday," I said.

"Don't you think you're a little busy to have a dog?"

"I, um, hadn't thought about it."

She looked at Maria. "Where's Nate?"

I waggled my eyebrows at Maria in a "tell her" kind of way. Maria shrugged. "Working," she said. "Getting ahead so he doesn't have to worry about the office while we're on our honeymoon."

I groaned.

My mother lifted the top off the rice, stirred it. "Looks good," she said.

"It's burned," Maria chimed in behind her.

"Posh. It just adds flavoring."

I couldn't help comparing her to Roz. Even if my mother had hated what I'd made, she'd eat it with a smile.

She looked around. "Who else is coming?"

A drawer closed behind me. "What do you mean?" my father asked.

"The table. It's set for eight."

Maria blinked. "Why *is* it set for eight?"

The doorbell rang. I longed to hide out in Mr. Cabrera's gazebo.

Gracie yipped and yipped, and when I pulled open the door, she peed on the floor. I sighed.

"Mrs. Krauss, come on in. I'm glad you could make it," I said, steering her around the puddle and into the kitchen where everyone had gathered. Gracie followed us, sniffing Brickhouse's ankles as we walked.

This, in my humble opinion, was a stroke of genius. There's no way my mother would kill Aunt Rosa if there were nonrelatives present. I'd called Mrs. Krauss on my way home from Verona Frye's. Luckily, both she and Mr. Cabrera had agreed to an impromptu dinner party.

"Ach. Well. I miss him." She squinted. "Is that a rat?"

Maria said, "I told you so."

Introductions were being made when the doorbell rang again. I darted for the door, grabbing some paper towels to clean up after Gracie on the way. I let out a deep breath when I saw Mr. Cabrera on the front porch.

"Is she here?" he asked, peeking around me.

I nodded. "In the kitchen."

He kissed my cheek. "You're a peach, Miz Quinn. A peach!" he said, hurrying through the kitchen doorway.

I looked out into the darkening night. Where was Ana? Aunt Rosa?

I closed the door, leaned against it. So far, so good. No bloodshed. How long would it last, though?

With Gracie's mess cleaned, I went back into the kitchen. After washing up, I dumped the rice into a glass bowl and set it on the table. I transferred the stir-fry from the wok into a teak salad bowl—the only thing I had that was big enough. Out of the fridge, I grabbed fresh pineapple slices that I'd gotten already cut at the grocery store and put them on the table.

I'm not a cook. Far from it. But even I was happy with the way the dinner had turned out, rice and all.

The doorbell rang. Everyone looked at me.

"I'll, um, get that."

My aunt Rosa was on the porch, and I hugged her tight. She looked a lot like my grandma Ceceri—except with boobs. Her long black hair was streaked with silver and cut into a stylish shag. She looked great.

"Where's Ana?" I asked, leading her inside.

"I don't know. She called and told me to meet her here."

I bit my lip. I hope she wasn't bailing on me, the coward! "Well, come on, we might as well get this over with."

She chuckled. "It's okay, Nina Bo-bina."

"Not the Bo-bina. Please." It was a childhood nickname given to me by my brother, and every so often it reared its ugly head to torment me.

"Everyone," I said, entering the kitchen, sounding like a perky morning TV show host, "Aunt Rosa's here!"

My mother's gaze shot to the butcher block. Thank God it was empty. My father put his arm around her. To hold her down, I was sure.

Brickhouse and Mr. Cabrera introduced themselves, and Maria gave her a big hug and kiss. My father looked like he wanted to, but didn't want to let go of my mother.

My mother who was staring at me.

Ack.

"What is this about, *chérie*?"

I pulled out the chair across from my father for Aunt Rosa. "A nice dinner."

"Celeste," Aunt Rosa said. "You're looking well."

"Rosetta," my mother said to her sister-in-law. "You're looking well."

"Let's eat!" I urged. The sooner they ate, the sooner they would leave.

I'd just doused my stir-fry with soy sauce when the doorbell rang. I jumped up. "That's gotta be Ana!"

"I should have known she was in this with you!" my mother said under her breath.

Aunt Rosa pointed a fork at her. "Don't you say anything bad about my Analise!"

My mother looked innocently at my father. "Did I say something bad?"

Like a tortured man, he said, "Celeste . . ."

"Is something wrong?" Brickhouse asked. "I feel tension."

As I scooted out of the room, I heard Mr. Cabrera say, "Rosetta is Tonio's sister. She and Celeste have a long-standing feud . . ."

I didn't even want to know how he knew that.

I pulled open the door. "Thank God you're—"

"I knew you missed me," Kevin said.

He leaned against the doorjamb, a folder in his hands.

Ana stepped out from behind him, looking contrite.

I let them both in, shot a nervous glance toward the kitchen. "Maybe you shouldn't come in," I said to Kevin. "My parents are here, and you're not exactly on their list of favorite people right now. There's no telling what my dad might do to you."

Kevin looked over my head, toward the doorway. Loud voices filtered out as my mother and Aunt Rosa bickered.

Grimly, Kevin said, "I'll have to take my chances. This is important."

"Oh?" I said. Ana wouldn't look at me. *Uh-oh.* "What's going on?"

Kevin tapped his chin. Dark stubble covered his jaw, his cheeks. "Funny thing happened today."

I noticed he'd lowered his voice. A good idea. My father knew where the knives were hidden. "What's that?" I asked.

"John Orlenke paid me a visit."

My gaze slid to Ana. A while back she dated John Orlenke, a rookie patrol officer. Ana had to feel my glare, but she apparently found something interesting in the carpet and wouldn't look up.

"Oh?" I said.

"Let's say," Kevin gestured, "hypothetically, an old friend of his came in and asked him for a favor."

"Oh?" I said again.

"Not a big deal." He tapped the folder against his palm. "Just to run some prints. See what comes up."

"I'd say that would be nice of him." I needed to sit. The arm of the couch seemed like a good spot.

The arguing from the other room escalated. Maybe this was the best thing for Mom and Aunt Rosetta. Get things out in the open.

"Yeah, it would be. And let's say he does it, thinking maybe he'd do *this* favor and the old friend would offer him a favor or two."

Ana's head snapped up. I couldn't tell if she was appalled or excited.

Kevin continued. "Imagine John's shock when the FBI

calls him. Wants to know how he obtained a certain pair of prints."

Gulp.

"Scared, he comes to me. See, I know his friend quite well, and he wants me to take care of this for him."

Something crashed in the kitchen and Gracie came bolting out. She bumped into the chair and darted under the couch.

Ana jumped, lifting her feet up onto the chair. "What the hell was that?"

I rubbed my temples. "Gracie."

Kevin glared at me. "You got a dog?"

He'd always wanted a dog, but I'd argued we weren't home enough.

"It's not a dog," I said. "It's a rat."

He narrowed his green eyes.

"Can we just get to it, please? World War Three is raging in my kitchen."

"Do you know her?" he asked me, pulling a picture from the file.

I took it, examined the face. The hair was definitely different, and she looked somehow younger, but it was Stella Zamora, the blue-haired lady from the Kalypso. I told Kevin about my run-in with her.

He just kept nodding.

"Is that Chinese I smell?" Ana broke in. "I'm hungry. Haven't eaten since Mom got here. She never stops long enough to. And sleep? Hah! She was up all night on the computer. Tappity-tap-tap. It's driving me nuts." She eyed the couch. "This pulls out, right?"

"It's taken," I said.

"Food?" she whimpered.

I motioned to the kitchen. "Have at it. And try to keep

them from coming in here, will you? I really don't want to see any bloodshed."

When Ana disappeared through the doorway, the arguing reached fever pitch.

"Is she wanted by the FBI?" I asked Kevin, handing the picture back to him.

"Nina, she *is* FBI."

Ack.

"Her real name is Fran Cooper, and she's been missing since yesterday morning. Needless to say, the FBI is very interested in her whereabouts."

"I don't know where she is." It was the truth, as lame as it sounded.

"So Ana told me. She filled me in on the pictures Nate sent you too. Can I have them now?"

Out of the coat closet, I grabbed my backpack. I thrust the packet of pictures and the guest list at Kevin. "I don't know why he sent them to me."

"Probably figured you were safe."

"Safe from what?"

"I honestly don't know. The FBI doesn't like to share. I need to turn these over to them." He flipped through them, whistling under his breath.

"I don't recognize him," I said. "Do you?"

Kevin shook his head.

Maria came running in with rice stuck in her hair. She collided with Kevin and the pictures scattered. "It's getting ugly in there! Don't worry," she said to me. "I'll call the painter first thing in the morning."

I didn't want to know. Really, I didn't.

Gracie came out, sat at Maria's ankle. She was eyeing it like she was going to take another bite, but Maria gave her the Ceceri evil eye and she slunk away.

Kevin hurriedly grabbed the pictures and tried to sound low-key. "Looks like a Chihuahua to me," he said.

"You want her?" I asked.

Maria was shaking her head no, warning Kevin off. The backstabber.

"No thanks," he said.

"Oh, you missed one." Maria scooped a Polaroid from beneath the chair.

Kevin reached for it, but she didn't let go. I peeked over her shoulder and breathed a sigh of relief. It was the picture of the man from chest up. No gun. No Claire. No blood.

Maria looked up at Kevin. "I didn't know you were working on his case."

Kevin and I looked at each other. Kevin said, "*His* case?"

"Brian Thatcher. I hope you catch whoever did it. It was quite a shock."

"You know him?" I asked, shocked myself.

"I told you about him," she said to me, acting put out. When I looked blankly at her, she sighed. "You know, my boss . . . at Phineus Frye. He was carjacked a few months ago . . ."

This was Brian Thatcher? I tried to remember everything I'd been told about him, but all I came up with was his death and that he'd been Maria's boss. I thought these pictures certainly proved that he hadn't been carjacked.

Brian Thatcher had worked *at* Phineus Frye. Claire Battiste worked *for* Phineus Frye and, it turns out, *was* a Phineus and *related* to a Frye. And Nate? How did he tie in other than he worked for Claire?

Maybe it was enough.

Another crash came from the kitchen.

"That's my cue to leave," Kevin said. "We need to talk about this," he said, holding up the file. "I'll be in touch."

"Can't wait," I said.

Kevin darted for the door as more glass shattered. I ran into the kitchen.

Serenely, Ana sat cross-legged on top of the island, my father was on the floor picking up pieces of wineglass, and my mother and Aunt Rosetta were facing off across the table from one another, each holding a fork at arm's length.

"Who was here?" my father asked.

"The paper boy," I lied.

"Hmmm," he said as he picked up shards. I thought it was a good thing Kevin had left when he had.

"Where are Mr. Cabrera and Mrs. Krauss?" I asked.

Ana dipped her fork into her bowl. "They slipped out the back when the soy sauce started flying." She gestured to her bowl. "This is good, by the way."

Dryly, I said, "Glad you like it."

"Nina!" my mother shouted. "This is unforgivable!"

"Don't blame her for you being too stubborn to let by-gones be bygones!" Rosa yelled.

"Really, Nina. You *could* have warned us," Maria chimed in.

Oooooh. My blood pressure jumped. "Mom," I said childishly, "Maria has something she needs to tell you. About Nate."

My mother looked at Maria. "Oh?"

Maria shot me a dirty look. Then she lifted her chin, drew her shoulders back, and smiled evilly. "Actually, I do. Nina thinks Nate and I should elope."

My father quickly sidestepped and caught my mother as she fainted.

Seventeen

I looked up from my sketch pad at the knock on my door.

"I can't sleep," Maria said, coming in.

"Maybe you should go sleep at Mom's."

She pulled back the covers. "You're not still mad about earlier, are you?"

I went back to sketching, my colored pencils spread out around me. They rolled when Maria crawled into the bed.

Gracie hopped up and snuggled next to her. Maria nudged her away and Gracie slunk down to the end of the bed, circled five times and settled down.

I gaped at the two of them, but they were oblivious to the fact that this was *my* room. *My* bed.

Maria yawned. "I'm really worried about Nate, Nina."

Which is exactly why I was keeping my mouth shut on the matter. She didn't need to know about Nate's frightened phone call, or what really happened to Brian Thatcher. Not yet, at least. Honestly, I wished I didn't know about any of it.

"He'll be fine."

"You're lying."

"How do you know?"

"Your nostrils flared."

"Don't look at my nostrils," I said, covering them up. "That's gross."

"Tell me about it. But it's the only way I can tell if you're lying."

I pinched my nose closed. "He'll be fine," I said in a squeaky Donald Duck–like voice.

"He didn't kill Claire."

"I didn't say he did."

Gracie inched her way up the bed. I watched her with a wary eye. I hadn't had a waterproof mattress cover on my bed since I was four.

Picking up a black pencil, I drew in a wrought-iron chaise lounge on the Frye's design board. I hoped I'd be able to find one on such short notice. "What do you think happened to him?" I asked her.

"I thought he ran away with Claire. But Claire's dead, so where's Nate?" She pulled the covers up to her chin. "Would I know if he were dead? Have some sort of feeling?"

"I think that only happens in movies."

A tear slipped out of her eye. "I love him, Nina."

A lump formed in my throat. Jeez. I'd gone to bed early to escape this. "I know."

Her eyes shut and within minutes she was snoring. Worrying had apparently exhausted her. If Nate was my fiancé, I'd be up all night giving myself ulcers. It was only one of the many things that made us different. Sighing, I drew the covers up under her chin.

As I went back to sketching, I kept an eye on Gracie. I noticed her surreptitiously inching her way up the bed. Curious, I watched to see what she'd do.

Once she was finally nestled between Maria and me, she snorted and snuffed, trying to lift the covers with her nose.

In amazement, I watched as she burrowed beneath the covers and settled in. From my point of view, Gracie's small shape made Maria look like she was hunchbacked.

I grabbed my pencils and sketch pad and headed for the living room. This drawing needed to be done for Verona Frye before tomorrow. Apparently, her sister's death hadn't put a damper on her plans. She'd called the office after Kevin and I left her house and told Tam as much.

To my eyes, it seemed as though Verona had wanted nothing to do with Claire. Why? Because she wasn't a full sister? Or for some other reason?

When I dropped off this sketch, maybe I could pry the information out of her. All right, so I was hoping for more cookies. I admit it.

Way past midnight, I put the finishing touches on my sketch. I'd run it by Verona, get final approval, have her sign the contracts. I'd then round up the materials we needed to get the job done.

Upstairs, I pushed open Riley's door. He'd come home and laughed until he cried when he saw the soy sauce on the walls. But he did help me clean it up, which gave me hope for our future.

I knocked softly on the open door. A large lump rested in the middle of his bed.

Feeling oddly maternal, I crept over to give Riley a kiss. I pulled the covers down and gasped when all I saw was pillows.

"Riley Michael . . . !"

What was he up to? I wouldn't even consider that he was the panty thief, so my mind jumped to the next logical conclusion. He was out *looking* for the panty thief.

I'd wait up for him, then ground him until he left for college.

I went into my room to grab a robe. Gracie shimmied out from under the covers. She saw me and started whimpering.

"Oh no," I said. I grabbed her and made a run for the back

door. Once outside, I set her down. She wandered around the house, looking for a good place to do her business.

It was quiet, and I heard the sound of voices.

It was the middle of the night. Who on earth was out?

Gracie followed me as I backtracked to the house to grab Riley's hockey stick from the laundry room. After all, there was a burglar creeping around these days and I needed to protect my bikini briefs.

Slowly, I crept back out into the night. Gracie stayed at my heels. I followed the voices to Mr. Cabrera's gazebo.

I inched forward, poised to strike.

Gracie started barking. *Yip yip yip.* So much for sneaking up on anyone. In the moonlight, I saw Riley's head pop up.

"Nina?" he said.

I leaned on the hockey stick. "Riley? What're you doing?"

"Uh, keeping watch?"

Had he fallen asleep on the job? Maternal instincts reared up. It was a school night. What was he thinking, being out here this late? And what was Mr. Cabrera doing, *letting* him be out this late?

He stood up, tugged on his shirt.

"Do you know what time it is?" I asked.

Gracie milled around, her snout to the ground, probably looking for more food. Her stomach had to be the size of Maria's suitcase.

Riley shrugged, kept tugging.

Getting a strange vibe, I put my hands on my hips. "*What* is going on?"

Riley shifted back and forth, looking everywhere but at me. Then it hit. I'd heard *voices* when I came out. More than one.

"Olly olly oxenfree," I snapped, all patience lost.

Long dark curls trailed down the girl's back as she popped up next to Riley. "Uh, hi, Mrs. Quinn."

Oh-ho! This certainly explained Riley's nighttime forays. "And you'd be?"

"Katie Coughlin," she said brightly.

Gracie continued yipping. I wished she had batteries so I could take them out and toss them far, far into the woods.

Mr. Cabrera's floodlights flashed on.

Oh, here we go.

"Take her home," I told Riley. "We'll talk about this in the morning."

"Uh, Nina, it *is* morning."

"Riley . . ." I warned.

"All right." He took Katie's hand and they disappeared into the woods behind the gazebo. There was a trail there that led to the neighborhood behind ours.

Mr. Cabrera's door creaked open. "Who's back there?" he called out.

"It's okay, Mr. Cabrera. It's just me." I winced at the sight of him in a pair of boxer shorts and black socks pulled to his knees.

Too much information.

He stepped out. "Miz Quinn?"

"Really, Mr. Cabrera, I'm just out here with the dog."

My jaw dropped when Brickhouse appeared behind him, wrapped in a bed sheet. I quickly looked away before I saw something that would send me directly into therapy without passing Go.

"Donatelli?" she said to Mr. Cabrera, her loud voice carrying easily in the quiet night. "What's going on?"

"Go in," I urged. "Go back to—" The word lodged in my throat and I forced it out. "—bed."

I tightened my robe, warding off heebie-jeebies.

"You sure you okay?" he asked.

"Right as rain."

He said good-night, and I heaved a sigh of relief when he closed the door behind him.

I fought a yawn, but I knew I couldn't go back to bed until I knew Riley was home safe and sound. I'd kill him in the morning.

"Gracie, come on."

Looking around, I didn't see any ratlike dogs. "Gracie?"

Oh no. I'd barely had her two days and I'd already managed to lose her. This is why I didn't have a pet. I was lucky I hadn't lost Riley during the last eight years.

"Gracie!" I said in a loud whisper.

A yip pierced the silence. It came from my right.

I started to follow it, then stopped. Why? Wouldn't it be easier to let her go?

Guilt nudged me forward. That, and the image of Kit's face when he learned I'd lost the stupid dog.

"Gracie!"

I cut across Mr. Cabrera's backyard, through the next two yards, trying to spot any movement in the moonlight.

I raised my voice. "Gracie!"

Two yips punctuated the night.

A light flashed on. Mrs. Daasch opened her window. She tossed something out, yelled, "Now let me go back to sleep," and slammed the window closed.

I stooped to pick up what she'd tossed. In the pale moonlight, I made out a pair of flowered panties.

"Eww!" I let them drop, wiped my hand on my robe. But I hated to leave them there, on the ground. I snatched them up, held them at arm's length with two fingers, and hung them on her back-door knob.

"Gracie, I'm going to ring that little canine neck of yours!"

I heard a long, prolonged *yiiiiiip* and took off, grass squishing between my toes, the dew nearly making me slip.

I zigged and zagged through trees, rounded the corner of

Mr. Weatherbee's house and stopped so fast my feet went out from under me.

A man dressed all in black stood in the shadows of the house, as if he'd been there watching me the whole time.

"Eee!" I cried as I went down. On the ground, I backpedaled, not caring that my robe had fallen open.

I opened my mouth to scream again, but my voice had gone AWOL. I assumed no one had heard my initial scream since no lights were coming on. I cursed hearing aids and searched the ground for something to protect myself. Stupidly, I'd left Riley's hockey stick back at the gazebo.

The man stepped forward, out of the shadows, and moonlight cut across his face. Mr. Weatherbee.

"Does this, Mrs. Quinn, belong to you?" he asked, holding Gracie out like I'd held Mrs. Daasch's underwear.

My voice still missing, I nodded.

"I'll thank you to keep . . . it . . . out of my garden."

I nodded again.

He stepped over to me, dropped Gracie. I caught her, felt her shaking.

I was surprised she didn't tuck her tail and do the pee thing, since Mr. Weatherbee had certainly scared the piss out of me.

"Thank you," I managed, scrambling up. "Um, Mr. Weatherbee, what are you doing out here, dressed all in black?" I asked, keeping the "and scaring poor innocent landscape designers to near death" to myself.

He laughed. Gracie and I backed up, inched toward home. "You think I'm the panty thief?"

"I didn't say that."

After a moment he said, "I'm on watch tonight."

A flashlight beam cut through the night, shined on us.

"What's going on here?" Mr. Mustard demanded.

Flash Leonard stood behind him looking at my legs. "Great gams," he said.

"Uh, thanks."

"An explanation is needed," the Colonel said. He was dressed all in black too. I supposed older people had a lot of it, what with all the funerals they had to go to.

Even Flash had on a black robe. Of course, it was open, but so was mine. Balancing Gracie, I managed to tighten my sash.

I held out Gracie. "She got out." Gracie yipped as if in agreement. "Mr. Weatherbee found her."

"I heard a scream," the Colonel said.

"I, uh, fell."

"What're you two doing out this late?" I asked them.

The Colonel bristled. "I heard commotion, including a scream."

"I'm on duty tonight," Flash said. "Thought I saw someone and followed him over here."

"Really? Who?"

Flash frowned. "Don't know. Lost him. Then I heard your scream."

At Flash's pace, he could lose track of a snail.

"It's late," Mr. Weatherbee said. "Why don't we all turn in?"

There were murmured agreements all around. Except from me. I kept feeling like someone wasn't telling me something.

"I'll walk you home," Flash offered me.

I tucked Gracie into the crook of my elbow and slipped my other arm through Flash's.

As we walked down the street, I looked back over my shoulder. Mr. Weatherbee and the Colonel were watching us go.

I shuddered, and I wasn't quite sure why.

Eighteen

As I closed and locked my door early the next morning, I found myself worrying about Gracie. She hadn't inhaled her food like she usually did. And through the front window, I saw that she was walking in circles.

Maria promised to look after her, but I doubted the closeness of her watching. She was fast becoming addicted to TV. Everything from *Regis and Kelly* and the *Young and the Restless*, to *Dr. Phil* and *Judge Judy*.

My truck beeped as I unlocked it. I was running a little behind thanks to my early morning talk with Riley.

"I hope you weren't too hard on him."

My sketch pad went flying as I covered my pounding heart with my hand. I turned to face Mr. Cabrera. "Jeez!"

"Sorry," he said, not looking the least bit contrite.

Once my heart settled down and I gathered up my sketch pad, I asked, "Weren't too hard on who?"

Today Mr. Cabrera wore a pair of black cargo shorts and a white button-down with yellow ducks on it, left open to reveal a plain white T-shirt beneath. "Riley. He really likes Katie."

I shaded my eyes against the sun. "You knew?"

He nodded.

Silly me. I should've known. Mr. Cabrera knows everything. "You should have told me. I was worried about him."

"Us guys have to stick together."

"He's fifteen!"

"Exactly."

"Men," I muttered. Riley had explained to me that Katie's father didn't want her to date until she was sixteen—a little over six months away. A lifetime to a teenager. Riley hadn't liked me saying he had to abide by her father's rules.

The, er, conversation hadn't been pretty. Even Gracie hadn't stuck around.

"Did you hear that Mrs. Walker got broken into last night?"

"What?!" Mrs. Walker lived four doors down. I gasped. Right next door to Mr. Weatherbee.

"Guy broke in, but something apparently scared him off."

"What time?" I asked, feeling slightly sick.

"'Bout one-thirty or so. Mrs. Walker heard the glass break in the front door and hid in her closet."

I frowned. "Who was on watch?"

He scratched his chin. "Flash had duty last night."

"Not Mr. Weatherbee?"

"No."

"Not the Colonel?"

"Not that I know of. And I'd know," he said, thumping his chest.

Hmmm. Mr. Weatherbee had told me he was on duty . . . The Colonel had merely said he'd heard commotion . . . From five doors down? My eyebrows started twitching.

"Do you think it's a good idea to have Flash out alone?"

"His bones don't work so well, but his eyes are fine and so're his ears. That's all that really counts."

I remembered what Flash had said the night before: He'd seen someone go by and followed.

And what about the Colonel? He said he'd heard me scream, but honestly, I hadn't screamed *that* loud. It was more a squeal than anything, maybe even a squeak. He'd had to be really close by to hear it. Like at Mrs. Walker's front door.

The Colonel, Mr. Weatherbee. They'd both lied to me. Why? I even had doubts about Flash's story. He could barely walk, never mind run. How did he get to Mr. Weatherbee's so fast after he heard my scream?

"You're right, Miz Quinn."

Lost in thought, I jumped. I'd forgotten he was standing there. "Right? About what?"

"We need to beef up security, add more patrols."

Had I said that? Still, it was a good idea, and I had an even better one. "Let's call a meeting together," I suggested. "Here, around four or so, so we can all talk about it."

"Good idea, Miz Quinn. I'll set it up."

As I drove toward work, I couldn't help but wonder what Kevin would think of the plan I'd just hatched . . . and how it involved him.

As I was turning left onto Jaybird, my cell buzzed. After checking the caller ID, I flipped it open. "Hey."

"I think my mother's got a secret boyfriend," Ana said.

"Jealous?" I asked.

"Ha. Ha."

"What makes you think so?" I asked.

"You know how she's been on the computer a lot since she got here?"

"Yeah?"

"Well, I caught her instant messaging someone last night. When she saw me, she signed off real quick."

"That doesn't mean much. She could be talking to anyone."

"With the screen name 'hunkoburninglove'?"

I let that one sit for a minute.

"Maybe she's got a friend who's an Elvis nut."

"You're not helping."

"So what if she does have a boyfriend? Good for her."

"She should tell me. I'm her daughter. I'm supposed to know these things. I mean, who is this guy? He could be any nut off the street? What if he's after her money?"

"Does she have money?"

"No, but that's not the point."

I sighed.

"I need to make sure she's safe, Nina."

I could understand that.

"I'm going to find out who this hunk o' burning love is. Run a background check. Before she signed off, I saw that they're meeting tonight at nine at Arello's."

I knew better than to try and talk her out of it.

"So, are you gonna come or not?"

I smiled, not even bothering to mention that she hadn't asked me to come. "I'll be there," I said. "As long as you come dress shopping with me beforehand."

"Is the wedding back on?"

"Well, it's not off! What if Nate turns up and the wedding is still on? Then I'd be stuck in that . . . that . . . thing."

"Good point," she said. "I'll pick you up at seven. Gotta go, Mom's coming!"

She hung up before I could say good-bye.

I turned into the TBS lot, full of energy to work. I'd never attempted to do a mini this quickly before. I had a zillion things to do to get ready for tomorrow's job at the Fryes'.

For the first time in days, I actually felt like I could focus solely on work. Now that Kevin had those pictures, I could stop worrying so much.

My to-do list was a mile long. Near the top of the list was Leo Barker. I couldn't dismiss Tam's negative feelings toward him, and I still didn't know how he'd come to TBS. I needed to get some answers.

So preoccupied with how to deal with Leo, it took me a moment to realize that the alarm system wasn't set. Odder still, no lights were on either, and the coffeepot wasn't perking.

"Hello?" I called out. The hairs on the back of my neck rose. Chills swept down my spine. "Tam?"

I inched inside, holding the door open with my foot. "Hidey, er, ho?"

Early morning light filtered through the wooden blinds on the front windows. Dim sunbeams limned the couches, chairs, books. Tam's desk was neat and tidy, everything in its place, including Sassy, her African violet.

I swallowed, trying to ignore the goose bumps on my arms. It was entirely possible Tam had forgotten to set the alarm the night before.

Ah. I caught myself breaking a cardinal commandment. The delusion one.

Tam had never once forgotten to set the alarm.

But . . . she *was* freaked out over Leo Barker. There was always a first for everything.

I set my backpack down, dropped my keys onto it. Tiptoeing, I grabbed an umbrella from the stand by the door and set about searching the office.

Ten minutes later I'd found nothing that indicated TBS had been broken into. I couldn't shake the feeling, though, that someone had been inside.

Looking for what? I wondered.

But I knew.

The pictures.

Thankfully, they were now Kevin's problem.

Grabbing a Dr Pepper, I headed into my office and called Verona Frye. It was early, but she'd insisted I call first thing.

After the usual hellos, she said, "I don't think coming here this afternoon is a good idea. Roz is suspicious, and Colin said something about working at home this afternoon, getting ready for his trip."

Nothing about Claire. I wondered about a memorial service or funeral, and finally asked.

"Oh. That. Well, the medical examiner's office is holding her body until Monday. Something about the investigation. So, there will be no service until next week."

"You didn't like her," I said, then thumped my forehead with the butt of my hand. Open mouth and all that.

Inwardly, I groaned. I was even starting to *think* like my mother! I shuddered.

Verona said, "I'm that obvious, am I?"

I winced. "Just a little." I was hoping she'd fill me in on why, but no such luck.

"I won't miss her, and I'm not going to lie about it. And if that makes me cold, then so be it."

All-righty.

"I can scan the sketch and e-mail it to you for final approval. And I'll fax the contracts to you."

She gave me her fax number, and I asked her to electronically transfer the deposit I needed to the TBS account, since we were on a tight deadline. I couldn't get started without it, and it amazed me how often my wealthy clients tended to hem and haw about paying me.

"I'll do that now," she said. "I'll see you tomorrow, Nina. Thanks so much."

I set the phone in its cradle and wondered what Claire had done to Verona. Immediately, my mind jumped to Claire and Colin and how closely they worked together.

Maybe I was just projecting, because I'd been cheated on. But still, it made sense.

And had to hurt like hell. At least Ginger Barlow, Kevin's lover, wasn't my *sister*. I'd have probably killed Maria if that had been the case.

In shock, I sat back.

Verona obviously hated Claire. Now Claire was dead. What if she *had* been having a fling with Colin and Verona found out? That would explain why Verona hadn't seemed all that surprised to learn her sister had died.

And Roz too. I couldn't rule her out either. I couldn't imagine what it would be like to have to work with the child conceived from your husband's affair. Did it drive her to murder, though?

Shaking my head, I decided not to go there. Let Kevin deal with it. He was a good detective. He'd find out who killed Claire, why, and lock him—or her—away.

As I pulled an Almond Joy from my desk for breakfast, my gaze fell on the stack of message slips Tam had put on the desk. All from Robert MacKenna. All marked "Urgent" and "Call back ASAP."

Trying to ignore my guilty conscience, I crumpled them up and dropped them into the waste can. Thankfully, I didn't have time to dwell because my cell phone buzzed. My home number flashed on the ID screen.

"Maria?"

"Nina, Gracie's acting crazy."

"More than usual?"

"She keeps barking like someone's here, but no one is. Unless you have ghosts?"

"No, no ghosts."

"Then she's acting crazy."

I'd known something wasn't quite right this morning.

"Take her to the vet," I told Maria. "He's got an emergency entrance."

Great. This was just like Kit, to give me a defective dog.

"What? Me?" Maria cried.

"Yes. You."

"I don't want to miss *The Price Is Right*!"

"Kit won't like it if something happens to Gracie," I warned.

"All right," she muttered.

I gave her directions to the vet. Luckily, the office was next to a mall so she knew right where it was.

"Eww, Gracie!" I heard her say. "She just upchucked. Do I have to clean that up?"

"Yes."

"Nee-nah," she whined.

" 'Bye!"

I quickly hung up before I volunteered to come home. I had too much to do, and Maria was more than capable of taking care of a five-pound dog.

And I hated that I worried about Gracie. She was starting to grow on me in a moldy kind of way. I called the vet we used for Riley's snake Xena and warned him that Gracie and Maria would be in, and then I went to work on the supply list I'd need for the Frye job.

Tam was due any minute now, and the office would jump to life. Kit and I would need to make a run to the garden center—probably more than one. I'd let Deanna and Leo hit the Frontgate Outlet. I really hoped they'd find a wrought-iron lounge chair and a matching table. I planned to send Jean-Claude out in search of a pad for the chair. He had the best eye for fabrics.

I added lantern lights to my list, which already included pond supplies like liner, submersible pump and waterfall attachment, and I tried to think of everything from fieldstone to the type of aquatic plants that would work best for this job.

As I worked, part of me couldn't dismiss the alarm not being set. I couldn't help but look for things that might have been out of place or even missing around my office. But like I'd told Tam the other day, I didn't think I'd notice.

My desk seemed the same, nothing missing, at least. My stash of Almond Joys was still in the bottom drawer, which reminded me that I couldn't avoid Robert MacKenna forever. My conscience wouldn't allow it.

Unfortunately.

I dealt much easier with avoidance. Confrontation? Ugh. He was married. *Married.* No matter how cute he was, or how his odd quirks were growing on me, there could never be anything between us.

The cowbell jangled, and I jumped up, spooked. "Who's there?" I called out.

No one answered.

Unable to shake the heebies, I grabbed the umbrella just in case. Swallowing hard, I tiptoed to my open office door. The little hairs on the back of my neck told me someone was out there. Well, okay, that and the cowbell. Those things just didn't ring on their own.

Keeping tight hold of the umbrella, I poked my head out to look around.

"Eeee!" I screamed when I saw someone standing outside my door.

A hand shot out, grabbed the umbrella. "Hello, Nina."

Nineteen

I tugged on the umbrella, but he wouldn't let it go. Probably a good thing, because I was planning on stabbing him with its sharp tip when he did.

"Why didn't you say anything when I called out?" I asked.

"Didn't hear you," Kevin said.

"Why'd you grab the umbrella like that?"

He arched an eyebrow. "I didn't want to get hit with it. I know how you are."

One incident with a hockey stick! Jeez!

Kevin pulled the umbrella out of my hands, leaned it against the wall.

"What are you doing here?" I asked, noticing how good he looked. Too good. Ugh. I needed to get over him.

Kevin tucked his hands in his pockets. "A couple things, actually."

Reluctantly, I motioned him in, went around my desk. It was safer back here. That kiss yesterday had really knocked me for a loop.

He sat, leaned forward. "About yesterday . . ."

"What about it?" I knew exactly where he was going with this, and I didn't want to make it easy for him.

"That kiss," he said.

"Kiss?" I feigned cluelessness. I did it quite well, if I say so myself. "Oh! That. I'd forgotten."

His face hardened. "Well. I just wanted to be sure we were clear that it was a mistake. Since you seemed to enjoy it so much."

"Me?" I said innocently. "You were the first one in with tongue."

"To keep up the act," he said.

I shrugged. "If that's what you want to tell yourself."

"Nina, seriously, we should talk about—"

"Why else did you come by?" I asked, cutting him off. Talking about it was the last thing I wanted to do. There was no need. I'd already stuffed those feelings it had dredged up into the Do Not Go There corner of my brain.

Looking like he wanted to argue, he leaned back in the chair. I held my breath.

"Nate's car was found this morning."

"Where?"

"A tugboat operator spotted it in the Ohio River, in Lawrenceburg. Looks like it went over an embankment."

Oh no. I swallowed hard, spoke over the lump in my throat. "Near the Kalypso?"

He nodded. "You should probably know the FBI is handling the case now. They've been nice about it, though, and are actually sharing info."

Kevin hated losing a case to the FBI. "I'm sorry." When he didn't say anything more, I found the courage to ask. "Did they find Nate?"

"No." His eyebrows dipped as he frowned. "But, Nina, there were bloodstains all over the car. And bullet holes too. Preliminary tests say it's Nate's blood. Of course, that won't be definite for weeks. It doesn't look good."

I swallowed hard. "Has anyone talked to Maria?"

"No. Not yet."

"I'll do it."

He nodded. "Soon, Nina. The media has gotten wind of it. It will be on the news tonight."

I groaned. "All right."

He stood up, stretched his arms overhead. "I better go."

My cell phone buzzed. I reached for it, but stopped when I noticed Kevin staring at me from the doorway.

"What?"

"Nothing," he said.

The phone rang again. Still staring after Kevin, I answered it. "Hello?"

Noisy static filled the line.

"Hello?" I said again. Damn, I'd forgotten to check the caller ID. I needed to add "Thou shalt always check your caller ID display before answering the phone" to my list of commandments, but I was afraid I'd continuously break it. I tended to only make commandments I could keep.

"Nina."

Ohmygod.

My head snapped to the doorway. I covered the mouthpiece. "Kev!" I called out in a loud whisper.

"Nate?" I said, really loud. I heard the cowbell jingle. Jumping up, I went after Kevin, only to trip on the umbrella.

Holding in a groan, I covered the phone again. "Kevin!" I yelled.

A second later he filled the doorway.

I scrambled to my feet while motioning to the phone. "Nate? Where are you?" I said.

Kevin was mouthing "speakerphone."

I didn't know if I had it on my cell phone. I shook my head and held the phone out so both of us could listen with our heads pressed together.

Now wasn't the time to notice how soft his hair was, or how good he smelled, but apparently I couldn't help myself.

A long breathy sigh came across the line. "Hurt," Nate said.

Oh God, oh God.

Empty static echoed on the line. "Nate," I said, my throat clogged. "Are you still there? Nate!"

"Maria." The word seemed ripped from his soul, each syllable sounding like it took such effort to say. "Love," he said.

"I'll tell her," I said. "Where are you?"

"Nate," Kevin said, his voice forceful. "It's Kevin. Where are you, man? We can help."

The line went dead.

Kevin said a word that would have had my mother washing his mouth out.

"He's alive," I said.

"Not for long by the sounds of him."

"What do we do?" I asked.

He stared at me, his green eyes hard as stone. " 'We' do nothing. *I've* got to make some calls."

"What about Maria?" I asked.

He dragged a hand over his face. "You decide," he said. "You know best how she'd react."

How would she react? I wondered. Images of Maria out on a ledge somewhere came to me. "Think I'll wait on the phone call." But I had to tell her about the car. I didn't want her hearing it on the news.

"I'm okay with keeping her in the dark for now," he said. "I've got to go." He took me by the shoulders and stared down at me. My traitorous knees shook slightly.

After a second he let me go, turned and walked out. A moment later the cowbell jingled.

I was not disappointed he didn't kiss me.

Not at all.

I slumped in my chair. That was twice today I'd broken a cardinal commandment. The same one too.

Tam came rushing in, her hair bobbing, her smile wide, her face flushed. "Was that Kevin pulling out?"

I nodded.

Tam shook her head as if trying to clear it. "I want to know, but I have to share first."

Excited, she was talking so fast her words slurred.

"Share what?"

"I found it!"

"What?"

She set a paper on my desk. "The proof I need to show that Leo is a phony!"

Picking up the paper, I scanned it. "What is this?"

"An obituary. For the real Leo Barker."

Twenty

I should stay out of it.

I knew I should. This whole Nate/Claire mess was best left to the police, the FBI, heck, even Mr. Cabrera. I had no desire to cross paths with any homicidal maniacs running around out there.

I'd had my fill of those this year, thankyouverymuch.

So what was I doing driving down Leo Barker's driveway?

Good question. One I couldn't quite answer, so I avoided it. Hey, avoidance wasn't one of my commandments—yet.

Leo wasn't Leo. Tam had explained to me the whole identity theft process over a doughnut. Tam was convinced Leo was wanted by the FBI, and her saying that had my mind veering left of center.

I'd have confronted Leo at work, except—surprise surprise—he'd called in sick.

I turned up the driveway of the small farm Leo had given as an address on his application form. Who knew if it was even his?

There were no cars parked in front of the quaint two-story farmhouse, but the front door was open beyond a screen door.

Once again the thought that I shouldn't be there flitted

through my head and flitted out just as fast. If my hunch was correct, I had nothing to fear.

If.

Using one of Maria's tricks, I lifted my chin, pulled my shoulders back, and walked toward the house.

Out of nowhere a pack of dogs came galloping around the corner of the house, toward me.

At least I thought they were dogs. They kind of looked like horses.

"Eeeee!" I screamed, breaking into a run.

Leo bolted out the front door, a dish towel slung over his shoulder. "Nina?"

"Eeee!" The dogs were gaining fast.

Leo let out a shrill whistle just before I hurtled his front steps and leapt into his arms. The dogs stopped immediately, huge tongues lolling out the sides of their mouths.

I squirmed out of Leo's arms, pushed a lock of hair behind my ear. "I wasn't really scared," I said.

"Of course not." He frowned. "What are you doing here?"

"I—" I struggled with how to phrase what I wanted to say. "I mean—" I bit my lip. "I came to ask . . . Are you . . ."

He motioned to the top step. We both sat. The dogs pranced around.

Pulling the towel off his shoulder, he said, "When did you figure it out?"

I let out a deep breath. "I didn't. Not really. I knew something was up, since Ana hadn't sent you to me, but I never had the chance to ask you about it. But really, with Tam's reaction, I was thinking more along the lines of felon rather than FBI."

"I must be getting sloppy," he said.

"Tam found out the real Leo Barker died twenty years ago."

"She's good. Real good. The Bureau should give her a job."

No wonder Tam hadn't liked him. Tam and law enforcement didn't get along. Deep down she must have sensed he carried a badge. "I couldn't do without her. Actually it was her comment about you probably being an FBI fugitive that made the pieces finally fall into place. You're working Nate's case, right?"

"Nina, I really can't—"

"Can't or won't, Le—" I broke off, realizing that Leo wasn't his name. Not anymore.

"Ian," he said. "Ian Phillips."

"Ian," I said, testing it out. "Well, Ian, I didn't come all this way to get the shaft. I turned in the pictures, I've reported the phone calls, my office has been broken into—twice. By you, I assume?"

He nodded. "Sorry about that. Just part of the job."

Hmmph. "I'd really like to know what's going on and why."

He twisted the dish towel. "*We'd* like to figure the why too."

"Huh?"

"We don't *know*, Nina. We don't know why all this is happening. Nate does, but as you know, he's missing."

"So you don't think he has anything to do with Claire Battiste's murder?"

"Personally, I don't think so, but I have no evidence to back that up."

I rubbed my temples. "Nate must have contacted you, right?"

He sighed, long and heavy. "I shouldn't be telling you anything."

I fluttered my eyelashes. "Please?"

Groaning, he said, "Only since you've been so cooperative, I'll tell you what I can."

Meaning, not everything. *Damn.*

"Nate called the Bureau about a week ago. The minute he mentioned the Kalypso, he was transferred to Fran Cooper. She's the go-to person for the casinos."

The blue-haired lady.

"He said he had evidence we would be very interested in involving the Kalypso, but he wouldn't say what. He was scared, though, and thought he might be in danger. Fran agreed to meet him that afternoon, but he never showed, and from what we learned, no one has seen him since."

"Is this where you come in? You obviously found out he'd sent a package to me, so the FBI planted you in my office—to what? Intercept it?"

"Yeah, but I was foiled by Tam. Unbeknownst to us, she took the package home."

"You searched the office that night," I said, vowing silently to never doubt Tam again.

He nodded. "I can't believe Tam noticed. I had to be very careful after that. I didn't want her to blow my cover."

"I didn't connect you to being an agent until I realized you saw me put the package in my backpack that day in my office. I was wondering how the blue-haired lady knew I had it."

The sun dipped behind a puffy white cloud as he stared out across the yard. "I called Fran to tell her you were on your way to the Kalypso. That was the last time anyone from the Bureau talked to her."

His somber tone told me what he thought had become of her.

"I don't understand any of this," I said. "Why would Claire kill Brian Thatcher? And who killed Claire?" A lump formed in my throat when I thought of Nate, of how he'd sounded on the phone that morning.

Looking like he was debating telling me anything more, he paused for a moment. Finally, he said, "It all ties in with

Phineus Frye and the Kalypso, that's obvious. But how, we haven't figured out."

"Do you know if Claire Battiste was sleeping with Colin Frye? Her sister's husband?"

He shrugged.

"Does that mean you don't know, or you won't tell me?"

He shrugged again.

Try, try again. "Do you know why Nate sent the gala guest list in the package?" I asked. "Have you figured that out yet?"

"We're working on it, Nina. This case is priority one in the office, especially since Nate's father got involved."

"Then why call in sick today?" I asked. "And why are you home and not out there looking for Nate?"

"I realized I forgot to reset the alarm last night. My supervisor thought it best for me to lay low today, but stay here in case you called to check on me. Knowing Tam's suspicious mind, *I* thought it best to show up to work as though nothing unusual had happened, but I was overruled."

I watched the dogs, five of them, race across the yard. And was glad I was up here, safe and sound. I thought about Verona and Claire. About Verona's hatred. Because Claire was sleeping with Colin? Or for another reason? When her father died, had he favored Claire more than Verona in the will?

Did killing Claire alter his will somehow? I ran that by Ian along with my ideas about Verona and Roz.

"His will is airtight. Phineus was an intelligent man who definitely knew what he wanted. When he was diagnosed with cancer, he sold off his lesser holdings and kept only the two biggest moneymakers: the PR firm, and his holdings in the Kalypso. He then established a trust that oversees several charities he created. He put the trust in Verona's charge. When he died, all his money and his stakes in the Kalypso were given to the trust to continue his philanthropy."

"And the PR firm?" I asked, trying to absorb everything Leo, er, Ian was telling me.

"Phineus willed the PR firm to Verona."

"Verona? But she doesn't know anything about PR!"

"Exactly why Phineus gave Colin Frye creative control so long as he's married to Verona. And, Phineus added that Roz be appointed co-CEO so she could make a living."

I let his words sink in. "Wow. So, essentially, except for the PR firm, no one got anything."

"Except," he said, "for the—"

"Charities," I finished. "He's very generous."

"He came from nothing to become something. He was a big believer in giving back."

It was all very interesting in a *Dynasty* kind of way, with lots of motive for murdering Alfred Phineus but not each other. Certainly not Brian Thatcher. Or Claire. Or Nate.

Sighing, I asked, "What now? I've got the Frye job lined up for tomorrow. Do I cancel?"

He thought for a second. "No," he said. "It might be the perfect time for me to get into the Frye house, snoop around."

"Don't you need a warrant for that?"

"Officially."

Oh-kay. I'd leave that one alone.

"What's with the dogs?" I asked. "And what're you feeding them?"

"They're English mastiffs. They're naturally that big. I breed them." He pointed. "Those three are actually puppies."

"Shut up!"

"I'm serious. They're almost ready to go."

I looked up at him, an idea forming. "How ready?"

* * *

I tried Maria on her cell phone, but her voice mail kept picking up. It was just past four and my living room was filling with neighborhood watchers.

After seeing Leo, er, Ian this morning, I'd spent most of the day at the office, getting things together for tomorrow's job.

Kit and I had made several runs to the garden center. I'd decided on a greenish flagstone for the Frye's little nook, and found just the right plants for the pond. Deanna, working with Jean-Claude, had found a lovely old iron lounging chair at an antique mart near the Tri-County Mall. She was still at TBS working the rust off and touching it up with paint.

I'd left Kit in charge of the little odds and ends that still needed to be done while I took off for home.

There was nothing to worry about.

Nothing at all.

So why was I worried?

I attempted to push the image of Leo/Ian sneaking into the Fryes' house out of my head. If he got caught, my reputation would be shredded, even if he was FBI.

I felt a headache coming on as I tried calling the vet's office, but it had closed for the day at four. I didn't want to call the emergency number so I hung up, not sure what to do next.

Where had Maria and Gracie disappeared to?

Dragging his feet, Riley came into the kitchen. He looked so . . . forlorn.

It was pitiful.

He caught me staring at him and batted his long lashes. "Couldn't you just let her come over?" he asked.

"If her father says it's okay."

He muttered something under his breath that sounded like a curse word, so I let it be. I figured he was suffering enough. He didn't need me grounding him on top of everything else.

"Miz Quinn." Mr. Cabrera hurried into the kitchen. "Everyone's here."

He'd gotten here twenty minutes ago carrying a large whiteboard with a fancy graph of schedules drawn on it.

I looked at Riley. "You ready?"

Briefly, his eyes lit. I'd roped him into helping me out with my little entrapment. Not very motherly of me, but I hadn't given birth to him, so I figured it wouldn't hurt all that much.

Maybe.

I tried not to think about it as I loaded glasses onto a tray. No paper cups today.

As Mr. Cabrera droned on and on about beefing up patrols, I kept a close eye on those glasses.

Flash had barely touched his—only to put it down on the table after Riley handed it to him.

The Colonel had yet to let his go, and I began to think that maybe he was planning on taking it home with him "by accident."

Mr. Weatherbee had frowned at his as soon as Riley gave it to him, and I swear I saw him check the bottom of it, looking for a marking. Not likely to find one since I'd gotten them on sale at Target. He'd also put a folded paper towel under his to catch the condensation.

He glanced up, looked right at me. With the amount of disappointment I saw in his eyes, I felt like I'd failed some sort of test.

Almost made me want to run out and pick up some Waterford tumblers.

Almost.

Where was Maria? As hard as I tried to focus on the meeting, I couldn't. I shouldn't have made her take Gracie to the vet. I should have done it myself. Then, at least, I'd know where she was. I glanced at the clock. Yep. *Oprah* was on, and ordinarily Maria would be camped on the couch watching her. Something drastic must have happened for Maria to be missing *Oprah*.

Forcing myself not to think about guns and bloodstained cars, I watched Mr. and Mrs. Mustard.

Outwardly, they seemed like a happy old couple. But looking closer, I noticed they never touched, not even a sleeve, even though they were sharing the love seat. And I swear I caught the Colonel ogling Mrs. Johanssen.

Odd.

Even odder was that Mrs. Mustard kept ogling *me*. I looked away when she caught me staring. Again.

I turned my gaze to Mr. Weatherbee. He kept looking at the clock as if wishing he didn't have to be here.

I knew that feeling.

He was barely paying attention to Mr. Cabrera, and I think I heard him groan when Mr. Cabrera launched into his buddying up program.

And Flash? Well, he was staring at my legs again. Maybe it hadn't been such a good idea to change into shorts when I got home.

But I'd been hot and sweaty and covered with dust. I smiled, quite pleased with my crew and the work they'd done today. Criminal backgrounds or not, they were the best.

I just hoped and prayed Tam would still be working for me tomorrow once she found out about Leo Barker and who he really was. I hadn't told her about Ian—by his request. I hated keeping secrets from her, and I know she hated not knowing *everything* going on.

She was going to hold this against me for a long time to come.

I snapped to attention when a round of hearty applause broke out. I clapped too, unsure why until I saw people standing to leave.

Riley quickly collected Flash's and Mr. Weatherbee's glass. I lunged for the Colonel's. Mrs. Mustard grabbed it before me. "I'll set this in the kitchen," she said.

"No, really. No need. I'll get it," I said, playing tug-of-war. I was holding on tight, hoping she wasn't smudging any prints.

Riley caught sight of us and rushed over. "Excuse me, ladies," he said, and plucked the glass out of both our hands. Hurrying, he rushed off to the kitchen.

Mrs. Mustard fluffed her hair. "Yes. Well."

"Thanks for your help," I said, trying not to snarl. "But we have it under control."

Her head snapped up and she stalked out the door.

I blinked after her, not sure what to make of all that. I'd never known her to be so . . . helpful before.

Flash shuffled over to me, cleared his throat. "I, um, wasn't being honest last night."

My jaw dropped. "What? When?"

"I said I was following someone and lost them . . . I didn't lose them."

"You didn't?" This could be the break we were looking for. "Who was it?"

He blinked sheepishly. His fuzzy salt and pepper eyebrows waggled. "You."

Twenty-one

 "Me!?"

He shrugged. "I saw you out by Donatelli's gazebo, and thought you might need some help looking for your dog. By the time I caught up to you, you were at Mr. Weatherbee's."

"Why didn't you tell me this last night?"

"Didn't want you to think I was a stalker! But after another burglary happened last night, I didn't want you to think I had anything to do with that either."

I wasn't sure what to believe. Before I could ask more questions, Mr. Cabrera grabbed my arm and shooed Flash off.

"Mr. Ca—"

He interrupted. "I've got you on the schedule for Saturday, Miz Quinn. That okay with you?"

Inwardly, I groaned. The last thing I wanted to do was be part of the neighborhood watch. I couldn't even keep tabs on Riley.

"Everyone's taking part," Mr. Cabrera added.

I caved under his pointed stare. "Oh, all right. Who am I paired with?"

He smiled. "Ursula."

"Brickhouse? What? Why? She doesn't even live in this neighborhood."

"We're shacking up," he said, grinning so broadly I thought his dentures were going to come loose. "On a trial basis."

Oh dear God.

I opened the door to see him out, and Maria came up the steps, grinning broadly. *"Bonjour!"* she cried.

I sniffed the air, wondering if I should have been calling the local taverns looking for her.

"Where have you been?" I asked.

She sighed, slipped off her heels and sank onto the sofa. "At the spa." She held up her hand. "Look at my manicure! Isn't it fabulous?"

I should have known. Even *Oprah* couldn't compete with paraffin.

"Where's Gracie?" I asked.

She scrunched her nose.

"Maria?"

"Oh, stop with the worrying. She's fine. The vet wanted to keep her overnight." She looked down at the floor.

"Maria . . ."

She looked up at me. "Oh, all right. I talked him into keeping her for the night. It's only sixty dollars, Nina, and I really need to get some sleep."

My sixty dollars, at that. I wanted to yell at her, but I couldn't. Reluctantly I admitted—only to myself—that I might have done the same thing if I'd been there. "Well, did he say what was wrong with her?"

She was studying her pedicure. "Hmm? Oh, she's going blind and has bladder problems."

Where on earth did Kit get this dog?

"Oh yeah, and something about poison."

I shook my head, thinking I didn't hear her right.

When she didn't say anything else, I waved a hand in front of her face. "Poison?"

Her nose wrinkled again. "Yeah?"

I sighed, went to the phone to call the vet.

I couldn't be mad at Maria even if I wanted to. Not when I knew what I knew. My stomach twisted. How long did Nate have? We needed to find him. Silently, I begged him to call me again.

I looked up the vet's number, then remembered that the office was closed. Before I could decide whether to have him paged, my phone rang.

Startled, I jumped back. It rang a second time. I ducked my head and looked at the caller ID. My mother. I didn't pick it up. Two rings more and it stopped.

A second later Maria yelled into the kitchen, "Your cell phone's buzzing. I'll get it."

"No!" I darted into the living room. It had to be my mother. Maria had my backpack open and my cell phone in her hand.

I lunged for the phone. "Don't answer it!"

"Why?" Then she looked at the caller ID screen. "Oh." She dropped the phone back onto my backpack and stared inside as though something had caught her eye.

Oh no! The copies I had made of those pictures were in there. Wrapped in an envelope, yes, but still in there.

I lunged again, but it was too late.

"What's this," Maria asked, pulling out the PCF gala guest list.

Thank God it wasn't the pictures. I wouldn't know where to begin an explanation.

She flipped through the pages, her eyebrows furrowing. "Where'd you get this?"

Oh jeez. "I . . . um—"

"This is the guest list Verona Frye needs . . ."

I grabbed onto an idea for dear life. "*That's* the guest list?"

"Yeah. Where'd you get it?"

"Nate left it at my office." Close enough.

"He did?"

"Yeah. When he came by to drop off some papers for your backyard. It must've gotten mixed up somehow." *Liar, liar, pants on fire.* I nudged her over on the couch, sat down. "I've been carting it around, waiting to give it back to him."

"He probably doesn't know where it is."

Now that she had it, I thought this was a good time to pick her brain. "What are those columns?" I asked. As an event planner, she'd know, right? Nate's weird shorthand and all . . .

"This," she said, pointing to the first column, "is that the invitation was sent." Her French manicure slid to the next column. "This is the RSVP column. An X means no, a Y means yes."

On the page we were looking at, almost all of the RSVP column had some symbol or another in it. "What's the third column for?"

"Double-checking. People who haven't RSVPed are notified . . . usually a telephone reminder."

Now that I looked more closely, I saw that when the middle column was blank, there was a check in the third column. Very confusing.

"Now this is strange," she said.

"What?" She was looking at the bottom of the last page.

"There's about twenty names here that look to have been added on to the master list."

"How do you know?"

"Not alphabetized."

"That's unusual? To add a last-minute guest?"

"Not so much. What's odd is that there's no mark in the RSVP column and no reminder mark either. Wait . . . and there's a circle around the checkmark in the first column."

She was seriously losing me. "English, please?"

"These last twenty invitations were returned unopened."

I scanned the names and was surprised to realize I recognized some of them . . . kids from the PCF website. I shared this with Maria, and she smiled. "I know what he did," she said.

"What?"

"He must have invited some of PCF's beneficiaries to the gala, as guests." She looked at me. "He's so sweet."

I thought about his phone call and my stomach turned. "He loves you, you know." I'd promised him I'd tell her.

"I know. I just wish I knew what was going on . . ."

She wasn't the only one. My gaze slid to the guest list. "If these names are PCF beneficiaries, why did all their invitations come back?" I asked.

"Good question," she said. "I'll ask Verona when I call to tell her I have the list."

"No!" Maria looked at me strangely, and I said, "I, um, am going to see her tomorrow. I'll bring the guest list with me. No need to bother her."

Nate was hiding that list from someone, and I wasn't letting it out of my sight until we knew who it was.

"All right." Maria stood. "I'm going to take a long bath. I've had a rough day."

A rough day at the spa. I could just imagine.

She headed up the stairs and I called out to her. "Maria . . ."

"Yeah?"

I needed to fill her in about Nate's car, but oddly enough, she did look like she'd had a rough day. No doubt Nate's disappearance was taking its toll on her, though she put up a good front.

"It can wait till later," I said.

She tipped her head. "You sure?"

"Yep."

"All right."

I moseyed into the kitchen and caught sight of the three glasses on the kitchen counter. Riley had put them into big gallon-size Ziploc bags and written whose was whose on the plastic.

Maybe there was a little bit of detective in him after all.

I heard Maria on the stairs. "Oh," she said, coming into the kitchen, a thick bathrobe over her arm. "Gracie."

"What about her?"

"I forgot to tell you that the vet thought she might have gotten into something around the house."

I wondered if Gracie had been sniffing around Riley's room. Who knew what toxic things lurked in there?

"He suggested you dog-proof this place."

I looked around. There wasn't really anything for Gracie to get into here. Not only that, but she hadn't been out of our sight, except when she was under the couch—and the only things under there were harmless dust bunnies.

I slapped my forehead. Gracie *had been* out of my sight—when she'd escaped last night.

Mr. Weatherbee had found her in his *garden*.

Ugh. "Come on," I said, pulling Maria to her feet.

"Where are we going?" She hung her robe over the back of the stool.

"Mr. Weatherbee's."

"Oh, the gay guy?"

"What?!"

She slipped on a pair of my flip-flops and pulled open the back door. "The older man with dark wavy hair, green eyes, clean shaven? Wears Bruno Magli loafers, Hugo Boss clothes?"

"Mr. Weatherbee is not gay." What was it with my family

and thinking everyone was gay? Between Maria and Ana, I was starting to look twice at everyone I knew.

We cut across Mr. Cabrera's and Mrs. Daasch's yards. Her panties were gone from her doorknob. As we passed through Mrs. Walker's yard, all I could imagine was her hiding in a closet while someone was breaking into her house.

This guy needed to be caught.

"What are we doing?" Maria asked.

"Look around. See if you see anything dug up or half eaten. Bulbs, especially."

Day lilies and daffodils were beautiful—and very deadly to dogs. If Gracie had nibbled on one, she was lucky to be alive.

I wracked my brain, trying to remember what other plants were toxic to pets. There were so many, and I hadn't needed to brush up on it lately.

"And you're trying to tell me this man isn't gay?" Maria said, looking around.

I hated to stereotype, but I had to admit she had a point. The lawn was meticulous, Mr. Weatherbee's garden filled with pastels. From pink canterbury bells to purple sage. And his house? A pretty salmon color with cream and tan trim.

"But he's divorced!"

"Did you ever wonder why?" Maria asked with a "duh" look on her face.

"But he gets *Playboy* in the mail," I said weakly, not believing that a juicy tidbit like Mr. Weatherbee being gay could be kept secret in the Mill. The Mill!

Maria kept her gaze on the ground. "Maybe it's a decoy."

"You think?"

She shrugged. "A friend of mine once dated a guy who

had an above-average porn collection only to find out he was gay."

"How'd she find out?"

"He wouldn't put out." She sounded seriously miffed by this. "Then a couple years later, she saw him and his boyfriend at the Home and Garden show."

"Oh my God! Derrick? Derrick Brandt?"

Maria's mouth dropped. "How did you know that?!"

Maria had dated Derrick for two months her freshman year of college. I'd never seen her so angry over a breakup . . . and Derrick Brandt—and his partner Sean—owned the nursery where I had an account.

She hmmphed. "Never mind. I don't want to know."

We continued to search the area. Gracie had definitely been here. Signs of trampling were everywhere. The garden would spring back with a little TLC, though.

A broken stem caught my eye. I wandered over to the trellis attached to the back of the house. Morning glory vines were working their way upward. The plant was pretty young, not yet three feet, but it had a fair share of buds, and several closed blooms.

Bending over, I picked up the stem. It hadn't been cut with shears. Looked like small little dog teeth to me. "I found it," I said to Maria.

"What is that?"

"Morning glory. Gracie must've eaten one of the blooms."

"So?"

"It's poisonous to dogs," I said. It explained a lot too, like why Gracie was walking in circles this morning. "It causes hallucinations and an upset stomach."

"That explains the yakking this morning."

"And the ghosts. She should be okay, though." Thank God. I could just imagine explaining all this to Kit.

"Mrs. Quinn?"

Maria and I jumped. Mr. Weatherbee stood on his back deck.

"What are you doing back there?"

"Looking for evidence," I said.

Now that I looked a little closer, I can't believe I'd never noticed the way he dressed. I suddenly remembered how he'd held his glass of lemonade too, and how he'd checked for a mark on the bottom of the glass.

I shook my head. I was doing it again. Stereotyping. Straight men did those things too.

Lots of them.

All right, all right. Some of them.

"I can assure you," he said, "that I am not the panty thief."

Maria snorted. "I should say not. He's obviously—"

"A very nice man," I put in quickly. "Here," I said to Maria, handing her the morning glory stem, "chew on this for a while."

Maria folded her arms over her chest. "Hmmph."

"I was looking for something our dog might have eaten. She got sick."

"Oh."

"But now that you mention it—why were you out last night?" I asked.

He looked irritated that I even asked. "I told you, I was on thief patrol."

"You weren't scheduled," I countered.

He arched an eyebrow. "Do I have to be?" he said. "To be looking out for my best interests?"

I tipped my head. Looking out for his best interests? What did that mean? I peeked over at Maria. She was admiring her manicure. She'd said something about a decoy earlier. Was it possible Mr. Weatherbee was acting suspicious to make us think he was the panty thief? All so we wouldn't suspect he was gay? Why? Why not just come out?

"Is there anything else, Mrs. Quinn? My mother and I are trying to eat."

I shook my head, completely confused.

"Then might I suggest you go home and mind your own business."

Twenty-two

I raised my hand to knock on the closed door and pulled it back again. Did I really want to do this?

With my other hand, I clutched the paper bag that held the three lemonade glasses Riley and I had collected.

This was like dealing with the devil. Maybe even worse than that.

Taking a deep breath, I knocked.

"Come in," he said.

I stuck my head in first, making sure he was alone. An arm lamp glowed bright over his desk. A bottle of Advil sat next to an open can of Mountain Dew.

It was just past five, and with the stack of paperwork in front of him, it looked like he'd be here until well after dark.

"Got a minute?" I asked.

A slow smile spread across Kevin's face. "For you? Always."

Oh jeez. My knees went all spongy. This little game he was playing was wreaking havoc with my hormones.

If it weren't for Mrs. Warnicke, I'd backpedal out of there and run for the nearest loony bin, which is where I needed to be since I was actually heading toward a chair.

But—I pushed the chair back away from the desk an extra foot. Closer to the door. Closer to an escape if I needed one.

"Any more calls from Nate?"

I shook my head. The FBI had been in the office all day, going over my computer and tapping my phone. Tam had nearly gone into labor right then and there—so I'd finally sent her home.

"I need a favor," I said.

A dark eyebrow lifted. "Oh?"

Uncomfortable, I cleared my throat. "Hypothetically, what would you do if a friend came to you and asked you to run some prints for her?"

His gaze shot to the bag I held. I clutched it like it was my very last roll of refrigerated cookie dough.

"Is this about Nate?" he snapped. "Because you should have turned everything you had—"

"It's not about Nate," I snapped back.

He pulled a hand over his face. "Sorry. I'm a little stressed."

I knew how he felt, but I wasn't about to offer any sympathy.

"What's this about, Nina?"

"The panty thief," I mumbled.

Again his gaze went to the bag. "You got those red lace bikinis of yours in there?" he asked, his eyes hooded. "I've missed them."

I gritted my teeth, trying to muster up some anger, instead of the heated desire taking over. *Ginger Barlow,* I kept repeating to myself.

Ignoring him was the best way to keep my sanity—and my vow never to sleep with him ever, ever again. I set the bag down, took out the glasses.

It took me fifteen minutes to explain about the panty thief, the neighborhood watch, Flash, Mr. Weatherbee, and the Colonel.

I finished up with, "I have no proof at all. It's all gut instinct."

He looked at the glasses, then slowly glanced up at me, all sorts of innuendo in his eyes. "Sometimes instinct is the best gauge."

Now, what in the hell did that mean? Was he trying to tell me something? Was I supposed to have ESP?

All I knew was that he was looking at me the same way I looked at . . . well, cookie dough.

Danger! Danger!

I jumped to my feet. "Well, thanks," I said, beating a hasty retreat. "I appreciate your help." My hand settled on the doorknob.

"Whoa," he said. His chair creaked as he stood.

I didn't turn around. Didn't dare. I felt his breath stir the hairs on the back of my neck as he stepped up behind me. A shiver shot down my spine.

"What," he whispered, "would you say—hypothetically—to a man who thinks he made a huge mistake. That he gave up something he needs desperately?"

Oh good God.

I swallowed hard. "I wouldn't know what to say." I squirmed. Tugging on the door, I said, "I really have to go."

He put his hand out, kept the door from budging. "Wait. We haven't discussed payment."

"Payment?" I squeaked.

He turned me around, nudged up my chin so I had to look him in the eye. I kept my hand on the doorknob.

"You know," he said. "One favor for another? I'm sure Ana filled you in on how that works."

"Uh-huh?" I said weakly. My hand was cramping, I held onto the door so tightly behind my back. It was my lifeline.

"Actually," he looked over his shoulder, "it's one, two, three favors."

My gaze flicked from his eyes to his lips and back again. Dear God, he was one sexy man. It would be so easy to let go of the door, fling my arms around his neck, and let him do what he pleased. Which happened to be what pleased me.

Ack!

Mistake, he had said.

Ugh. Could I forgive him? Let him come back?

I just didn't *know*.

I held onto the door even tighter. "A case might be solved using those prints."

"That's one," he said, leaning in, his lips thisclose to mine. "What about two and three?"

I wet my lips, stared at his. *Oh boy.*

Warning bells blared in my head. My hand began to shake from the cramps.

"Well?" he said, leaning in.

Twisting the doorknob, I ducked under his arms. "Number two is Ginger, and number three is Barlow," I said in a shaky voice I wished sounded firmer.

I dashed out the door, my cheeks flaming, my heart pounding, and my libido begging me to Turn Around. Now.

I kept going, but I distinctly felt Kevin's eyes following me. Following me as if he somehow *knew* I was wearing those little red bikinis today.

Kit's garage door was open when I pulled into his driveway. His bright look-at-me yellow Hummer was parked on the left half, Daisy's sleek red Jaguar was on the right.

I put my truck into park, wiped the doggy drool off my arm with the hem of my shirt. "You ready?" I said to the horse of a dog next to me.

I'd been calling her Black Beauty, BeBe for short, even though she wasn't black, wasn't a beauty, and of course, was a dog.

Her giant head had hung out the window most of the thirty-minute ride from Ian Phillips's farm in Lebanon to Kit's huge Tudor-style house in West Chester. The rest of the time she'd spent drooling on me.

I wrestled BeBe out of the car. Keeping tight hold of her leash, I led her up Kit's front walkway. All right. She led me. Semantics.

I pushed Kit's doorbell.

BeBe pranced around, nearly taking my arm from its socket.

The beautiful stained-glass door opened. Kit's eyes widened.

"Her name's BeBe," I said. "Here are her papers. Here's her leash." I rolled my shoulder once I was free of the leash. I was going to be sore tomorrow.

Kit was still staring at me.

I shrugged. "I figure scary deserves scary." I turned and walked down the walkway.

"Nina!"

I turned back. BeBe had settled at Kit's feet like she'd known him all her life. Her massive tail thumped happily against his legs. Anyone else, and they'd be swept off their feet with one swipe. They were obviously meant for each other. It did my heart good. "Yeah?" I said.

He smiled wide. All right, when he grinned I could understand why women went all gooey over him. "See ya tomorrow."

Tomorrow.

The Frye job. I wasn't looking forward to it.

Not at all.

Twenty-three

"You had to do it," Ana said to me as we hid behind two giant Arello's menus.

"I know. It's just—you should have seen how pathetic she looked."

Once I'd gotten back from Kit's, I'd forced myself to tell Maria what I knew—up to a point. I'd told her about the car, and about Claire and Verona being sisters, but I'd kept my big fat mouth shut on Nate's phone calls. And the pictures.

"Not as pathetic as you trying on those dresses."

"I was not pathetic," I whispered, peering over my menu. Aunt Rosa sat at the bar with her back to us. "Hunk o' burning love" had yet to show.

Dress shopping hadn't gone so well. Not well at all. Seemed all that was left on the racks were the prom rejects. Rejects that made my dress look positively lovely.

Shopping also hadn't taken my mind off my troubles, like I'd hoped it would. My mind kept skipping back to Nate's phone calls . . . and Maria.

"I'm doing the right thing, right?" I asked Ana.

She sipped a gigantic Cosmopolitan. "About not getting any of those dresses? Definitely. And you look really good as a redhead."

I fluffed my wig. Ana had brought them with her so we could go fully incognito. Personally, I thought that the wigs made us stand out even more since they were so obviously fake.

"About Maria. Not telling her about those phone calls? Would *you* want to know?"

With the little information I'd given her, Maria dove into her Louis Vuitton handbag and came up with two Dramamines. She was out like a light, and with the way she was snoring, there would be a ticket for disturbing the peace on my door when I got home.

Ana didn't even think about it. "No."

Me either. Which was why I wasn't telling Maria. It would only add to her stress. Telling her wouldn't help Nate, and it would only make her worry more. Still, I felt a little bit like I did when she told me she'd broken up with Derrick Brandt. Guilty. Because I'd known all along that he was gay.

And maybe, just maybe, I could have saved her some of that pain.

Or maybe, my inner voice said, *she needed to live her own life, one that I needed to stay out of.*

I doused that voice with a generous sip of white wine and let myself wallow.

Sighing, I looked over the edge of the booth toward the bar. Aunt Rosa was twirling the little pink umbrella that came in her frothy drink. Still no sign of "Hunk o'."

Ana swung her phony long blonde curls, propped her elbow up on the table, and dropped her head into her hand. "Did you ever call Hubba Hubba MacKenna back?"

"No," I said, taking a sip of my drink. I needed fortification. There was no way I could get through a conversation about Robert MacKenna without it.

"He likes you."

•

"He's married."

"So are you."

"Don't remind me."

"Maybe he's getting a divorce too?" Ana said, draining the rest of her Cosmo.

My eyebrows dipped. "You think?"

"Why not?"

I'd never thought of that as a possibility. If he was separated, he was fair game. However, did I really want to get involved with someone who was separated? That was just screaming Heartache.

Whoa. *I* was separated. Did I want men running from me?

That would be a big NO. The only man I wanted running from me was Kevin, and it seemed he kept inching closer, like a worm. I asked Ana about that.

"Guilt," she said. "He's regretting losing you. Probably wants you back."

Again I thought of Kevin's hypothetical. *If a man had made a mistake . . .*

One hell of a mistake.

Ana's jaw dropped. "You wouldn't, would you?"

"What?"

"Take him back?"

I shrugged and looked away.

"Nina!"

"I don't know. I don't think so."

"Oy," Ana said.

"Oh my God," I gasped, ducking under my menu.

"What?" Ana said, looking around. "Oh my God!" she screeched, ducking under her menu.

I elbowed her. "Shhh!"

My mother stood near the hostess desk, looking around.

Ana reached for her silverware, grabbed the knife. Sat on it.

I did the same.

Fortunately, my aunt Rosa had spotted my mother too. She spun so fast on her stool, she nearly toppled off.

"What should we do?" Ana whispered.

"Call 911?"

Ana reached for her cell. Before she could punch in any numbers, though, my mother zeroed in on us. We slunk lower, but she barreled down on us like a category 5 hurricane.

One thin blonde eyebrow arched as she stood poised over our table. "*What* are those things on your heads?" she asked. Before we could answer, she held up a perfectly manicured hand, her white tips smooth and gleaming. "No, don't tell me. I don't care."

Ana and I shared a look. What was this about? "What're you doing here, Mom?"

"Looking for you, of course."

Of course. Like I came here all the time.

"Riley told me where to find you."

Grrr.

My mother motioned for me to scoot in.

"Yow!" I cried.

Heads turned. I pulled the knife out from under me. Thankfully, it wasn't a steak knife.

Ana laughed.

I gave her the Ceceri evil eye.

It didn't affect her in the least.

Again my mother arched an eyebrow, but she didn't say anything. Something important had to be weighing on her mind if she had nothing to say about me sitting on cutlery.

She flagged down a waiter. "Bourbon. On the rocks." He turned to walk away. "Make it a double."

Oh boy.

"Nate," she said, giving Ana and me her full attention. "I heard on the news he was missing! Is this true? Is it? Is it?"

I pushed the rest of my wine over to her before she burst a blood vessel. I told her what I'd told Maria. My mother had notoriously loose lips. I didn't trust her with the full story.

She leaned back, fanned herself. "He must be found. The wedding is in less than a week. A week."

"Yeah, that's what we're worried about," Ana said.

My mother arched both eyebrows.

Before a catfight broke out, I said, "Maybe we should focus on Maria right now."

"Yes, we must talk to Maria. We've got to talk to the florist and the caterer and the wedding planner and the baker, and—"

"Mom."

"What?" she said. "Oh," she snapped her fingers, "and Uncle Giuseppe and Aunt Rosetta are flying in tomorrow, can you pick them up?" she asked me.

"I've got a job tomorrow."

Her gaze slid to Ana, who tossed back a blonde curl. Mom opened her mouth, snapped it closed again. She turned back to me. "I," she thumped her ample chest, lowered her lashes, "need your help, Nina. Your ma-ma. Please don't disappoint me."

Ana snorted.

I sighed. "I really don't have the time," I said.

"*Chérie . . .*" she began.

I tuned out her guilt trip. My gaze wandered over her shoulder. I gasped and grabbed Ana's arm, motioning.

Ana's eyes went wide. "Ohhh noooo."

My mother stopped mid-guilt trip. "What?"

Ana cleared her throat. "Nothing. I'm just sympathizing."

"Well, yes. As I was saying . . ."

Behind my mother's head, my father was scanning the restaurant. He obviously didn't recognize us in our hootchie mama getups.

Ana and I watched in horror as Aunt Rosa rushed over to him. She motioned toward us, and my dad's bulldog eyes went all round and wide. *He* was Hunk o' Burning Love?

I made the international shooing sign with my hands.

"What are you doing, *chérie*?"

I breathed a sigh of relief when my father and Aunt Rosa ducked out the door.

"Nina?"

"Me?" I said, folding my hands into fists. "Nothing."

"Filing," Ana piped in. "Her nails."

My mother's eyes lit. "I'll do that!"

Before I could protest, my mother had my hands held hostage. She'd been trying to get me to have a manicure for years now and probably saw this as her only change to rid me of my ragged cuticles. As she pulled a file out of her purse, my cell phone rang. She pouted as I tugged my hands free and checked the phone's readout: *Home*.

"Hello?"

"Nina?"

"Kevin? What're you doing at my house?"

His long sigh echoed across the line. "You need to come home. There's been a break-in."

Red and blue lights bathed my house. Two patrol cars were parked diagonally at the sidewalk and Kevin's 4Runner was in my driveway. I pulled in behind it, and Ana and my mother jumped out before I could even get my truck into park.

Kevin had been waiting on the front porch talking with one of the uniformed officers when we pulled in. He came to the top of the steps when he spotted us.

My mother teetered on the flagstone path in her stilettos. "Where's Maria?" she cried. "My baby! Mar-eee-ahh! Bé-bé!"

Kevin said, "She's inside on the couch. Resting. She's a little dazed."

Ana gasped. "Did the intruder hurt her?"

Kevin shook his head. "No. She's still a little woozy from her, uh, sleep aid."

My cheeks heated, and I was glad I could blame the color on the strobe lights. "What happened?" I asked after my mother and Ana rushed inside.

"Nice hair," he said with a sly smile.

Ack! I whipped the wig off.

"Something I should know about?" he asked.

"Ana . . ."

"Enough said."

"What happened here?" I repeated. "Is Riley okay?"

"Maria said he's at a friend's house, left a few hours ago. Do you know which one?"

I had a pretty good idea. "Katie."

"Katie?" Kevin asked.

I quickly explained that whole situation. Kevin smiled smugly when I got to the part about Riley and Katie in the gazebo. I fully expected a "That's my boy" to come out of his lips any second now. I cut it off at the pass. "What happened here?" I asked again. "Is Maria really okay?"

He motioned to the porch swing. The uniformed officer disappeared into the house. "She's fine. Though I highly recommend she never takes two Dramamines ever again."

Through the thin walls I could hear Maria saying, "Poop on, poop on." I shot a look at Kevin. "What's she talking about?" Gracie was still at the vet—or I'd have assumed the worst. "And what are *you* doing here?"

Kevin chuckled.

"What?"

"The security company called the department after someone tripped the alarm here because apparently when they called the house, a semiconscious woman kept saying, 'Poop on, poop on.'"

I dreaded going inside. What in the world was I going to find?

"The 911 operator recognized it as my address and let me know what was going on."

I didn't correct him that it was his former address. Although I wanted to.

"I was second on the scene, and came in to find Officer Frennell trying to coax Maria off of your neighbor, Mrs. Mustard. She was saying 'poupon.' As in Grey Poupon. The mustard."

I gasped. "Is Mrs. Mustard all right?"

"Depends."

"On what?"

"Those fingerprints you asked me to run . . . as a favor?"

My cheeks heated again at the memory of favors. "Yes."

"Turns out Jake Jones has an outstanding warrant out for his arrest in Oklahoma."

"Jake Jones?"

"Aka Jacob Mustard."

"What!?" I said, shocked. Straight-laced Colonel? A fake name? An arrest warrant?

"Peeping Tom. He skipped bail."

My jaw dropped.

"But that's not all," he said, just like a perky talk show host.

I didn't think I could take any more. I could still hear Maria whining about Poupon. I was tempted to give her another Dramamine to knock her out for the night.

"He's never been in the military, and he's not married. Margaret Mustard, aka Margaret Jones, is his sister, or as we're now calling her, his accomplice. He's skipped town again, and she's not talking."

Sweet Mrs. Mustard?

"She was breaking in here to find that glass from this afternoon. She'd apparently figured out what you were up to."

I remembered Mrs. Mustard trying to wrestle that glass from me. I couldn't believe her sweetness and light act fooled me!

"The alarm woke Maria, and she came down to find Mrs. Mustard in the kitchen."

He laughed again.

"This isn't funny!" I snapped. Maria really could have been hurt.

"I know, I know," he said, but he was still laughing. "Old habits must die hard for your sister, though. She brought a can of Aqua Net down with her. She got Mrs. Mustard but good, then sat on her until we arrived. I still haven't been able to get that can of hair spray out of her hand."

Oh dear Lord.

"I think," he continued, "that we might have to have her register that can with the department as a licensed weapon."

"Ha. Ha."

He stood up. The swing swayed. "You better go in," he said.

I nodded.

I was bone tired, needed to get up early, and was stressed beyond my limits.

At the sound of footsteps, I looked up. Mr. Cabrera was hustling up the driveway. It was going to be a long, long night.

"One other thing," Kevin said.

I arched an eyebrow.

"Mr. Weatherbee?"

"Yeah?"

He stepped down. "Thought you might be interested to know that he was arrested in 'ninety-four in Boston at a gay rights rally."

Twenty-four

Kit's Hummer and Tam's Cabriolet were in the lot when I pulled in early the next morning.

I'd left Maria at home fighting a terrible headache. She looked like death warmed over. At noon she was due at the police station to give her statement from last night (what she could remember). She'd also promised to pick up Gracie from the vet.

Physically, she seemed okay, but mentally . . . I was worried. Since waking up that morning, she'd been pretending she wasn't waiting to hear news about Nate. And *I* pretended not to notice how she jumped every time the phone rang.

Tam was at her desk when I came in, all smiles at Leo/Ian, who was sitting across from her. I arched an eyebrow, said hello, and walked on past without stopping to chat like I normally would. For one, I didn't want to know why she was being so friendly, and secondly, I didn't want to accidentally let it slip that Leo was FBI.

It was just after 6:30 A.M. and the office phone was already ringing. It was always like this on the morning of a job.

I had to admit I jumped every time the phone rang too,

hoping it was Nate calling. I feared the worst, but was trying to think positive. For Maria's sake.

Tam came wobbling in. "About Ian . . ." she said.

My head snapped up. "Ian?"

"He told me everything," she admitted, sitting across from me. Her helmet hair stayed put as she shook her head. "I should have known. I must be losing my touch."

"It's not lost," I said. "Just a little fuzzy."

"He brought me éclairs," she said.

"Oh?"

She blushed. "And V8."

I shuddered at the combo.

"We have a date this weekend," she said.

I gaped. Really I did. It wasn't pretty, I was sure.

"I know, I know." She struggled to her feet. "Don't start the lecture. I know what I'm getting myself into, and using my own advice about taking chances. I really tried not to like him, but there's only so much willpower I have."

"You don't have to explain anything to me," I said. "So, éclairs and V8, huh? That's all it takes to get on your good side?"

"Nina, I'm seven months pregnant, thirty-two years old, and single. He had me at the wink."

The phone rang as she waddled out the door, and I grabbed it on the first ring.

"Nina?"

I smiled. "Hunk o' Burning Love, is that you?"

My father groaned. "It's my secret screen name. Your mother checks my other one."

Oddly, I wasn't at all surprised my father had a secret screen name . . . I tsked. "You're lucky you didn't get caught. Because, really, there's no more room in my house."

We purposely avoided the big issues about Nate and

Maria and the Wedding That Might Not Be. We Ceceris are notorious at denial.

Secretly, I thought my dad might be happy the wedding was in jeopardy. He never liked Nate. It wasn't Nate personally; it was anyone who dared take his baby away. Sometimes it paid to be a middle child.

We said our good-byes and I hung up. I looked at the picture of Riley on my desk. He'd been nine when it was taken. He was pudgy back then, and full of anger and hurt. Six years later he'd lost the pudge but was still fighting against the anger and hurt.

After my house had cleared out last night, I'd thrown on a light coat, grabbed a flashlight and trekked through the woods behind the house in search of the Coughlin residence. I'd found the address in the phone book, and Katie's dad was very surprised when I showed up on the doorstep, and even more surprised when I explained why I'd come.

Ian poked his head in my office. "Got a minute?"

"Sure," I said.

"I need a favor," he said as he sat down.

"You mean more than me letting you break and enter while I'm working on a client's yard?"

"I gave you a dog," he said.

"I bought that dog," I countered. He laughed, and I added, "What do you want me to do?" Despite myself, I was kind of excited to be in the middle of all this.

"I'd really like you to keep Verona busy while I'm inside. Chat with her or something."

"About what?"

"Anything."

"Can I ask her if she's a murderer?"

His eyebrows dipped. "No."

"Can I ask leading questions about Claire and Nate and the Kalypso?"

"No."

Well, this wasn't going to be any fun.

He stood, headed to the door.

"Oh, Ian?"

"Yeah?"

"If you hurt her you'll be sorry."

He looked over his shoulder toward Tam's desk. He winked at me. "I have no doubt of that."

It was chaos at the Frye house.

Just the way I liked it.

My adrenaline was high as I walked around the site, double- and triple-checking the materials and making sure everyone knew what they had to do.

The Frye driveway was a mess, between the pallets of fieldstone and flagstone and the load of topsoil that had been delivered bright and early.

I hefted a piece of the patio's flagstone that was in the shape of Nevada, turning it over in my palm, loving the cool smooth surface. Muted browns and soft golds flowed over it. The fieldstone for the pond ran more toward dark grays and subtle browns, which I knew would only be enhanced by the pond water, deepening the hues and creating depth.

Deanna hustled up the driveway, Coby and Jean-Claude behind her, carrying the iron chaise she'd found.

"Nina! Don't you love it? I absolutely love it!" I opened my mouth, but she rushed on before I could get a word out. "Isn't it perfect?"

She was one of the best up and coming designers I'd ever met. Despite never having any formal training at all, she had a natural talent for design that was rare. One day soon I was sure she would quit working for me and move on to her own business.

Her blue eyes went wide as she waited a half second for a response from me. "You don't like it," she said.

"I love it. I just wasn't sure you were done talking."

"Oh! I'm so glad you like it! Jean-Claude and I looked forever before we found it. You know, he's not so bad to work with, once you get over the smell."

"Smell?"

She leaned in. "He swims in cologne."

"I can still hear you," Jean-Claude said in an all-American voice. His name was French through and through, but he'd been born and raised in Cleveland.

Deanna smiled at him. "I know. I'm hoping you take the hint."

I rolled my eyes and plotted how I was going to escape. Deanna was a talker and I had things to do. I sent her in search of the chaise's cushion, asked Coby and Jean-Claude to start hauling the stone into the backyard, and went looking for Kit.

I found him marking the pond area with paint. Orange for the pond, pink for the patio. I looked around. He'd already started the electrical work.

"Yo," Kit said when he spotted me.

"Hey. How's BeBe?"

He grinned. "Great. How's Gracie?"

Ack. Lie, definitely lie. "Great. Perfect. Very healthy."

A dark eyebrow with a horseshoe-shaped silver piercing shot up. "What did you do to her?"

"She's, er, fine. Just fine." That wasn't a lie. She was fine. *Now.*

I spotted Ian lurking near the house. I waved him over. "You might as well start digging the pond until Verona comes out."

He looked like he wanted to argue, but didn't say anything as he picked up a shovel.

I took a step back, already envisioning the transformation. The water garden would be exquisite. This little nook was the perfect place for it. I couldn't wait to see the end result.

My crew milled around, everyone focused on their individual tasks. It wasn't long before Verona came out with a plate of cookies. I pulled off my gloves and took two. Okay, three, but I don't think anyone noticed.

Verona looked scared. "It's such," her nose wrinkled in dismay, "a mess. You really think it's going to be done by tonight?"

"Positive." I was used to dealing with shocked homeowners. "It's going to be beautiful."

Out of the corner of my eye I saw Ian set his shovel down and mosey toward the house.

To stall, I took Verona around, introduced her to everyone. Kit mentioned he remembered her, and she blushed. He took four cookies, so I felt less guilty about my three. After inhaling them, he picked up Ian's shovel and took up where he left off.

Over my shoulder, I glanced toward the house. No sign of Ian yet. I steered Verona toward Deanna. Deanna could keep Verona busy for hours.

"I heard about Nate's disappearance on the news," Verona said. "I'm so sorry. Has anyone heard from him?"

Ack. Ian had said for *me* not to mention Nate, but he didn't tell me what to do if *Verona* mentioned him.

"I, er . . . No," I said, lying. Ian never said anything about telling people about Nate's calls. And it would be just like me to blab something I shouldn't.

"Oh." She kept tight hold of the cookie plate with one

hand, but the other went to her neck, straight to her pearls. "That's too bad."

I kicked the ground with my toe.

"Maria sounds like she's holding up well."

I felt my eyes widen in surprise. "You talked to her?"

Verona nodded. "Last night. She said you found the guest list. I can't tell you how relieved I am. Do you have it with you?"

I was going to kill Maria with my bare hands. I'd told her *I'd* take care of the guest list. I couldn't very well give it back to the Fryes when I didn't know why Nate was hiding it in the first place.

"Actually, I don't . . . I gave it to—"

"Nina!"

I spun, my pulse kicking up a notch at the tone of Kit's voice. He was leaning on the shovel, muttering under his breath.

Verona and I rushed over. "What's wrong?" I asked.

Kit nodded downward.

I followed his gaze, gasped when I spotted the upper torso of a body lying facedown in the ground.

I gasped, recognizing that blue hair.

Looked like Kit had found Stella Zamora, aka Fran Cooper, FBI.

Swallowing hard, I wished I hadn't eaten those cookies.

Verona screamed and dropped the plate. She backed away in horror.

Coby came running. "Holy—"

"Go find Ian," I told him. "Now."

"Ian?" he asked, confused.

I'd forgotten about the alias. "Leo! Leo! Find Leo."

Something red near Stella's hair caught my eye. I knelt down.

"Dude," Kit said to me. "Don't get too close."

I'd been a cop's wife too long to go touching anything. But I didn't need to. I recognized immediately what that bit of red was.

Roz Phineus's fingernail.

Twenty-five

Two hours later it was chaos of a different sort at the Frye house. Somber FBI agents swarmed the property, cordoning off the crime scene and questioning everyone, including me. Twice.

Verona hadn't let go of her pearls since Stella's body had been found. She stood just inside the French doors at the back of the house, peering out.

I wondered what she'd had to say about all this, but I wasn't privy to that kind of information, and really, I didn't want to know. All right, I'm lying. I wanted to know, but I hated that I wanted to know so I was lying to myself.

I tended to do that, lie to myself, which was why I hadn't made it a commandment, because I knew I'd never be able to keep it.

And I was rambling to myself too, which was never a good sign.

Biting my lip, I wondered at the coincidence of my crew finding Stella's body. Had it been a mistake? Or planned all along?

Again I questioned Verona's innocence in all this. She brought me here, to this spot, and she had motive to kill Claire. How involved was she? Had she killed Stella?

Or was she truly innocent? Completely oblivious to the evil around her?

One thing I knew for certain was that Roz Phineus had been involved—information I gladly passed on to Ian's superiors.

An APB was out for Colin and Roz, so far with no luck. Verona had said they were off to New York for a business meeting, but all attempts to reach them had failed.

I'd questioned whether they were even *in* New York, but apparently they were, having landed at LaGuardia late last night. The hotel staff where they were staying also confirmed that they had checked in.

So much for my detective skills.

How involved was Colin? I wondered. Was he as clueless as his wife seemed to be, or was he up to his eyebrows in murder?

Or were all three of them in it together for some reason? One happy murdering family?

I shook my head, sick of thinking about it. There was a lot to be done, cleaning up the supplies we wouldn't be using and figuring out what to do with everything.

What a nightmare.

My cell phone buzzed. *Freedom, Ohio.* Frowning, I flipped the phone open. "Nina Quinn."

"Mrs. Quinn, this is Vice Principal Robert MacKenna at Freedom High."

Oh no. His icy tone coupled with his full title told me all I needed to know. "Is Riley in trouble?"

"I have him in my office. I need you to come down here as soon as possible."

Ack. This didn't sound good. Not good at all. If Robert had put a little warmth into his voice—after all this was the same man who sent me Almond Joys on a regular basis—I wouldn't have been so worried.

"I'm at a site," I said, looking around for Kit's bald head, "but I can be there in forty minutes or so." If I ignored the posted speed limits.

"We will be waiting." He disconnected. Without even saying good-bye. Dear Lord, what had Riley done now? And after I went to bat for him with Katie's father and everything.

I found Kit, begged him to take care of everything here, found Ian/Leo and asked him if I could leave.

His eyes were haunted, and they snapped me out of my denial. Stella was dead. Claire was dead. Brian Thatcher was dead. And Nate . . .

I swallowed hard, took a deep breath, and forced myself back into oblivion. The FBI would find Nate. Everything had a good explanation, and everything would be fine. Just fine.

"If I find anything out, I'll let you know," he said.

"I'd appreciate it."

I watched him walk away, toward Verona, who was still watching from the doorway. She looked my way and quickly turned from me.

I tried not to take it personally.

Hurrying, I sprinted down Verona's narrow driveway. Thankfully, I'd had the foresight to park on the street instead of running the risk of being blocked in again.

As I drove toward Freedom, thoughts swirled in my mind, giving me a headache. Attempting to drown them out, I flipped to the Oldies station on the radio. Within minutes I was singing "Do You Want to Dance?" at the top of my lungs.

When the song ended, I turned the radio down and realized my phone was ringing. I made a grab for it. *Maria.*

"Nina," she said in a loud whisper. "I think someone's trying to break in. I keep hearing noises and Gracie keeps coming out from under the couch to bark. Do you think my stalker is back? Do you think maybe Mr. Mustard has come for my lace panties?"

"How many Dramamine have you had today?"

"None! Seriously, Nina, someone's out there."

"Is the alarm set?"

"Yes, but I'm freaking out."

"Go to Mom's."

"Okay, so maybe I had one Dramamine . . . I don't think it's a good idea to drive."

"I think it's time to throw the Dramamine away, Maria. Obviously, you don't tolerate them well."

"But—"

"No buts."

She whimpered.

I sighed. "I'm on my way to get Riley. I'll swing by to check things out at home." I couldn't dismiss her worries. After all, the last time she thought she heard someone outside, a dead body had turned up.

"How long?" she whimpered.

I could picture her crouched behind the couch with a can of hair spray.

"Thirty minutes."

"That long?"

A girl could only do so much. "I'm going as fast as I can."

"All right. Just hurry."

She genuinely sounded freaked. But between the alarm and the hair spray, I figured she'd be okay until I got there.

Tucking my phone away, I turned the radio up again and sang away some stress.

Twenty-eight minutes later I pulled up next to Maria's Mercedes, and frowned when I spotted Ana's SUV at the curb.

Ana was holding a cloth to Maria's head when I went inside. Gracie raced around, her sharp *yip yip yips* making me question why I had actually missed her cold snout last night.

"I looked around," Ana said, "but I didn't find anything. Or anyone."

I looked at Maria. "I told you I'd be home. You didn't need to call Ana."

Maria pouted. "*She* came in five minutes."

Argh. "I don't have time for this. I need to go pick up Riley." I relayed the message I'd gotten from MacKenna.

Ana grabbed her purse. "Hubba-hubba? I need to see this."

Maria sat up. "What? You're leaving me?"

"You're welcome to come," I said.

She looked like she was going to argue, but had the good sense not to, Dramamine and all. She grabbed her keys. "I'll drive."

I snatched the keys away from her. "Dramamine," I reminded.

She pouted.

Dread filled my stomach as I paced the high school office. Maria and Ana were flipping through dusty yearbooks, making fun of old hairstyles.

Riley had been doing so well. School was out in less than a week . . . Why would he mess up now?

The secretary said, "You can go on back, Mrs. Quinn."

Ana jumped up and followed me. I turned to her. "Maybe you should stay here with Maria." I peeked over Ana's shoulder. Maria had gone more than a little pale, and was currently muttering about bad perms.

"What? And miss all the fun?"

Maybe reinforcements weren't a bad idea. After all, there

was no telling what I would do if left alone with Robert MacKenna.

My cheeks heated just thinking about what kinds of things. I grabbed Ana's arm. "Don't leave me alone with him." A physical relationship between us would only complicate my life. Which was already complicated enough, thank you very much.

MacKenna's door was open. He behind his desk, his back to me, tossing a baseball from hand to hand.

I felt my eyebrows dip. "Where's Riley?"

He jumped up, dropping the ball, and spun around.

MacKenna shrugged as he walked toward me.

Flabbergasted, I barely noticed him nudge Ana out the door.

"Wait a minute," I protested.

Ana beamed. "Don't do anything I wouldn't do." She finger waved to me as MacKenna closed the door, leaned against it.

My mind searched for something Ana wouldn't do and couldn't find a single thing. Ack.

I looked up at MacKenna, trying to ignore the way my heart beat triple-time. "You set me up, didn't you?" I accused.

He treated me to a half smile. "You've been avoiding me. I had to think of some reason for you to come in."

"So Riley isn't in trouble?"

"Not that I know of."

"I'm leaving," I said, though I didn't know how since all six feet of him still blocked the door.

"Nina, we really need to talk."

He wore a baby blue button-down that matched his eyes, light brown twill pants that weren't creased, and a pair of soft suede shoes.

I kind of missed his snakeskin cowboy boots.

His blond hair had grown out since the last time I saw

him, falling in soft waves onto his forehead and over his ears.

My palms started to sweat. He looked even better than I remembered, and I remembered him looking damn hot.

Taking a big step away from him, I asked, "Are we going to sit down?"

He didn't budge. "I don't trust you not to bolt."

Damn. How did he already know me so well?

I was still grimy from working at the Fryes'. I wish I'd taken some time to, oh, I don't know, shower?

"Robert, there's really nothing to say." I gestured between us. "This, whatever this is, isn't going to work. You're married. Off-limits."

He looked down at me, his eyes all soft and warm and inviting. I took another step back, out of the danger zone.

"Nina, there's four things I want you to know."

Four? I swallowed. "All right."

"One. My friends call me Bobby. Feel free to call me that anytime. Or plain old Robert is fine."

Bobby. Oh my God, how the name fit. All-American with just a hint of mischievousness.

"Two," he continued, "this wedding ring is my father's. It came to me after he died. Mostly I wear it because I miss him. Partly I wear it to keep the horny divorcées at bay."

I wasn't sure if I should be offended, considering I was somewhat (all right, a lot) horny and an almost divorcée, but he didn't seem to mind, so why should I?

"Three?" I asked weakly.

He stepped toward me. I went to take a step back, but somehow (imagine my surprise!) I went forward, straight into his arms.

"This." He cupped my face, leaned in and kissed me.

When we finally broke apart, my heart was hammering, my knees were weak, and my brain was screaming, *Kevin, who?*

He didn't let go of my face. "And four . . . I like you, Nina. Like you a lot."

"It'll be complicated. And messy. I'm on the rebound," I felt necessary to explain, though I didn't want to.

He grinned a sheepish smile that had my heart flopping. "I was the best rebounder on my high school basketball team."

"My family is crazy," I said.

"My aunt Renee runs a halfway house."

"So?"

"For squirrels."

I smiled. "My cousin Rocco swears he can communicate with stuffed animals."

He laughed. "Well, my uncle Joe is a cross-dresser. He gives flamenco lessons out of his basement studio."

"Could we get lessons?"

"Name the day," he said softly.

I backed up again. "I just don't know," I said, trying to be as honest as I could. Well, kind of. If I were being really honest, I'd admit to thoughts that would make Ana blush.

My cell phone buzzed. "I'm sorry," I said to him, pulling it out of my pocket and looking at the caller screen. My mother. I tucked it back into my pocket. There was only so much I could handle.

"Just think about it, Nina. Okay?" He leaned in again, and I felt myself meeting him halfway.

The door opened, pushing Bobby into my arms, nearly knocking us both over. Maria looked between the two of us, saying nothing. She held out her phone. I took it, and she turned and walked away.

"Hello?" I said.

"Nina Colette Ceceri! How dare you screen *my* calls?"

"Hi Mom." She must have called Maria after not reaching me.

"Don't you 'Hi Mom' me. Aunt Carlotta and Uncle Giuseppe are at the airport waiting for you to pick them up. Why aren't you there? You knew you were supposed to meet them. What will they think of me? What kind of hostess leaves her guests stranded?"

"Mom, I told you I had to wor—"

"I know you're not making excuses to your ma-ma!" She launched into a long string of French. I was beyond glad that I had no idea what she was saying. "Tonio," she called out.

A series of bells toned as I sighed. Kids' voices in the halls filtered into the office. Bobby came around me and started to rub my shoulders.

"Nina."

"Yes, Daddy?" I tried not to moan as Bobby's fingers pressed into that sensitive area at the nape of my neck.

"You're mother is on the edge, and she's driving me so crazy that I'm tempted to push her over. Be a good girl. Just. Do. What. She. Says."

Ducking out of Bobby's reach, I tensed as Dad hung up. I clenched Maria's phone so tight my knuckles turned white.

"Nothing serious, I hope," MacKenna said.

"Life or death as far as my mother is concerned. Namely my death if I don't do what she wants. I better go."

I paused in the doorway, looked back at him. "I—"

"Just think about it," he murmured.

Nodding, I closed the door behind me.

Twenty-six

I took I-75 south to 275 west/south, a route that looped around the city, by dipping into the corner of Indiana and curving through northern Kentucky. Taking I-75 through the city to get to the airport would have been faster—if there wasn't any traffic, which wasn't likely considering the construction going on.

While I was in MacKenna's office, school had let out, and Riley managed to spot Ana and Maria in the office and bum a ride home. Anything to avoid the bus.

Unfortunately, I didn't dare take the time to drop off Riley—or Ana—so they were coming for the ride. Maria hadn't had a choice. If *I* had to pick up Aunt Carlotta and Uncle Giuseppe, then so did *she*.

"You know, Nina," Ana said, "how are Uncle Giuseppe and Aunt Carlotta gonna fit in here?"

I drove fast, too fast probably (which was rather easy to do in Maria's Mercedes), but I just wanted to get to the airport, gather my wayward relatives, and go home. I seriously needed a date with the bathtub and a roll of cookie dough.

"Yeah, Nina," Maria chimed in. "Uncle Giuseppe isn't the slimmest of guys."

I hadn't thought about getting them home. Hadn't

thought about much except getting to the airport before my mother imploded.

I frowned. "I don't know." The trunk was probably out of the question.

"Maybe you can put them in a taxi?" Riley suggested.

I imagined my mother's reaction to that. "Maybe I should put Ana and Maria in a taxi—"

"This is *my* car!" Maria cried.

"How about," Riley said to me, "I put you, Ana, and Maria in a taxi, and I'll drive Uncle Giuseppe and Aunt Carlotta home?"

"No!" we all said at once.

"Hmmph." Riley glared. "I *am* getting my permit soon."

"No!" we all said again.

In the rearview mirror I saw Riley fold his arms and stare out the window. It was amazing. He and Maria shared no blood, yet they pouted exactly the same.

"We'll figure something out," I said.

"Well," Maria snapped, "I'm not sitting on Giuseppe's lap. He always smells like sausage."

Personally, I didn't think Giuseppe had a lap.

Maria and Ana lapsed into a discussion about body odors that I did my best to tune out. I-275 west turned into I-275 south and merged with I-74 west. We were about half an hour from the Greater Cincinnati airport, which was located in, of all places, northern Kentucky.

My mind spun as I tried desperately not to listen to the B.O. conversation. Little snippets made their way through, though. When I heard catfish and curry in the same sentence, I let myself think about Nate.

How was he involved in Claire's murder? Or Brian Thatcher's? Not to mention Fran, the blue-haired FBI lady. And what about the bullet holes in his car? He'd said on the phone that he was hurt, but had he been shot? If he was shot, who'd pulled the trigger? Claire? Roz?

Fighting a growing headache, I tried to separate everything I knew.

Three people were dead. Why?

Had Stella/Fran died because someone found out she was FBI? Had she found out the truth about what was going on?

The truth of what, though?

Of what happened to Brian? Claire? Nate?

But wait. Ian/Leo had said that Nate called the FBI saying he had something they'd be very interested in. The pictures and the guest list, I'd assumed.

The pictures were obvious enough, but I still didn't understand the guest list . . . According to the day-planner in his office, Nate had been double-checking the gala guest list on the day he disappeared. Did this all have something to do with those invitations that had come back?

I just didn't know.

Indiana welcomed us. In another ten minutes we'd be in Kentucky. I drove past the Lawrenceburg exit, the one that led to the Kalypso. Nate would have driven this route every day. He was familiar with this area. Very familiar. He could be anywhere.

My mind flitted to the Kalypso, and the pull of the casino called to my inner gambler, especially now that I was so stressed.

I sighed, almost in withdrawal. It was almost like I could hear the bells, the whistles, the *shush* of the cards.

The bells . . . the whistles.

With a jerk of the steering wheel, I swerved left, into the breakdown lane.

Conversation about cabbage and garlic broke off.

"Nina? You okay?" Ana asked.

"Bells," I said.

"As in you're hearing them?" Maria asked. "Have you been into my Dramamine?"

Bells. When I'd talked to Nate the first time, I'd heard bells in the background.

I'd heard them before! The monorail tones at the Odyssey, the hotel next to the Kalypso.

Ohmygod! "I know where Nate is!"

"What!?" Maria shrieked.

Riley leaned forward. "Where?"

"Are you sure?" Ana asked.

"No! I'm not. I need to call Ian."

"Ian?" Maria asked.

"FBI," Ana said.

"You know an FBI agent?" Riley asked.

"He works for me," I said, fumbling with my cell phone.

Riley's eyes went wide. "Sweet."

Cars zoomed past as I reached Ian, who was still at the Fryes' house. I told him what I suspected, and hung up with his promise that the Odyssey would be crawling with FBI agents as soon as possible.

I avoided looking at Maria, knowing my throat would clog if I did. My conversation with Ian was the first she'd heard of Nate's injuries—and that I'd been in touch with him over the past couple of days.

She was probably royally ticked at me.

I couldn't help myself—I peeked over at her. It just wasn't like her to be so quiet, especially when she was mad. Instead of finding her angry, though, she simply looked lost.

I had to do something. Anything.

Shifting into drive, I said, "Let's go find Nate."

Maria's head snapped up. "Then what are we waiting for, slowpoke?"

At her cranky tone, I smiled. Bracing myself, I jerked

hard left and bumped over the median. Horns blared as I swerved into westbound traffic.

"Sweet," Riley shouted. "Will you teach me how to do that when I get my license?"

"No!" we all said at once.

We had beat the FBI to the Odyssey, so we took matters into our own hands and started asking everyone and anyone if they'd seen a man fitting Nate's description. Ana had even roped S. Larue, Security, into helping as well.

When FBI agents started arriving, however, all we could do was stand back and wait while they conducted a room by room search.

An hour later we were still waiting.

Onlookers milled around, not sure what was going on, but curious anyway.

Ana had one of Maria's hands, and I held the other while we waited. And waited.

Just when I thought I'd been totally wrong, Ian came striding up to us.

"Ms. Ceceri?" he said to Maria.

Her lower lip trembled. "Yes?"

"We found him in a janitor's closet on the second floor. He's unconscious, but he's alive. We're airlifting him to the hospital; there's not enough room on the helicopter, but we thought you might want a ride with one of our agents . . ."

My stomach was in my throat when Maria turned to me, looking scared and lost. "Go!" I said hoarsely.

She took Ian's hand and they sprinted away.

On one hand I was thrilled Nate was found, on the other, Ian had looked grim. Nate must be in bad shape.

With a heavy heart, I called my mother. I suffered through ten seconds of complaints about Giuseppe and Carlotta (who had given up on me and taken a cab) before I was able to get a word in edgewise. Finally, I took a deep breath and filled her in.

"Oh dear," my mother said before hanging up.

"We should go," I told Ana. "There's nothing we can do now but wait."

She gathered up her purse, looked around. "Where's Riley?"

Great. I'd finally gone and lost him. Ana and I split up to look for him.

Ten minutes later I found him in the casino, near the Big Bang. The whole Nate thing had severely tested my will not to gamble, and I tugged on his arm before I ended up plunking down all the money I had on a blackjack table.

"Let's go," I said.

"I need this car," he said. "Look at it."

I looked. I drooled. It was the same car that had been there a few days ago. A red BMW convertible.

Sighing, I tugged on his arm. "Let's go."

"Please! One pull?"

"You're underage!"

"You can do it for me, right?"

I'm sure there was some law against it, but I felt the adrenaline kick in. One pull. What could it hurt? It wasn't like he was going to win. And it would go a little bit toward helping us bond. Right?

"Please?"

I wavered. It would be so easy to fish in my backpack for a five dollar bill and feed it into the machine. After that drunken night eight years ago and that trip to the Chapel of Forever After, I'd made a commandment never to gamble again. So far I'd stuck to it. I couldn't break it now.

The old woman behind us tapped her foot. "You going or not?"

I pulled Riley out of the line. "Go ahead," I said to her.

"Oh man," Riley whined.

As we walked away, a loud siren whooped. We turned to find the woman jumping up and down. Three BMWs were aligned on the screen.

Ack!

Riley looked at me, mouth open, an accusation in his eyes.

"Don't say it," I warned.

"But—"

I shot him a look. He closed his mouth. "Besides," I said, "if I had won it, I would have kept it."

"You would not have!"

"Would have."

"Life's not fair!"

"Nope. Come on," I told him. "Let's go find Ana."

He was still brooding, but managed a smile. "That could take a while. There are lots of single guys here."

Ack. And hotel rooms.

We broke into a run.

"So, he said, "you'll buy me a car when I get my license, right?"

I shot him a look. "Keep dreaming, kid."

Twenty-seven

If the puddle that appeared on the floor was any indication, Gracie was very happy to see me.

I bent down, rubbed her smooth head. She snuffled and raced around in circles, before bouncing into a wall and diving back under the couch.

Riley hadn't bothered to come in—he'd made a beeline toward the path in the woods, no doubt to tell Katie all the latest news.

In the kitchen, I grabbed a box of Nilla wafers and checked my messages. I had one from Mr. Cabrera that said he'd heard the Colonel had been picked up in Cleveland.

I didn't doubt it was true. Mr. Cabrera was usually quite reliable when it concerned gossip.

There was a message from my father telling me that Nate was in surgery and it was touch and go. He hadn't regained consciousness yet, so no one knew what, exactly, had happened to him. He'd call back when he heard something.

I had a message from Bobby MacKenna too. "I hope you're thinking."

I smiled in spite of myself. I had mixed feelings where the good vice principal was concerned. Oh, I liked him. A lot.

But I still loved Kevin.

And I didn't know what to do about it.

I stuffed a wafer in my mouth, sat on the counter. All I wanted to do was go to bed.

I checked the cat clock that hung on the kitchen wall. It was only seven. Not even dark out.

Beyond that, I was expecting my uncle Giuseppe and aunt Carlotta to show up at the door any minute now, once they realized my parents weren't home.

My only hope lay in the fact that they didn't know where I lived. Maybe, just maybe, they'd call Aunt Rosa and decide to stay at Ana's with her.

A girl could dream.

In case I was being delusional, I threw some musty smelling sheets in the washer, and before I knew it I found myself in a full cleaning frenzy.

I, unfortunately, tended to clean when I was stressed. Which, these days, was often. Honest to goodness, I needed to get another neurotic pastime.

Gracie stayed under the couch while I cleaned and waited, waited and cleaned.

By nine, dusk was settling into a muted darkness and Gracie had decided not to be such a scaredy-dog of the vacuum. She came out, pranced around.

I knew that prance.

Scooping her up, I raced toward the back door. I flung it open and gasped when I saw Mr. Weatherbee on the back step, hand poised to knock.

"Mrs. Quinn," he said. He looked as uncomfortable as I felt.

"Do you want to come in?" I asked.

"No."

"Oh."

Gracie squirmed. I set her down next to the washing machine and kept an eye on her.

"I heard," he said, arms folded, "that it was fingerprints that led to the Colonel's arrest. Seeing as how I know you also suspected me . . ."

Ah. He was fishing. He wanted to know if I knew of his arrest record. "And?" I asked, being petty enough to want to see him squirm.

"And, ahem, there are things that . . ." He frowned. "My mother," he said softly, "would never understand . . . or accept."

Jeez. My heart wasn't made of stone, for crying out loud. It wasn't my place to judge.

"Mr. Weatherbee," I said, watching Gracie circle my feet, "as I recall, you drank out of a paper cup yesterday, didn't you?"

The barest hint of a smile broke on his face. "Thank you," he said. He turned to go, but stopped and looked back. "For the record, Mrs. Quinn . . . I detest paper cups."

I scooped up Gracie. "Good to know," I said.

As he walked away, I looked out into the dark night. Mr. Cabrera's back floodlights were mysteriously dark, and I admit to being a little freaked out, especially after Maria had been so positive someone had been out there earlier.

I looked around but couldn't find Maria's can of Aqua Net. I grabbed a can of Pledge instead, and Riley's hockey stick from the closet.

The minute I set Gracie down, she took off, her little snout to the ground like a bloodhound on a trail, stopping every few feet before rushing on. I chased after her as she darted into the shadowy woods.

I followed her in. "Gracie!"

I heard a loud *yip* and spun toward the sound.

"Looking for something?" a voice said. I spun. In the pale moonlight, I saw Roz Phineus holding Gracie in one hand and a gun in the other. A gun that looked suspiciously like a Smith & Wesson pistol with a four-inch barrel and a black polymer grip. *Uh-oh.*

"Hot dogs," she said, rubbing Gracie's head. "Worked like a charm."

I glared at Gracie, somehow feeling betrayed. Sold out for a few pieces of hot dog. Hmmph.

"Put the stick down," Roz said.

"What are you doing here? How was New York?" I said, trying for nonchalant. Another minute or so and I'd invite her inside to share my Nilla wafers.

Roz pointed a red talon at me. "I spoke with Verona earlier. Seems there was some excitement at home."

I shrugged, acting as though finding a body wasn't all that out of the ordinary for me.

"I want that guest list and those pictures," she demanded. "I know you have them."

Uh, uh-oh. "I don't," I said.

Roz waved the gun. I tried not to cringe. "Maria called last night and said you *did*. If you have the guest list, you have the pictures. Nate said he had them both right before Claire shot him . . . May he rest in peace. Now let's get them before I shoot you."

I really didn't think my legs would move. Claire had shot Nate . . . And obviously Roz didn't know Nate was alive.

"Why kill Nate?" I asked. "He'd never hurt anyone."

"Hah! He was about to hurt my livelihood!"

Huh?

"Mr. Goody-two-shoes couldn't leave well enough alone." Roz set Gracie down. "If he'd minded his own business, none of this would be happening. He just had to go and invite those *sick* kids. All my hard work, including having to cozy up with my husband's bastard child . . . down the drain."

My thoughts whirled, and snippets of conversations I'd had over the past few days haunted me.

PCF was founded by Roz after Alfred Phineus's death.

PCF is Roz's baby.

Roz didn't inherit anything after her husband's death.

•Nate had called the FBI saying he had information they'd be interested in . . .

Like fraud?

Had Roz, with Claire's help, pulled the scam of the century? Had she invented a phony charity just to rake in millions? I wouldn't put it past her.

She'd been cheated on by her husband, but then he'd left her absolutely nothing . . . except instructions to look after his love child.

Talk about a woman scorned. The ultimate payback, that's what this was. And Nate had found out about it—all because he was trying to do a good deed for some sick kids. Kids, I suspected, who didn't even exist. And to think I'd almost given PCF some of my money!

Money. That's what all this had been about. Alfred Phineus hadn't left any to his wife—or to Claire—so they'd teamed up to get some of their own, using his name.

"Why kill Claire?" I asked, hoping to stall some more.

"Bringing Claire in on this was a mis—"

"For God's sake, write her a book!" someone said. "Just shoot her and be done with it."

Gracie set off on a barking frenzy as Colin Frye stepped out from behind a tree. "This whole thing is your fault," he said to Roz, "trusting Claire to get the job done. Getting those pictures back from Biederman was her job."

My eyes widened. *Colin* had been in on all this too? Then I thought about it and realized he'd have to be. He worked too closely on the events at Phineus Frye not to know what was happening. My mind jumped to Brian Thatcher, the senior event planner at Phineus Frye—the one Claire had killed. Had he been in on it too? Or been an innocent bystander like Nate?

Roz hissed, "And if you hadn't been sleeping with her, then maybe you'd have had more control over her."

So Colin *had been* sleeping with Claire. I wondered if Verona knew . . . I suspected she did.

"She killed him," Colin said, "didn't she? Got that FBI agent's number out of his pocket too."

I gasped. Poor Fran Cooper!

"Yes, Claire was *perfect*," Roz said. "That must be why *you* killed *her*."

"Claire got sloppy, leaving those pictures in her office where Biederman could find them—and then not getting them back. Sloppy like someone who had the brilliant idea to bury an FBI agent in our own backyard!" Colin snapped.

Roz waved her gun around as she talked. "Well, pardon *me*. It wasn't as if your idea to drop Claire's body in that pond was the best of ideas either! *I* didn't know what Verona had planned! If she'd stop trying to please you and kick you out, then that FBI agent would be resting in peace."

Ohh-kay. I took stock. My hockey stick was out of reach, but I still had my Pledge. But getting away when both of them had guns didn't bode well for me coming out alive.

"If you recall," Colin explained to her in a chilling voice, "our plan was that *Nate* would take the blame for Claire's death."

I wanted to ask a few questions, but it seemed like they'd forgotten I was here, and I kind of liked it that way. I took another small step backward. Gracie moved with me.

Roz snorted. "*Your* plan. *I* never thought anyone would believe that he'd kill someone."

Colin calmly raised his gun and fired twice, the silenced bullets hitting Roz in the chest. She fell to the ground.

Gracie yipped and yapped and circled Colin's legs. "Ah," he said. "Much better."

He turned to me. I tried not to wet my pants. He was obviously on the wrong side of crazy. I stalled. "I, uh, er, was it you who took those pictures of Brian Thatcher?"

He laughed. "Do you think this is some ridiculous episode of *Law and Order* where I'm going to spill my guts to you?"

I didn't point out that his bickering with Roz had pretty much told me what I needed to know.

"I was hoping," I said weakly.

Gracie started yipping again. Colin reached down and picked her up. She squirmed as he held her snout closed with two fingers. "Let's get those pictures now. They're the only things that tie *me* to this whole mess. Poor Roz will take the blame for everything else. Including your death."

How did those pictures implicate him? I wondered. Then I remembered the bookcases in the background. Had they been taken in Colin's office?

When Colin took a step toward me, Gracie shook in his arms, tucked her tail, and did what she does best.

"What the hell?" Colin shouted, dropping her.

I stepped forward, pulled my Pledge out of my robe pocket. I aimed and fired. Colin dropped his gun and went down on his knees, crying out in pain as he held his hands over his eyes.

I grabbed my hockey stick and slap-shot his gun away, then hit him over the head for good measure.

Before I knew it, I heard someone crashing through the brush. Brickhouse Krauss came barreling toward us, her silky knee-length robe flapping, revealing more than I ever wanted to know. She was brandishing a wine bottle and made no bones about smashing it over Colin's head. Then she sat on him.

He wasn't going anywhere.

"Where did you come from?" I asked in awe.

"Gazebo. We heard the commotion."

Mr. Cabrera came puffing up, his banana-covered shirt unbuttoned, his shorts too. He took one look at the situation and said, "I'll go call the police."

I didn't want to envision exactly what Brickhouse and Mr. Cabrera were doing in the gazebo, her in a nightie, his clothes askew, and wine involved. My mind had had enough horrors for one day.

"Thanks for the help, Mrs. Krauss," I told her, though I'd pretty much had the situation under control.

She clucked. "No problem, Nina Ceceri. But you do owe me twenty bucks for the wine."

Twenty-eight

"Your mother is behaving quite well," Ana said in between sips of champagne.

It had been three weeks since Nate was found.

We leaned against the brand-new railing of the half-moon footbridge that straddled the koi pond in Maria's backyard. "I think she got hold of Maria's Dramamine."

We looked toward the patio, where most of the reception guests were gathered, watching Maria and Nate open gifts. My mother was sitting calmly next to them, taking notes on who had given what.

I looked around. Maria's yard was incredible, if I did say so myself. This garden was the epitome of serenity and simplicity. Winding gravel walkways lit with tall granite lanterns snaked around the pond. Groupings of plants were sparse and simply elegant. Azaleas, boxwoods, rhododendrons, Japanese maples, honeysuckle, and wisteria all lent to the beautiful landscape.

Along the paths, benches were tucked away in hidden nooks, perfect for reflecting back on a hectic day. And Nate and Maria had plenty of those in their futures now that Nate had taken over Claire Battiste's job at the Kalypso and

Maria had been promoted at the newly renamed Alfred Phineus Public Relations.

Ana took a big swallow of champagne. "My mother's threatening to move here. She wants to live with me."

My eyes widened. "You're joking?"

Grimly, she shook her head. "Not."

"Well, don't tell my mother. Not today. Things are going so well right now."

My father had the buffet table manned. My mother wouldn't be allowed near the knives. And Aunt Rosa, who flew back for the reception, had promised to be on her best behavior.

My brother Peter hadn't been able to change his vacation days but promised to come home for Christmas. I was personally holding him to it.

Laughter erupted on the patio, and we turned to see Maria smiling up at Nate as they opened yet another wedding gift, this one a set of his and her thongs.

Personally, I'd had enough talk of underwear in the past month to not even want to wear it anymore.

There were subtle differences between *want* and *need*.

I smoothed my dress, a clingy red chiffon thing that Ana had picked out for me.

"You look amazing," Ana said, noticing. "Aren't you glad you didn't have to wear that hideous matron of honor dress?"

"Glad doesn't begin to describe it." I still had nightmares about that dress.

Ana motioned toward the deck. "He hasn't been able to take his eyes off you."

I'd been in a quandary for weeks trying to make a decision between Bobby and Kevin.

Kevin . . . I loved him. I did. I couldn't help myself. And Bobby? He was amazing. Giving and caring . . .

With Kevin, there was history, but with Bobby there could be a future. "Did I make the right decision?" I asked.

"Time will tell."

"What kind of answer is that?"

"Hey, I have my own problems. My mother moving here puts a serious damper on my love life. I finally find a steady guy and we have to sneak around!"

My gaze shot to S. Larue, Security, who was talking to Verona Frye. Her right hand had yet to let go of her pearls, and I gave her credit for being here, for showing the world that she wouldn't let her S.O.B. of a husband ruin her life any more than he had.

Once Nate came to, he'd explained everything. From deciding to invite some of the Phineus foundation's beneficiaries to the gala only to find out they didn't exist, to snooping through Claire's office in hopes of finding evidence that PCF was a phony charity. That's when he'd stumbled on the pictures of Claire killing Brian Thatcher.

He'd called the FBI, sent the package to me for safekeeping just in case, and had convinced Claire to turn herself in. Only, she'd turned a gun on him instead.

Turns out, Verona didn't know anything about the phony charity—but she had known about Colin's affair. And overlooked it in the name of love.

On the patio, Verona said something to S. Larue that had him smiling. "Come on," I said to Ana, "tell me what the *S* stands for!" They'd been on five dates and I still didn't know.

"*I* don't know!" she said. "He won't tell me."

"There's got to be a way to find out."

She gave me a secret smile. "I think it's kind of mysterious in a sexy way."

"You're insane."

"They look good together, don't they?" Ana asked, looking toward the patio.

"Larue and Verona?"

She elbowed me. "Ow!"

"Maria and Nate."

I turned and looked back at Nate and Maria. After all the fuss and muss, the Wedding of the Century had been canceled. Nate had barely come to before Maria marched in a justice of the peace and married Nate right there in his ICU room.

My mother had needed resuscitation, which was somewhat fortuitous, seeing as how she was, after all, at the hospital when she found out.

In between doctor's visits and physical therapy, they'd spent their honeymoon locked in their new house. In time, Nate would be just fine.

"Yeah, they do," I said. "Happy too."

"Until she opens your present."

I smiled. "She'll get over it." I hoped.

Ana laughed. "Well, I'm going to go up and get a front row seat."

"Think I'll stay here out of harm's way."

"Smart idea."

I bent over the railing, watched the koi swim. Fountain grass swayed in the breeze and the black pebbles in the pond sparkled beneath the water.

Warm hands settled on my hips. "You look beautiful."

I turned around, looked up. "So do you." He was wearing a dark navy suit, tailored to fit his broad shoulders, and a soft blue button-down, left open at the collar. The colors set off his blue eyes, made them seem darker and deeper.

"I'm glad you came," I said. "Are you?"

Bobby took my hand. "I could do without the murderous stares from your husband, but seeing you in this dress makes it worth it."

"He's almost my ex-husband."

"Can't happen soon enough for me."

"Slow," I reminded.

"How slow is slow?" he asked.

"Snail slow."

He moaned. "You're killing me."

"Sorry."

"Don't apologize," he said. "I can wait."

For how long? I wondered, but didn't voice the thought.

I glanced toward the porch. Sure enough, Kevin was staring. I finger waved. I couldn't believe Maria had invited him in the first place, but then again, she always did have a soft spot for him. And my father was behaving amazingly well, considering. Still, I was keeping a careful eye on those knives.

Kevin turned away, said something to Riley and Katie that had them in smiles, as if to prove that my being here with someone else didn't bother him.

It was Verona, really, who had helped me decide between Bobby and Kevin. I didn't want to be that woman who continually wondered where her husband was, or who he was with . . . Living a lie just because it was easier.

Kevin had taken my decision relatively well. And as far as I knew, he was still living with Ginger.

"Oh no," I muttered.

"What?"

"Maria. She's opening my gift. And it's not the Egyptian cotton sheets she wanted."

I ducked behind Bobby, peered around him.

Maria lifted the top off the box, peeked in. A series of *yip yip yips* filled the air.

I couldn't help but smile at the look on Maria's face when she pulled Gracie out of the box, set her down.

A collection of *awwwws* quickly turned into a collective *ewwww* when Gracie tucked her tail.

Maria jumped up, scanned the crowd. When she spotted me (darn this red dress!), she crossed her arms and stamped her foot. "Neeee-naaah!"

Take Your Garden by Surprise
by Nina Quinn

"Curiosity and the cat, *chérie*," as my mother would say. For the rest of us, that translates to "Curiosity killed the cat."

The same, unfortunately, holds true for dogs. Recently, I learned this the hard way while I had temporary guardianship of a slightly crazy Chihuahua who decided to eat a very dangerous snack—a morning glory blossom.

Those gorgeous plants and flowers we work so hard to grow can cause serious illness or death to our canine companions. Every year, more and more cases of dogs dying from eating poisonous plants are reported. With a little know-how, you can help prevent this from happening to your four-legged best friend . . . and create a beautiful garden at the same time.

Know your plants. There are many, many types of poisonous plants with varying degrees of toxicity. Some common yet dangerous plants and shrubs include holly, hydrangea, oleander, azalea, foxglove, and morning glory. Certain bulbs are toxic too, like amaryllis, lily of the valley, tulips, daffodils, and day lilies. Bulbs are especially tempting—and hazardous—for dogs who like to dig.

Plan ahead. There are several ways to protect your pets from these dangerous plants. Clearly defined pathways will help keep your dog on the right track—and out of your garden. Raised beds, hanging baskets, and containers will help keep your plants—and your puppies—safe.

Head them off at the pass. Beyond fencing, another good deterrent is mesh bags filled with mothballs tucked here and there between plants. Sprinkling granular laundry detergent or cayenne or black pepper throughout your garden will keep even the nosiest of dogs out. Also, covering bulbs with chicken wire when planting should keep them from being dug up and possibly eaten.

Uh-oh! If you suspect your mischievous mutt has nibbled on something he shouldn't have, contact your veterinarian ASAP, preferably with the scientific name of the plant if at all possible.

Compromise. For those of you whose dogs refuse to stop digging, I suggest creating a garden just for Fido. Set aside a spot in your yard filled with loose soil. Bury goodies like bones and other toys so your dog can feel like he's gardening too.

Forewarned is forearmed. For a complete list of toxic plants, shrubs, trees, and bulbs—and other helpful animal poisoning advice—check out the website for the American Society for the Prevention of Cruelty to Animals at *www.aspca.org*.

And as an added reminder, before you give a dog as a gift, make sure the recipient is ready and willing to become a puppy parent. Trust me on that.

Best wishes for happy gardening.

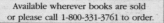

PERENNIAL DARK ALLEY

The First Cut: Award-winning author **Peter Robinson** probes the darkest regions of the human mind and soul in this clever, twisting tale of crime and revenge.
0-06-073535-X

Night Visions: A young lawyer's shocking dreams become terribly real in this chilling, beautifully written debut thriller by Thomas Fahy.
0-06-059462-4

Get Shorty: Elmore Leonard takes a mobster to Hollywood—where the women are gorgeous, the men are corrupt, and making it big isn't all that different from making your bones.
0-06-077709-5

Be Cool: Elmore Leonard takes Chili Palmer into the world of rock stars, pop divas, and hip-hop gangsters—all the stuff that makes big box office.
0-06-077706-0

Eye of the Needle: For the first time in trade paperback, comes one of legendary suspense author **Ken Follett's** most compelling classics.
0-06-074815-X

More Than They Could Chew: **Rob Roberge** tells the story of Nick Ray, a man whose addictions (alcohol, kinky sex, questionable friends) might only be cured by weaning him from oxygen.
0-06-074280-1

Men from Boys: A short story collection featuring some of the true masters of crime fiction, including Dennis Lehane, Lawrence Block, and Michael Connelly. These stories examine what it means to be a man amid cardsharks, revolvers, and shallow graves.
0-06-076285-3

PERENNIAL
DARK
ALLEY

An Imprint of HarperCollinsPublishers
www.harpercollins.com

DKA 0205

Investigate the Hottest New Mysteries!

Sign up for the FREE HarperCollins monthly mystery newsletter,

The Scene of the Crime,

and get to know your favorite authors, win free books, and be the first to learn about the best new mysteries going on sale.

To register, simply go to www.HarperCollins.com, visit our mystery channel page, and at the bottom of the page, enter your email address where it states "Sign up for our mystery newsletter." Then you can tap into monthly Hot Reads, check out our award nominees, sneak a peek at upcoming titles, and discover the best whodunits each and every month.

Get to know the magnificent mystery authors of HarperCollins and sign up today!

MYN 0205